I0742438

SIC TRANSIT TERRA 3

THE RELATIVITY BOMB

ARLENE F. MARKS

EDGE SCIENCE FICTION AND FANTASY PUBLISHING
An Imprint of HADES PUBLICATIONS, INC.
CALGARY

The Relativity Bomb
Sic Transit Terra Book 3

EDGE SCIENCE FICTION AND FANTASY PUBLISHING
An Imprint of HADES PUBLICATIONS, INC.
P.O. Box 1714, Calgary, Alberta, T2P 2L7, Canada

The EDGE Team:
Producer: Brian Hades
Acquisitions Editor: Michelle Heumann
Edited by: Heather Manuel
Cover Design: Lynn Perkins
Book Design: Mark Steele
Publicist: Janice Shoults
Copywriter: Myles McDonough

ISBN: 978-1-77053-168-0

EDGE Science Fiction and Fantasy Publishing and Hades Publications, Inc. acknowledges the ongoing support of the Alberta Foundation for the Arts and the Canada Council for the Arts for our publishing programme.

 Canada Council Conseil des arts for the Arts du Canada

Library and Archives Canada Cataloguing in Publication
CIP Data on file with the National Library of Canada
ISBN: 978-1-77053-168-0
(e-Book ISBN: 978-1-77053-167-3)

FIRST EDITION
(20180317)
Printed in USA
www.edgewebsite.com

Publisher's Note:

Thank you for purchasing this book. It began as an idea, was shaped by the creativity of its talented author, and was subsequently molded into the book you have before you by a team of editors and designers.

Like all EDGE books, this book is the result of the creative talents of a dedicated team of individuals who all believe that books (whether in print or pixels) have the magical ability to take you on an adventure to new and wondrous places powered by the author's imagination.

As EDGE's publisher, I hope that you enjoy this book. It is a part of our ongoing quest to discover talented authors and to make their creative writing available to you.

We also hope that you will share your discovery and enjoyment of this novel on social media through Facebook, Twitter, Goodreads, Pinterest, etc., and by posting your opinions and/or reviews on Amazon and other review sites and blogs. By doing so, others will be able to share your discovery and passion for this book.

Brian Hades, publisher

The Sic Transit Terra Universe Series:

Acknowledgements

I am grateful for the insights provided by the following people during the writing of this book: David Marks, Ken Haigh and my perceptive fellow authors in the Collingwood Writers' Collective, Bette Walker, and Adde Walker, my science guy. Many thanks as well to Heather Manuel, who actually made the editing process enjoyable.

PART I

THE MINTING OF JUNO VARGAS
EARTH, 2374 C.E.

Dennis René Forrand (b. 2320 – d. 2387 C.E.?) was the middle child and only son of pharmaceuticals magnate Gilles Forrand. Entering politics at an early age, he quickly rose through the governmental ranks, achieving the lofty post of Supreme Adjudicator for Americas just days before his fiftieth birthday. Available records indicate that he never married or fathered children. Although not the most popular of leaders, he was nonetheless respected for his political astuteness. Forrand was best known for his efforts to improve the public image of the Earth Relocation Authority. He is presumed to have perished when his personal vehicle ran off an ungridded road and tumbled down a cliff, bursting into flames; however, the remains found in the vehicle were too badly burned for a positive identification to be made.

— *Sic Transit Terra, An Unauthorized Planetary History*
   (2673 C.E.)

CHAPTER 1

"That is one very determined lady."

His attention snagged, Supreme Adjudicator Dennis Forrand leaned over his executive assistant's shoulder and took in the image on her light screen. A woman dressed in medical scrubs had stepped off the elevator and was now arguing with the guards at the floor reception desk. He didn't need to hear her voice to know what she was saying — the stiffness of her posture, the staccato motions of her arms, and the storm warning on her face were all quite eloquent.

"Yeah, she's feisty as hell," he said with a sigh. "She comes by it honestly."

The InfoComm buzzed. "They're calling through, sir. What do you want me to tell them?"

"Tell them I've been expecting her," he instructed, already strolling back to his office.

A minute later the door to the anteroom flew open as though kicked and the visitor barreled through it. She paused and glared briefly in the direction of the assistant's desk, then swept past her without a word into the Supreme Adjudicator's inner sanctum. This second door slid instead of swung, so she couldn't slam it shut behind her as she so clearly wanted to do.

Forrand gazed benignly at her from the other side of his large oaken desk.

"Doctor Caroline Townsend," he said in his most welcoming voice. "And what can I do for you today?"

Her hands curled into fists as she covered the distance to his desk in two furious strides and leaned ominously across it.

"You bastard!" she spat, then went on, thrusting each razor-like word at him as though hoping to draw blood, "You promised! You said that if I kept quiet— You swore to me that my family would stay together. Well, I've held up my part of the bargain, but we've just been posted off-world without our son."

"Drew is no longer Eligible. I told you that as long as you were all Eligible I could ensure that the Relocation Authority would not separate you. When Drew broke the law and lost his Eligibility—"

"He's only twelve years old. He's a child! What happens to him when we've gone? For godsakes, he's your—"

"He's under my protection," Forrand declared, loudly enough to drown out the rest of her sentence. He rose from his seat and locked eyes with her, facing down her reproachful stare. "Just as you've all been up until now. I give you my word, Caroline, he'll never lack for food or shelter. Your son will not come to harm. Now, I suggest you go home and finish getting the rest of your family ready to travel so you can make your scheduled flight to the transfer point."

"That's the other thing I needed to tell you." She was calmer now, but not by much. "Olivia is refusing to go with us. She says she won't leave her little brother to fend for himself."

Forrand sank back down, scowling. "You're her mother. Order her to start packing."

"I'd love to, but she ran out of the house shortly after we got the notice from the Relocation Authority and now I can't find her. I was hoping you would know where she is."

"I'm sorry, Caroline, I don't. However, I will do everything in my power to see that she is located. If I can't get her onto the same flight as yours, I'll put her on a later one."

"And you'll take care of Drew." It wasn't a question.

"I promise."

"Your promises aren't worth as much to me as they used to be, *Mister* Supreme Adjudicator. Just make damned sure you keep this one," she warned. With that, Caroline Townsend wheeled and stalked out almost as angrily as she'd arrived.

Forrand waited for the sound of the outer door closing. Then he swiveled his chair and rapped lightly on a wall panel behind him. "You can come out now, young lady."

The panel slid aside. A girl in her mid-teens emerged from the hidden compartment, straightening her clothing and patting her mop of short dark hair back into place. She marched to the other side of his desk, leveled cool gray eyes at him, and demanded, "So what's the big secret? It has something to do with Drew, doesn't it? Something you didn't want me to overhear."

There was a lot of her mother in her, he mused. And her grandmother, come to that.

"No, angel, it doesn't. And since my biggest secret right now is you, standing in my office, let's just focus on why you're here. It took persistence and ingenuity for you to get this far, so you must want something important. What is it?"

Olivia thought for a moment. "My mother says you're the most powerful person in Americas."

"I could be described that way," he conceded.

"Then I want you to teach me how to be as powerful as you are."

"If you want to run the world," he told her, "you need to get on that short-hopper with your parents. It's a lot easier to manage a hub or a colony than it is to control a planet like Earth."

"I didn't say I want to run the world," she corrected him sharply.

"I see. Well, you're still talking about amassing a great deal of political clout, and powerful people attract powerful and determined enemies. There's been a target painted on my back for the past thirty years. Are you sure you want to live like that, constantly on yellow alert?"

"Are you sure I'm your biggest secret right now?" she shot back, crossing her arms over her chest and raising her chin defiantly.

Forrand permitted himself an indulgent chuckle. Then he said, "Before I agree to go along with this, you have to understand a few things. Power may seem attractive but it comes at a price, and it's always going to be steeper than you expect. Once your guard goes up, it stays up. Once you're committed, there's no backing out. Are you absolutely certain, at the tender age of — what are you, sixteen?" She nodded. "Are you absolutely certain that this is how you want to spend the rest of your life?"

"I've been thinking about it for a long time," she told him, her voice sounding a lot older than sixteen. "Being Eligible seems attractive but it comes at a price too. If gathering political power is the only way for me to take back control of my life, then that's what I want to do. And you may have a target on your back, but you're still alive and kicking, so I figure you're the best person to teach me how to do it."

Her gaze had captured his as soon as she began speaking. Now he sat back in his chair, studying her expression as he digested her words.

"What about Drew?" he asked softly. "You told your mother you wanted to protect him."

"He's already taken control of his life by losing his Eligibility," she pointed out. "I know I can't shield him from the consequences of his choices. But he's still a kid, and he's going to make mistakes. I just want to be able to keep him alive so he can learn from them. Do we have a deal, Mister Supreme Adjudicator?"

Forrand smiled inwardly. Olivia was definitely her mother's child. "We have a deal. However, there's one thing I want you to do first. I want you to sleep on this and give me your final answer tomorrow morning."

She said nothing, just crossed her arms over her chest again and regarded him sullenly for several seconds.

"Humor me," he said. "I'm giving you a cooling off period. Whatever your decision is, I don't want you to have any regrets about it later on."

"Fine, then," she snapped. "But I'm pretty sure you don't want me going back home, so where exactly am I supposed to do all this sleeping? Am I camping out in your office?"

Forrand pressed an intercomm key on his desktop. "Nothing that dramatic." A moment later his executive assistant stepped through the door. "Mrs. Delgado," he told her, "this young lady needs a place to stay overnight, and I was wondering whether I could impose on your hospitality."

"It isn't a problem, sir. I'll have Estrella make up the spare bed."

"And someone will have to fetch her belongings from Clearmeadow Enclave and deliver them here."

"Already arranged. I've also contacted everyone on your list. Miss Townsend will be escorted to and from in secrecy."

"Hey, I'm standing right here," Olivia reminded them, impatience putting an edge on her voice. "I'm not just some parcel that you're moving around."

"Indeed, you're not," Forrand agreed. "What you are at the moment is a logistical nightmare, which I fortunately have the resources to manage. Meanwhile, there's something else I want you to think about tonight. If your answer tomorrow morning is still yes, you'll need to pick a new name, one that you're willing to live with from now on."

She stared a question at him. After a beat, he replied, "Anyone associated with me — and anyone associated with *them* — becomes a target. If you're serious about keeping your brother safe, Olivia Townsend will have to die."

"You mean my parents will think I'm dead? I'll never be able to contact them again?"

Her chin was wobbling, despite the determination that still filled her eyes.

"Not your parents and especially not Drew," he told her sternly, then added in a softer voice, "Sadly, it's part of the price I was talking about earlier. The easy part."

— «» —

There were two individuals waiting in Forrand's anteroom when Olivia was brought there the following morning, and she didn't like the way either one of them was looking at her.

The young woman talking with Mrs. Delgado was tall and sturdily built, with plain features. A rope of braided brown hair fell over her shoulder and nearly to her waist. As Olivia stepped into the room, the woman turned and impaled her with an icy blue stare.

Meanwhile, a young man with short, dark blond hair had claimed one of the matched chairs against the far wall. Wearing a ganger jacket and sporting a crown-shaped tattoo on his neck, he was scanning Olivia up and down with a calculating smile that made her skin crawl.

Fortunately, she didn't have to endure their attentions for long. Scant moments after her uniformed escort had departed, she was ushered by Mrs. Delgado into the Supreme Adjudicator's inner office.

Forrand sat watching her intently from behind his desk. His suit was rumpled, making her wonder whether he'd slept in it. Then it occurred to her that he might not have slept at all.

Breaking into her thoughts, he got right to the point. "Have you come to a decision?" he demanded.

"I have," she told him, managing to keep her voice steady. "I still want to go ahead with this."

He made an approving noise and pressed the intercomm key. "Send her in."

A few seconds later, the plain-faced, brown-haired girl strode through the door and took up a position beside Forrand's desk.

"All right, then," he said, addressing Olivia once more. "Your education begins right now. Before you can wield power, you need to understand it. Specifically, you need to understand its effects on the people who have it and on those who lack it. You've grown up with a great deal of privilege that you've never had to earn. So, I'm sending you on an extended field trip to places most Eligibles never see or even think about. This is Angeli. She will be your companion, guide, and bodyguard for the next twelve months." He indicated with a gesture the forbidding-looking young woman to his left.

Olivia's heart sank. A whole year? With *her*?

"The arrangements have already been made," he went on briskly. "All that's missing is the name you'll be traveling under. I trust you've picked one?" In the silence that followed this question, it felt to Olivia as if everything in the room was holding its breath in anticipation of her response.

Finally, she replied, "Juno Vargas."

Forrand considered this, then said, "Juno was the queen of the ancient Greco-Roman gods, and Adam Vargas was the primary architect of our current geopolitical system. That's quite a statement for a sixteen-year-old to be making. Well,

Miss Vargas, I recommend that you get as much enjoyment as you can out of this excursion, because once your name is linked to mine you won't be able to do much traveling."

He leaned forward and began speaking quietly into the intercomm. Meanwhile, the newborn Juno Vargas looked into the face of the woman who would be her guide and chaperone for the next year and saw a raised eyebrow and a mouth set in a hyphen of disapproval. However educational this trip might turn out to be, Juno very much doubted whether Angeli would permit it to be enjoyable. Forrand had probably selected her for that very reason. This "tour" was most likely intended to be a test of her stamina and commitment. All right, she decided grimly. She would pass his damned test with room to spare, even if she had to ditch her traveling companion and complete it on her own.

"Mrs. Delgado will be forwarding your bags to the first stop on the tour as soon as your new identity is official," Forrand announced. "Angeli has the itinerary...?" The young woman nodded once. "You'll remember what we discussed," he told her, and she nodded again, her expression matching the sternness of his voice.

As Angeli preceded her out of the inner office, Juno glanced over her shoulder and saw Forrand sink slowly backward in his chair.

— «» —

"So, that was the chosen one?" Forrand's remaining guest had been shown into his office as soon as the two girls had left the anteroom. Now, flopped down on one of the padded chairs to the right of the big desk, the ganger commented, "Twenty credits says she doesn't last a month in the boonies."

Forrand smiled thinly. He was the most powerful man in Americas. If this Tommy Novotny was everything he needed him to be, it wouldn't matter what the kid knew. If not, Forrand would make a commcall to the guards in the lobby. Novotny would disappear somewhere between the elevator and the front door, and any record of his visit to the building would be wiped clean — and it still wouldn't matter what he knew.

"I think you'd lose that wager, Tommy. She's a lot like her mother, who can be stubborn as hell. That being said,

I've decided to hedge my bet. That's where you come in. You and the Warrior Kings."

Tommy leaned forward. "I'm listening."

"There's a twelve-year-old boy, an Eligible who rebelled against the system and now has a juvenile criminal record. Sound familiar? He's being evicted from the family home in Clearmeadow Enclave as we speak, and I promised his family that I'd make sure he was protected after they went off-world."

"So, what? You want us to babysit this kid?"

"Not at all," said Forrand. "I want you to educate him. Take him into the gang and teach him everything you know about surviving on the streets. Don't let him get arrested. When he's eighteen, I'll take him off your hands."

"And what do we get in exchange for providing this service, Mister Supreme Adjudicator?"

Forrand leaned over his desktop. "How old are you now, Tommy?"

"Nineteen. Why?"

"Only nineteen and already at the top. You're Rex Regum, the King of the Kings. But what have you got to look forward to? Another ten or so years of playing hide and seek with District Security before someone rats you out so they can take your place? Spending the rest of your life in and out of detention and watching your crew age around you? It's not much of a future, is it?"

Tommy's expression hardened, as did his voice. "Make your point, Forrand."

"I want to offer you a second chance — a new name and a fresh beginning. You're strong and you're smart, Tommy, and you care about your crew. You must once have had ambitions that didn't include street crime. If you could erase the past and had access to large amounts of credit, what would you rather be doing with your life?"

Warily studying the other man's face, Tommy asked, "Are you serious?"

"Absolutely. I can set you up in whatever legitimate business you want, arrange for training for you and your current gang, give you all new identities. A clean slate. And all you have to do in return is keep Drew Townsend safe for the next six years and consider joining an organization that I'm putting together. Its purpose will be to protect the truth. We're going to gather, verify, and — if necessary — act on information that will make the various levels of Earth's government accountable."

"You're asking a bunch of criminals to help you keep a bigger bunch of criminals honest?" said Tommy with a grin.

Forrand gazed serenely back at him. "Can you think of anyone better qualified for the job?"

Still smiling, Tommy tilted his head in acknowledgment of the compliment. "So, you have big plans for this kid? What is he, the next in line for the throne after Miss Poutyface blows you off?"

"Possibly. It takes a special combination of qualities to aspire to that kind of power. Time will tell whether he has them. Right now, however, he's just a young boy waiting to be shaped by the world."

"And by the Warrior Kings," Tommy added after a beat.

"So we have a deal?"

"For the next six years and the fresh start for me and my crew," he confirmed, getting to his feet and extending his hand to be shaken. "About the rest of it, I'll have to meet with the Kings and get back to you."

Forrand stood up to seal the agreement. "Fair enough. They'll need to pick new legal names for the database."

"It's just as well," said Tommy. "I always hated mine — Tomasz Boris Novotny."

CHAPTER 2

Juno leaned her head wearily against the window of the Multi-Passenger Vehicle. It had been a very long and tiring day.

Her parents' short-hopper had lifted off shortly before noon, carrying the Townsends to the orbiting transfer station. From there, a deep-space transport vessel would take them to Sector 3 to join the staff of the research hospital on Schweitzer Hub. At least, that was what Juno had been told — the room where she had been made to wait until her new identity was integrated into the population database had been nowhere near the airfield.

Meanwhile, before their bags could be sent ahead, Angeli had insisted on personally inspecting every item in Juno's luggage. The older girl had pulled out and set aside anything that was too stylish or expensive-looking. Flaunting one's wealth to the denizens of the "industrial wilderness" was not a very smart thing to do, she had warned, her lips making an even thinner hyphen than before. Bright colors were risky. Anything metallic, such as glitter or sequins, was downright dangerous.

Juno had seen no sense in any of this, other than the fact that all the forbidden pieces of clothing were cheerful and attractive, while Angeli's own tunic and trousers hung shapelessly on her and were the color of dirt. There wasn't that much difference in their ages — five or six years at most, despite the severity of the other girl's appearance. And she clearly hadn't volunteered for this tour guide assignment — the byplay in Forrand's office earlier had been hard to miss — so her resentment at having to babysit a pampered Eligible kid for an entire year was understandable. Juno probably should have been grateful that Angeli was taking it out on her wardrobe instead of her person. At that point, however, she was too preoccupied for it to matter much. She'd been thinking about her parents and Drew, and how they would react when the news reached them of Olivia Townsend's untimely death.

Forrand had promised that it would be fiery and final, but he obviously didn't know her mother. Caroline Townsend would demand to see a body, and when presented with the corpse would then insist on personally cutting it open and performing tests to ensure that it was actually her daughter's. No body would mean no proof, and without proof there would still be hope to cling to. But for how long? How long would her parents teeter on the edge of that terrible drop, waiting for Olivia to join them as Forrand had promised? How long before they could bear to admit to themselves that she was really gone? And how long would it take her little brother to stop hating her for breaking her word and abandoning him?

Since early that morning, sadness had been seeping into Juno, settling like sand in her chest. She felt like a ghost attending its own funeral. How long until the pain of losing herself and her family dulled to an ache? When would Olivia Townsend fade to a memory?

Angeli stirred beside her, dragging her thoughts back to the present. They were traveling west and the sun was setting, its final rays burning the sky pink and orange ahead of them. Three hours earlier, the MPV had left the central terminus. Rapidly reaching the district perimeter, the longcar had then rolled for half an hour through circumference greenbelt on a two-lane ribbon of asphalt. The road surface had grown progressively worse, cracking and crumbling as it led Juno and Angeli farther away from the residential and commercial Urban District of New Chicago.

Greenbelt and paved road had both ended at the edge of a second buffer zone known as The Flats. Juno had studied this area in geography class. The weather was uncontrolled out here, which meant there were wide temperature swings and a lot of seasonal precipitation. It appeared they had just missed a cloudburst. The rutted dirt path ahead of the MPV was dappled with shiny puddles, and the brush and weeds alongside it sparkled as though strewn with diamonds. Farther removed from the trail, abandoned fields stretched away to both sides, their margins suggested by the occasional knob of wood sticking out of the tall, thick grass. No fences were visible here — the land lay flat, drowned by a sea of green. Only the occasional gnarled tree stood higher, lifting its foliage as though trying to keep it dry.

Staring out the window, Juno suddenly realized that she had seen no signs of Human life outside the MPV for more than two hours. Now the light was fading, turning the world shades of gray, and even though the temperature inside the vehicle was maintained at a mild 22 degrees Celsius, she felt a chill. They were in the middle of nowhere, carrying only the contents of their tote bags, and were about to be engulfed in utter darkness. Although the MPV was equipped with autodrive, traffic wasn't gridded outside of urban districts. They were relying on a Human driver familiar with the route to conduct them safely through the night to their destination. But drivers could become tired. Machines could break down. If the worst were to happen, the small group of passengers on this longcar would have only one another to depend on.

It wasn't a comforting thought.

Juno swung her gaze to the interior of the vehicle. There was room for up to twenty passengers in a standard-sized MPV. Including herself and Angeli, there were only eight on this run. That in itself was disquieting. Fuel was expensive. For that reason, interzone MPVs didn't depart until every seat was paid for. There was only one conclusion to be drawn here: Forrand must have bought up all the remaining tickets to ensure the "field trip" would begin on schedule.

Had the other six passengers come to a similar conclusion? While she'd been focused on the scenery outside her window or busy with the light meal of sandwiches and fruit that Angeli had brought along, had they noticed all the empty spaces, quietly compared notes, figured out who on this trip had to be the one with connections or wealth — or both?

Despite Forrand's assurances, was there already a target being figuratively painted on her back?

If there was, and if Angeli was supposed to be her protector, she would do a better job of it with her eyes open, Juno decided, poking her in the shoulder.

"So, what's our first stop on this magic carpet ride?"

Reclined and dozing on her half of their dark green padded bench, Angeli opened one eye and turned her head slowly toward her young charge. "Agricultural District."

"Gonna show me where all the food comes from?"

"No. Gonna open your eyes and knock that chip off your shoulder," she replied tartly. "Don't feel obliged to make conversation, Juno."

She put special emphasis on that last word, both judging and mocking Olivia's choice of names. But Forrand had been right — Olivia had stayed up late the previous night thinking about her future, and "Juno Vargas" was a statement of intent.

So, swallowing the first response that had popped into her mouth, she assured Angeli brightly, "Oh, it's no trouble. We still have a long way to go. Chatting will help to pass the time."

The "guide and protector" blew out a martyred breath, then pulled herself upright and straightened the back of her seat. "All right, then," she said, biting off each syllable. "What do you want to talk about?"

"I think we should get better acquainted, since we're going to be traveling together for a whole year. For example, is Angeli your first name or is it your family name?"

The other girl gave her a strange look. For a second Juno thought she would refuse to answer, but she turned away and replied softly, "It's my full name."

"And did you choose it, or was it given to you?"

The prickles and sharp edges instantly returned. "Both. And neither. Now, if you don't mind, I'd like to get a little sleep. You could use some yourself, Miss Vargas. As you said, this is going to be a long ride."

Evidently, Juno had touched a nerve. She turned and met her reflection staring uncertainly back at her from the inside of the window. It was nearly pitch dark outside. The pale overhead lights of the MPV had come on, filling it with ghostly shadows. Alone with seven silent companions and a driver who hadn't spoken a word from the moment he'd boarded the vehicle, Juno reluctantly lowered the back of her seat and closed her eyes.

A second later, it seemed, a hand was on her shoulder and Angeli's voice was urging her to sit up.

"We're almost there," she said.

The longcar was still in motion, but a glance through the front window revealed a cluster of lights in the distance.

"And where is there?" asked Juno.

"The Council refuses to give it a name because it's not inside an urban district, but the inhabitants call it Veggieville. We're in the heart of the Food Production Zone, where the agricultural workers live."

Juno sat on the edge of her seat, watching the lights of Veggieville grow larger and rise higher as the MPV neared the food workers' settlement. At last, the longcar pulled to a stop in a broad open area surrounded by tall lampposts. Their harsh white glow fell down and inward, creating an island of illumination in the darkness; and the noise made by the vehicle as the driver turned off the engine and opened the front door sounded just like a sigh of relief. Angeli put out her arm, keeping Juno seated as the other six travelers moved past them in weary procession.

"Wait," whispered Angeli as the last of them disappeared through the exit. "Listen."

Juno heard voices outside the longcar. She heard greetings exchanged and names being given. She heard billets being handed out and instructions issued to report for work assignments right after breakfast. Then came a medley of sounds that she'd only ever heard in flat-screen videos about the ancient west: the clip-clopping of horses' hooves, the creaking of leather, the low burring of wheels turning on axles. Simultaneously, smells began wafting through the open door of the MPV. Some she could guess at — the musk of living horseflesh, the sweet pungency of grass and trees that hung in the air after a rainfall — but others were completely unfamiliar, reminding her just how far away she was from home. From family. From everyone and everything she knew. Unease began stirring in the pit of her stomach.

No! she scolded herself. Forrand had been right — Olivia Townsend's life had been sheltered and complacent, hardly a life at all. Now Olivia was dead, freeing her to claim a much larger existence. And that was what she would do, just as soon as her queasiness subsided. Juno Vargas might be feeling a little disoriented right now, but she was no coward.

A stocky man with swarthy skin leaned into the vehicle and spoke to the driver in accented Ameranglo. "What's your fuel situation?"

Juno couldn't make out the driver's response, but it apparently satisfied the other man, for he nodded and said, "We've got a group that have been transferred to General Millstown. Three families, with young children. There's a shuttle service that can pick them up in Breadbasket and take them the rest of the way, but they need a lift to the transfer point. It's not that far — only fifty-five kilometers from here."

Again, the driver's reply was a murmur of sounds; but from the way the man's face fell, it wasn't hard to guess what the answer had been.

"Why won't he help them?" Juno whispered to Angeli.

She whispered back, "It messes up the bookkeeping. Forrand has chartered the MPV for our entire tour from this point on. Based on the itinerary, he's already calculated the total distance we'll be traveling and prepaid for the right amount of fuel for the journey. So, while he has no objection to our giving lifts to people as we go, we can't let them take us too far out of our way. The driver's been warned that any fuel shortfall will be coming out of his own credit account."

"You're saying the itinerary is set in stone? We can't make any side trips?"

"'Fraid not," Angeli said.

The man squared his shoulders and looked directly at the two remaining passengers aboard the MPV. "Angeli and Juno, I presume? I'm Carlos Calvera. Welcome to Veggieville. You'll be staying with my sister Isabela and her husband, who have their own house and are both very good at keeping secrets. Your luggage arrived during the dinner hour and is waiting for you in your room. Gather up your things and I'll drive you there now."

Carlos disappeared into the darkness, returning a moment later on a moto that even Juno could see had been frankensteined together into a patchwork of mismatched parts. Fortunately, it had a sidecar and a muffler. In only a handful of minutes, Juno and Angeli were quietly transported, warmly welcomed, and then firmly ushered to a room on the second floor of Isabela's home. There, they stripped off their outer clothing and slipped between the covers of a large, blissfully comfortable bed.

— «» —

The following morning, Juno got up and went directly to the window to take her first look at Veggieville in daylight. According to Angeli, Veggieville and places like it predated the Reorganization, making them over two hundred years old. Juno hesitated, thinking of the Zone in New Chicago. That area of abandoned factories, warehouses, and offices had fallen into ruin after only a few decades of neglect, and it had been protected by a weather control dome. Veggieville, on the other hand, had spent four or five times that long enduring the punishment of wind, rain, and snow.

She felt gooseflesh pop out along her arms.

The previous night's moto ride had been a race along a dark, unpaved road lined on both sides by indistinct shadows. When she'd chanced to wonder what sort of structures they might be, Juno's imagination had paraded burned-out shells and tumbledown ruins before her mind's eye.

This morning she would find out what those shadows really were.

Holding her breath, she pushed aside the heavy curtain. Instantly, golden sunlight flooded the bedroom, warming the air and energizing every color it touched. Even the peaked roofs of the houses across the road gave off a rosy glow.

If the view beyond this window was typical, then Veggieville was definitely not the sort of ghost town that her teachers had described in history class. Those benighted communities, finding themselves outside the boundaries of the urban districts during the Reorganization, had been vacated by their residents, gutted of their technology by looters, vandalized by gangs and drifters, and finally left to rot. The street Juno saw below her, however, was arrow-straight and lined with homes, about ten on each side, built of stone and brick in a variety of colors. Despite being weather-worn, each of these residences looked tidy and well-maintained. Every window was intact and glinting in the sun. Every door was painted a different hue. Except for their obvious age and the fact that the architecture varied from building to building, these houses might have been transplanted here from any urban district in Americas.

"It's an enclave," she breathed.

"It's a town," Angeli corrected her, and Juno could swear she heard a smile in the other girl's voice. "There are hundreds more just like it all across Americas. Now, you'd better shut the drapes and put on some clothes before Carlos gets here. It's a fifteen-minute walk to the dining hall. Remember what he told us last night: breakfast is served at seven-thirty sharp, tables are cleared at eight, and latecomers go hungry, no exceptions. So you'd better hurry up or we'll leave you to find your own way there," she concluded sharply.

Angeli was already dressed, wearing the same dirt-brown trousers as yesterday, paired this morning with a muddy-green long-sleeved top.

Juno flung her bag down on her side of the bed and began rifling through it for something appropriate to wear. Angeli hadn't left her much to choose from. Finally she settled on a pair of denim jeans and a mustard-colored blouse with matching sash.

The other girl stared critically at the shoes Juno had picked out. "Those flimsy things will be ruined in the first twenty minutes," she said, not unkindly. "I brought an extra pair of boots for you. Treated leather. If they fit, wear them. If they don't fit, wear them anyway. We're supposed to be blending in, and it's better if people are smiling to your face rather than doing it behind your back."

Smiling to her face? Juno wasn't sure about that.

Every Eligible schoolchild came out to the Food Production Zone on at least one excursion — to tour a greenhouse, pick some fruit, eat a specially prepared meal, and visit the souvenir shop before piling back on board a chartered MPV. Even as early as first grade, Olivia had suspected a hoax. The travel time had seemed far too short, for one thing, and the students had been met by too many manically grinning faces. It wasn't normal for anyone to be that happy about having MPVloads of little kids invade their space for a whole afternoon. And she couldn't recall a single person on those field trips, not the students and not the food workers who greeted them, having to wear treated leather boots.

— «» —

The dining hall was a low wooden building set in the middle of a huge muddy field on the southern edge of town. Beside each of the three entrances sat a row of bristly fiber mats. As Juno took a turn at one of them, scraping the worst of the dirt off her soles before going inside, she had to admit that Angeli had been right. The uppers were stiff and the heels chafed a little, but boots were the most practical footwear for a place like this.

The hall contained a dozen long tables flanked by wooden benches, and the benches were filling up quickly. As Carlos led the way to his personal table in the corner — this one square and surrounded by actual chairs — the curious looks Juno had braced herself to ignore never materialized. In fact, people seemed to be doing their best to avoid making eye contact with her.

"Are they afraid of us?" she wondered aloud once the three of them were seated.

"Some of them are," said Carlos. "When new workers arrive, it generally means others will be leaving. Anyone who has been here for more than three years is liable to be transferred. And Ineligibles have to pay full price when they travel or move house. It's written right into their work contract with the Regional Council."

"The workers are responsible for the cost of the move? But what if they don't have enough in their credit account to cover the expenses?"

Angeli replied after a beat, "Then they have a hard decision to make."

Juno's next question died on her tongue as the doors at the far end of the room burst noisily open. A platoon of servers marched through them in formation, carrying platters of food, metal mugs and plates, and white enameled pitchers.

Reflexively she looked downward. The servers were all wearing boots.

In less than a minute, each table had been loaded up with trays of thick toast, sliced fruit, creamed cheese, and sausages, along with jugs of water and juice. And every eye in the room had then turned toward the corner where Carlos sat, not yet touching any of the food in front of him.

Hands remained folded in more than two hundred laps. For a moment, Juno wondered why. Then, with a sudden lump in her throat, she understood. The workers were waiting for permission to eat. Those people who had pointedly looked elsewhere as the three of them had passed weren't just afraid of receiving a transfer order — they hadn't wanted to be seen as challenging the most powerful person in Veggieville. Carlos Calvera was clearly the ruler here, the man who provided the tables and everything on them, and every worker knew it.

"When I pick up my fork, the rest of them will scramble to fill their plates. Serve yourselves quickly," Carlos advised them in an undertone, "and take everything you need in a single helping. Breakfast is the only free meal of the day here, so the food tends to go fast."

"What about lunch and dinner?" asked Juno.

"Those have to be earned by putting in a day's work," Carlos replied. "I'll give you your assignments later. Now, no more talking. Let's eat." And he reached past her and speared two plump sausages at once.

— «» —

"You're splitting us up? That wasn't the deal, Carlos," Angeli informed him darkly.

He looked unconcerned. "Perhaps. But it's my standard operating procedure. Maybe, if you'd been a little more flexible about *your* standard operating procedure yesterday..."

"This is about those three families going to Breadbasket?" she sputtered. "You're punishing us for a decision our driver made?"

"I am," he replied, "and there's nothing you can do about it. Out of the goodness of my heart, I've given you breakfast. Now it's time for you to earn your lunch and dinner. Between now and eight-thirty, wagons are departing the plaza every five minutes for the fields. The overseer of field number twelve is expecting you, so don't be late. Meanwhile, I'll escort Juno to the schoolhouse to assist Isabela. Or would you rather the assignments were switched?" he added, raising a forefinger in warning when he saw Angeli opening her mouth to object.

Standing outside the dining hall with the two of them, being jostled by workers bustling single-mindedly around them, Juno listened to this exchange with a deepening sense of foreboding.

Dennis Forrand might be the Supreme Adjudicator for Americas and occupy a seat on the Earth High Council, but Carlos Calvera held the power in Veggieville, and he clearly enjoyed wielding it. Today he was using it to derail Forrand's carefully laid plans. He had to know there would be repercussions later on. At the moment, however, all that seemed to matter to him was that he was in control and Forrand's people were powerless to oppose him. Despite her brave thoughts earlier about abandoning her guide and striking out on her own, it was rapidly becoming clear to Juno that she and Angeli were not in friendly territory right now. They would need to stay together, relying on each other for safety, at least until Veggieville was behind them.

"Angeli?" she ventured.

"Go earn your daily bread, Juno," she replied, staring at Carlos with eyes that glittered like polished blue stones. "I'll see you later."

CHAPTER 3

Juno trudged along silently behind Carlos, out of one torn-up field and halfway across another, to the building that housed the Veggieville school. Like the dining hall, it was low and boxy and constructed of weather-beaten wood, with cross-bracing visible on the outside of each wall. Juno counted the windows as she and Carlos approached. There were four, most likely one per classroom; and judging by the mud that surrounded it like a moat, this school hadn't been standing for very long.

About twelve strides from the front door, Carlos paused to let her catch up.

"Let me give you the FAQs," he said briskly. "We have 146 students ranging in age from four to fourteen years old, and five teachers on staff, all Council-certified. This is not our first school. The original building was three stories high, stone-clad, and nearly an hour's walk from the current settlement. When that school burned down, about two years ago, we built this one using materials salvaged from the surrounding area. The first school was named for someone the residents evidently admired. We would like to continue the tradition someday, but for now it's just the Veggieville school. Shall we go inside?" he concluded, with an insincere smile and an ushering wave of his hand.

Juno had fully expected that it would be called the Carlos Calvera School. Fortunately, discretion prevailed and she kept this thought to herself.

After wiping their boot soles on the mandatory coarse fiber mat, they stepped through the front door into a narrow hallway punctuated with five more doors, all different from one another. The washroom door at the end of the hall was labeled with male and female stick figures. The rest were numbered from one to four. Two of these looked to be made of wood, and one had a faceted knob shaped like a huge transparent crystal. The second door on the right — a solid slab of metal, plaincoated dark green and fitted with a long, vertical steel handle — could have come from Juno's old high school in Clearmeadow Enclave. As if on cue, the door swung away, and Isabela Bakshi leaned through the opening and beckoned to them.

She stepped back to let Juno enter. There was room for Carlos to pass through as well, but he chose to remain out in the hall. He looked stiff and uncomfortable, Juno thought with surprise.

"Mrs. Bakshi, this is Juno Vargas," he said, introducing her as though they were strangers meeting for the first time. "She is going to be your classroom assistant."

His voice hardened abruptly around the last two words. Juno glanced up, saw Isabela's dark eyes shooting daggers at him, and repressed a shudder.

This was not shaping up to be a fun day.

Without another word, Carlos left. A moment later Mrs. Bakshi was walking a circle around her new assistant, looking her up and down. And frowning.

Juno's heart dropped. Her first meeting with Carlos's sister had been a rush to get the visitors indoors and settled for the night. Nonetheless, she had sensed warmth and kindness coming from this woman. Now it was gone, seemingly drained from her by the rough wooden walls and battered furniture of the classroom. In her small, cozy kitchen, Isabela had been a welcoming hostess. Here, she was clearly an educator, about to deliver a lesson.

Juno had a good idea what the gist of it would be. Like her brother, she had chafed under the demands and restrictions of the Relocation Authority, often trying the patience of the adults in her life. She had faced disapproving teachers before — and this one didn't even know her. Preparing herself for a barrage of criticism, Juno clenched her jaw and stared at the vinyl-covered floor of the classroom. She waited. At last she heard Isabela remark, "I guess you'll do."

Warily, she raised her eyes to meet Mrs. Bakshi's gaze.

"Well," Isabela prompted impatiently, "are you ready to be a teaching assistant or not?"

Carlos's sister was tall and slender, with elegant cheekbones and thick dark hair that today was gathered and twisted into a knot at the crown of her head. Even swathed in baggy clothing and without a trace of makeup on her face, she was a very attractive woman. Being related to Carlos also made her a powerful woman. While waiting for Juno's response to her question, Isabela had drawn herself up. She now stood regally erect, with her arms folded over her chest as though daring the new girl to disappoint her.

Juno stifled a knee-jerk moment of rebellion. "I'm ready to earn my dinner," she replied at last, wincing inwardly as the words came out a little more sharply than she had intended.

Isabela tilted her head and uncrossed her arms, but her lips were pursed. She'd caught the defiant tone of Juno's voice and obviously didn't like it.

"And you would prefer to do it in some other fashion?" she demanded. "Why? Do you feel this work is beneath you?"

"No, I just—"

"Or perhaps it's the whole idea of working that repels you. Is that it? Do you feel superior to the rest of us and resent having to get your hands dirty with any kind of honest labor?"

Juno's skin went prickly. Isabela's voice had risen, her cheeks were flushed, and her eyes were hard and glittering. Olivia Townsend had never been physically struck in anger; but for Juno Vargas here in Veggieville, anything was possible — especially now, with Angeli off in a field somewhere and not a witness in sight.

"That's not it!" she yelped, taking a step backward. "I don't mind the work!"

"Then why are you so ill-tempered? Be truthful, *chica*."

Recalling the tension that had earlier chilled the air between Carlos and his sister, Juno inhaled deeply and took a leap of faith. "I don't like being controlled. And I hate it when people break their word."

"Ah! So we are of the same mind. Tell me, have I made promises to you?"

"No."

"Then I cannot possibly have broken any. Have I demanded your obedience? Have I threatened you to get it?"

She was right — she hadn't. Carlos was the one who had done all that. In a flash of insight, Juno realized that it might even have been the reason his sister was so upset with him.

Isabela didn't wait to hear an apology. "In about twenty minutes this room will be filled with students," she pointed out, "and we are both going to be very busy. So, let us begin again. Are you ready to be a teaching assistant?"

Juno straightened her shoulders. "What do you want me to do?"

This time the head-tilt was accompanied by a smile. "That's much better. Each morning, I teach the thirteen- and fourteen-year-olds, and in the afternoons, I have the twelve-year-olds. These students are close to graduation. They spend half the day in school and the other half working to earn their keep."

Funny — Juno couldn't recall seeing any youngsters in the dining hall that morning. Then it hit her: there had to be a second breakfast service. That would explain why the tables were cleared at eight o'clock sharp, and why school didn't begin for nearly an hour after that.

"They earn their keep? Doing what?"

"Whatever they are good at. Some of them will never be more than general field hands. But students with useful talent are apprenticed out at the age of ten and, with luck and a lot of hard work, will have a trade when they leave us. Just as Veggieville and the other communities are not officially residential areas, our school is not part of a standardized educational system. We are lucky to have five teachers here. Some places have only one, or none at all. There is no prescribed curriculum to follow. We do our best to equip these children with literacy and numeracy skills, instill a work ethic, and go over all twenty pages of the Council's employment contract in class to make certain that students understand what they are signing."

"But what if some of them qualify as—" Juno hesitated. Angeli had threatened dire consequences if she so much as mentioned the 'E' word aloud. "—able to do more. To be more than a field hand or a tradesperson."

"You think our children are screened for Eligibility? I hate to disappoint you, *chica*, but that only happens in the urban districts. And any of our young ones who are urban-born, even to Eligible parents, are written off by the Council the moment they cross The Flats."

— «» —

It wasn't fair. Juno chewed slowly on her cheese and lettuce sandwich and thought about the students she had worked with in Mrs. Bakshi's morning class. Yelena with the dazzling smile, whose caricatures and cartoons made everyone laugh, but who was preparing to sign on as kitchen help for the next three years of her life. Terry and Mac, identical twin brothers with fiery red hair, who dreamed of exploring the oceans but would probably never get to see one. Rachel, who sang with such joy and with the voice of an angel, and who deserved to be heard by a much larger audience than her fellow field workers. An entire class of bright, curious young people who would never be able to realize their dreams or their potential because the Relocation Authority had deemed them unworthy of opportunity.

The morning's lessons hadn't been at all what Juno expected. She was accustomed to sharing a school with hundreds of kids fairly oozing the brash entitlement of Eligibility. Here in the "industrial wilderness", she'd been struck by the quiet respect these teens showed to their teacher as they filed in and took their seats, and by their shy politeness when Isabela introduced her as the new classroom assistant.

But there had been even more surprises to come.

The first subject of the day was literacy. Mrs. Bakshi reached into a desk drawer and pulled out something Juno had heard about but had never actually seen — a bound hard copy book. This one was dog-eared and blackened around the edges, and Isabela turned it briefly to show Juno the cover. She recognized the title. It was *Animal Farm* by George

Orwell. Olivia Townsend had once begun reading that novel but had found it boring and juvenile and had deleted it from her personal library.

For nearly an hour, this single book was carefully passed from student to student. Each of them took a turn reading a page aloud to the others, then summarizing what it said. Meanwhile, Isabela made a vocabulary list on the blackboard. After all the reading was done, she asked the students to come up with probable definitions for each word, based on the part of the story that they had just heard.

In an enclave school, there would have been follow-up questions requiring students to practice a whole raft of critical thinking skills; but Isabela had evidently decided to let these teens draw their own conclusions. Considering how closely their situation paralleled the one in the book, that was probably the wisest course to take. Olivia hadn't given herself a chance to fully appreciate the novel; Juno figured that the image of Carlos with the face of a pig was going to be difficult to erase from her mind.

Next on the schedule was numeracy. Juno recalled the math classes at Clearmeadow High School and couldn't imagine solving problems without a compupad in her hand. To her astonishment, the students in Mrs. Bakshi's class were able to estimate crop yields, figure out profits and losses, and manage a credit account, doing all the calculations in their heads. When Juno praised one of them for it, he shrugged and replied, "You just have to turn on the computer inside your brain."

Then came current events—a sharing of worldwide news items, not one of which Juno could recall seeing or hearing about on the InfoCommNet. A strike by waste management workers in a district in Indo-Asia over unsafe conditions that had already cost more than fifteen lives. A power plant accident that had killed forty people and injured many more in the League of African Nations. A storm that had ripped through a pineapple plantation in Pacifica, resulting in twenty-eight confirmed dead and another dozen missing and presumed dead. Every casualty was an Ineligible. A disturbing thought occurred to Juno then, but before she could examine it she heard Isabela calling her to the front of the room.

Smiling, Mrs. Bakshi explained to the students that the new teaching assistant was to be the highlight of today's current events class — a special guest speaker who would describe what it was like to be a teen living in an urban district. Juno's stomach turned a slow cartwheel as she looked at all those curious faces. They were thirsting to know what life was like on the other side of The Flats, and she had just begun to realize how little she could tell them about it.

Carefully avoiding the 'E' word — and anything else that might sound as though she were "flaunting her wealth" — Juno plucked an uneventful week from her memory and did her best to describe it. When she was finished, hands shot up in the air. The students had questions — well-framed, thoughtful questions. It embarrassed her now to recall them and admit to herself how poorly she had answered them.

These youngsters had intelligence and talent. Given a proper education, they might achieve great things. They could enrich the world. Instead, all they had to look forward to was spending the rest of their lives being shuffled around the various industrial zones like pieces on a game board, performing manual labor or — if they were lucky — working in the skilled trades. All because of the Relocation Authority.

Lunch had arrived promptly at noon, carried on a horse-drawn wagon. Eight boxes of sandwiches, four kegs of juice, and two large baskets of pears had been brought inside and parceled out to the four classrooms.

Juno had been surprised at how hungry she was. Nonetheless, "Have I earned this meal?" she'd wondered aloud.

Isabela had laughed softly. "Of course you have. Learning is hard work."

So that was what she'd been doing, Juno thought ruefully — learning what a privileged life she'd led, and how truly uneducated it had left her.

They ate in silence for a while. Then Isabela remarked, "You look very pensive, *chica*. You must have questions. This is the time to ask them."

Juno washed down the last of her sandwich with a swallow of apple juice. "The hard copy book the students have been reading — where did it come from?"

"I found it in the library of the old school building."

"The one that burned down?"

"Yes. It was struck by lightning, something you don't have to worry about under a weather control dome. Out here we need rain for the crops in the field, so we're at the mercy of the elements."

"But you could set up a weather shield and put in irrigation pipes," Juno argued. "Then you wouldn't have to worry about lightning either."

Isabela smiled indulgently at her. "There's a reason we remain low-tech, *chica*. Weather control technology is costly to run, and irrigation systems need to be installed and maintained. Why go to that much trouble and expense when Mother Nature provides the water for free? We're not stupid — we make sure all the structures of the settlement are grounded — but there's no point sticking a lightning rod on a crumbling old wreck located kilometers away down the road. That was what Carlos called it, anyway," she concluded, no longer smiling as a faraway look came into her eyes.

"All those books, printed in ink, on paper. Hard copy requires no special technology, only sufficient light to read by. That was why we set up our classes in that old school in the first place. Most of the electronics had been stripped out of it long before Veggieville was established, but the books on the shelves had been left alone. What a treasure! It gave me the idea for a community library — a meeting place that had nothing to do with sleeping or eating or working. A dining hall for the mind. So, I convinced Carlos to apply for a credit grant to erect a new building.

"Meanwhile, the five of us teachers began sorting through the school's collection to identify and pack up all the books that were still in good enough condition to be handled. Our plan was to move them to temporary storage near the construction site. But there were so many of them." She let out a brief sigh of regret. "We worked as quickly as we could. Unfortunately, we weren't fast enough."

"The lightning struck?" Juno guessed.

"Yes. As soon as we saw that orange glow against the sky, we knew. We raced to the fire and saved as many books as we could, but hundreds of titles literally went up in flames that day. Shortly afterward, our construction grant was approved. So, instead of a nearly empty library, Veggieville got a brand-new school."

"It's still a dining hall for the mind," Juno pointed out, "only the minds belong to children and the books are inside the teachers' heads. And Carlos must have seen the value in it, or he would have put the credits to some other use."

A smile tugged at the corners of Isabela's mouth. "Carlos didn't really have a choice in the matter. I told him that I held him personally responsible for the loss of the old school, and if he didn't replace it I was going to have the teachers conduct their classes inside his house instead. Did you enjoy *Animal Farm* this morning, *chica*? I made a point of rescuing that book. If you hold it close to your nose, you can still smell the smoke."

— «» —

"You don't look good."

"I'll live," muttered Angeli, easing herself onto the bench across the dining hall table from Juno. "It takes more than a loudmouth with a stick to put a Fo— to put a person like me off her game."

"Careful," Juno teased. "You nearly gave away your last name."

"I told you, I don't have one." Angeli glanced up gratefully as a server set a pot of something savory down in front of her and handed her the ladle. She quickly took two full scoops of what looked and smelled like a delicious beef stew before handing off the serving spoon to the man beside her. Then she grabbed one of the last chunks of bread off a tray that had just been delivered.

"Was the overseer expecting you, like Carlos said?" Juno wanted to know.

Angeli started to shrug her shoulders but apparently changed her mind. "He was waiting for me, all right," she replied darkly. "Made me cultivate a whole field by myself. Beets, I think. So that was my day. What was yours like?"

"I told a bunch of kids about a way of life that they'll probably never get to have. I felt really stupid a lot of the time. After school I helped Isabela clean up the classroom for tomorrow morning. Mopped the floor. Wiped down the blackboard. And I learned a few things."

"Oh? Like what?" she asked between mouthfuls.

The ladle had finally made its way around the table. As Juno leaned forward, a little surprised to find a full serving of stew still left for her in the pot, she commented casually, "I learned that Isabela doesn't like Carlos."

Angeli stopped chewing long enough to utter a snort of laughter. "Nobody likes Carlos."

"But she's his sister."

"We don't choose our family, Juno. Just because two people are related to each other, that doesn't mean they have to be friends as well. Finish your dinner," she urged. "We still have something to do before we can go back to the house." In response to Juno's blank stare, Angeli prompted, "Have you seen Ronny since last night?"

"Ronny?"

"Our driver. We're supposed to check in with him each day. We make sure he's all right, he makes sure we're all right, and then he uses the MPV's comm unit to update Forrand on our progress. You didn't think the Supreme Adjudicator would simply hand over a fully-fueled longcar and send us off to explore for a year without putting some sort of monitoring in place, did you?"

Guilt pierced Juno as she realized that not only had she not seen the driver all day, she hadn't even thought about him — or about Angeli, for that matter. She felt even worse an hour later, when they arrived at the debarkation point where the MPV was supposed to be parked.

The area was empty. Both driver and vehicle were gone.

CHAPTER 4

With daylight waning and the temperature perceptibly dropping, Angeli and Juno stood at the center of the area bounded by lampposts — the plaza, Carlos had called it — where they had disembarked from the MPV less than twenty-four hours earlier. The longcar was nowhere in sight, meaning that its driver was missing as well.

As Angeli had finally explained, Ronny was under strict orders never to leave the vehicle unattended — the synthesized fuel in its storage tank alone was worth a fortune. Equipped with a washroom and a sleeping alcove, the MPV was to be his home for the next twelve months. Forrand had even made provisions for all the driver's meals to be delivered to him at the various stops on the itinerary.

"He wouldn't simply abandon us here, would he?" A cool breeze swept across the plaza, raising gooseflesh on Juno's arms. And the thought of being stuck in Veggieville under the thumb of the universally disliked Carlos Calvera was sending additional shivers down her spine.

Angeli's scowl deepened. "No. Not without telling us where he was going and when to expect him back. Look," she said, and Juno stepped closer to see what she was pointing at. "The ground has been raked, probably to cover up tire tracks. Someone doesn't want us to know where the longcar has been taken."

"Maybe Carlos borrowed it to transport those three families to Breadbasket," Juno offered.

Angeli shot her a withering look. "Borrowing without permission is called theft. And if you're right and Ronny was a willing accomplice, then he's crossing a Supreme

Adjudicator and can expect to have his ass handed to him when Forrand hears about this."

"Are you sure he'll hear about it?" Juno asked nervously. As Isabela had earlier informed her, Veggieville was low-tech. She'd seen no evidence so far of the InfoCommNet, so the settlement had to communicate with the outside world in some other way, one that Carlos undoubtedly controlled.

Deepening shadows made Angeli's determined expression look even grimmer than Juno felt at that moment. "Trust me," she said, "Forrand has been watching over you your whole life. He's not about to lose you in a turnip field. Or a classroom. All right, let's get back to the house. We can't do much more in the dark, but I'll snoop around tomorrow morning and see what I can find."

— «» —

Angeli had already left the house when Juno opened her eyes the following morning. Her sleep had been rest-less, broken up by dreams that eluded her memory but had left behind a persistent residue of fear and indigna-tion. Yawning, Juno slipped out of bed and into the cloth-ing she'd laid out the night before. Then, pausing only long enough to brush her teeth — the rest of her morning toilette would have made her late for breakfast — she hurried to the dining hall, hoping to run into Angeli and hear some good news.

There was no sign of the other girl at any of the tables. Robbed of her appetite, Juno chewed thoughtfully on a cold sausage, took a few sips of apple juice, and waited until the last possible minute to head over to the schoolhouse.

Isabela kept her busy all day, giving her no chance even to think about anyone outside the classroom. Evidently, the time for friendly conversation was over as well. During the lunch break, Mrs. Bakshi graded students' tests while Juno prepared the room for the afternoon session. Any questions she might have had about Veggieville or its inhabitants were firmly put on hold.

By dinnertime she was exhausted. She dragged herself over to the dining hall and dropped down onto the bench nearest the door. Glancing up as another weary body sank with a groan onto the seat directly opposite her, Juno stared in shock when she realized who it was.

Angeli looked terrible. Her face was ghostly pale except for a splash of heat on each cheek. Her expression was taut, her mouth a short, straight line. And there were marks on her arms that might have been dirt but suspiciously resembled bruises. If she'd been in a fight, there were probably more of them beneath her clothing.

Swallowing hard to clear the lump that had risen in her throat, Juno leaned across the table and asked, "Did you have any luck?"

In response, Angeli straightened her shoulders and darted cautious looks at the rapidly filling benches around them. "Some. Then Carlos caught me poking around the machine sheds and personally escorted me to my work assignment."

"More beets?"

The other girl's lips quirked briefly. "Lettuce and spinach. The hydroponic greenhouses are even farther away from the settlement than the fields are. And just to teach me a lesson, he left orders that I was to walk back here instead of riding in the wagon."

"He was hoping you'd be too late to get any dinner."

"Or too tired to eat it." She shifted her weight on the bench, wincing with pain.

"What's the matter?" asked Juno, alarmed.

"It's nothing. A muscle strain," Angeli assured her. "I'll be fine. Stop looking so worried."

"Can I *feel* worried, at least?"

"You can feel whatever you want, as long as you don't draw attention to us. We need to take a walk after dinner, just you and I. I think I've found our MPV."

— «» —

Angeli was in pain. Juno could see it in the careful way she moved and hear it in every word she spoke. This was more than a simple muscle strain. It might be a broken rib, or internal bleeding, or both.

Dinner — a thick lentil stew containing barley, carrots, potatoes and onions — had been eaten in silence. Angeli had taken just a single ladleful. She'd chewed and swallowed each mouthful slowly, as though unsure whether it would stay down, and had wordlessly shaken her head when Juno had tried to pass her one of the fresh-baked rolls that accompanied the meal.

"You need to be seen by a doctor," Juno informed her as they pretended to stroll casually toward the rows of boxlike buildings where the field hands lived. Angeli kept her arms crossed while walking, pressing both hands to the sides of her ribcage as if she feared it might spring apart.

"Yes, I do," she agreed, speaking deliberately through clenched teeth. "And since the nearest real doctor is at the hospital in Breadbasket, fifty-five kilometers away, that makes finding our MPV and its driver our top priority at the moment."

"You're sure it's inside one of the big mechanical sheds?"

"I looked through a window and saw a shadow that was the same size and shape as our longcar. Then Carlos grabbed me. So, no, I'm not absolutely sure. But it's the best guess I've got."

Conversation ceased as they concentrated on moving unseen from shadow to deepening shadow. Once past the worker housing, they stole across a broad field conveniently studded with thick shrubs and the broken remains of stone fences. At last they came in sight of the three metal-clad sheds lined up beside the plaza, just in time to watch the circle of tall overhead lights turn on.

Angeli dropped down behind a slab of rotting wood that had once been a gate. It stood at an angle, its posts now leaning crazily in opposite directions.

Juno gasped as the other girl grabbed her arm and pulled her to her knees in the grass. "Is someone there?" she whispered. "Were we seen?"

"I don't think so," Angeli whispered back. "Those lights are probably on a timer. In any case, it'll be pitch dark soon, so we'd better move fast. According to the field hands, Carlos keeps the settlement's various vehicles in the two large sheds closest to the plaza. The smaller one at the end is the repair shop. It's supposed to be empty right now. But it's the one

I was peeking into when Carlos caught me this morning, so that's the one we need to get inside first."

"But if he knows you saw where the MPV was hidden, wouldn't he have moved it by now? Or drained it of fuel?" Juno added, recalling what Angeli had told her earlier.

"One problem at a time. Let's just focus on finding the longcar for now. These buildings are the only ones in Veggieville large enough to hold something that size. If it isn't in the third shed, then it'll be sharing space with a bunch of horse-drawn wagons in one of the other two. Let's go." With that, Angeli heaved herself back onto her feet and began to walk.

Night had fallen. By now it lay over the land like a blanket, admitting only the grudging light of a half-moon that made Angeli's pallor less startling and details like doors and windows much less distinct. In the absence of visual distractions, the older girl's strained breathing was impossible to ignore.

"You need to stop and rest," said Juno, trailing behind her and becoming more anxious with every passing minute.

"Resting won't help me. I need a trauma doctor. We have to find the MPV and make sure Ronny is with it, and then we have to get out of here tonight," she said in a voice so hoarse and labored that it was barely recognizable.

"What if he's not there? Can we leave without him?"

Angeli winced. "No. We need his thumbprint to unlock the starter."

By now, urgency was gripping Juno like a fist, making it difficult for her to take a full breath. The uneven ground around the sheds didn't help. It forced them to slow their pace, and that increased Angeli's distress. Every few steps she gasped with pain; and with each gasp, the fist around Juno seemed to tighten a little more. At last they arrived beside the building where Carlos had probably concealed their MPV.

"Well, the good news is that all the plaza lights are on the other side of the shed, so as long as we keep at least one wall between us and them, nobody can see what we're doing," Juno reported.

"And the bad news?"

"I can't see what I'm doing either."

Angeli's syllable of laughter died in a moan. Juno eased her down to the ground, then felt her way along the corrugated metal wall of the building. She stopped when she came to a window. Like the windows of the schoolhouse, this one had been transplanted from a much older structure. Juno's fingers found the ledge first, then the ridges lathed into the wooden frame of the sash. She pushed up experimentally and confirmed what she'd already suspected — the window was locked. Pressing her forehead to the glass, she strained to see inside, but it was too dark to discern anything.

Angeli let out a feeble groan, and Juno's heart rose into her throat. It was up to her now. They were each other's only ally in a dangerous situation and they had to get out of it together. Going back to the settlement to find help was no longer an option. Time was running out. Juno had to locate the longcar and take Angeli to the hospital right away.

She was sure there must be a people-sized door to this shed; and if it was as old as the doors in the schoolhouse, then it might not have a lock built into it.

"Stay where you are," she hissed to Angeli. "I'm going to look for an entrance."

Juno continued to feel her way around the exterior of the building. On the side facing the plaza, she found a large square piece of metal set into the wall — probably a way in, but it was useless without a knob or handle to open it.

And she was casting a shadow against it. Juno hurried to round the next corner. As she dashed into the inky space between the two structures, something hard smacked into her hip. Juno spun, lost her footing, and fell backward to the ground. She stayed down for a moment, catching her breath. Then she noticed a familiar silhouette above her, outlined by the glow from the lampposts.

Handlebars.

She'd run into Carlos's moto. Angeli had been right. The MPV had to be inside this shed, taking up all the room. There was no other possible explanation for someone like Carlos to leave his personal transportation unattended outside.

Her bumps and bruises forgotten, Juno scrambled to her feet. Like everything else in this town, the moto was a patchwork of old parts. With luck, it wouldn't be equipped with a thumbprint lock. She pulled the vehicle by its handlebars into the pale light bleeding off the plaza and pressed the starter, nearly cheering out loud when the engine rumbled loudly to life.

There wasn't a minute to spare now. Isabela would almost certainly have noticed their absence; and if Carlos had been alerted, he was already on his way to the sheds.

Driving the moto to the other side of the building, Juno found Angeli sitting against the wall. She assisted the older girl into the sidecar, moving her carefully to avoid worsening her injuries. It took long, agonizing seconds. Juno struggled to breathe normally as she made Angeli comfortable. Then she straddled the machine again.

"Juno Vargas! Show yourself!"

Carlos had arrived. For just a moment, she hesitated. Then she glanced at Angeli, who appeared to be losing consciousness, and made her decision. Borrowing without permission might be theft, but this was an emergency, and he'd left them no other choice. Juno turned the moto and steered it around the corner of the building.

Carlos was standing in the middle of the plaza, flanked by a couple of large male friends. Juno swallowed hard. She would have to dodge all three of them.

"Where do you think you're going with my property, *chiquita*?"

"I'm taking Angeli to the hospital. She needs medical care right away." Then, speaking privately to her passenger, she added, "When I get to the road, which direction? Left or right?"

Weakly, the other girl pointed right.

"You're not stealing my moto," warned Carlos. All three men moved a step closer to her.

"You're right," replied Juno with a firmness she didn't really feel. "I'm borrowing it, just like you've borrowed our MPV. So let's trade vehicles and Angeli and I will be on our way."

"No deal! The longcar stays here as collateral against the rent you owe me."

For Juno this was the final straw. She'd wasted enough of Angeli's precious time arguing with this jerk. "Fine," she spat. "Hang onto the MPV, then, and clear a path, because we're leaving. I'm not going to let this woman die just because you've decided to make a career out of being a cold-hearted son of a bitch." And with that, she put the moto in forward gear and drove directly at Carlos.

Like a matador in the bullring, he raised his arms and sidestepped her charge. Incredibly, Juno heard laughter behind her, and shouts of *"Brava!"*

What was wrong with these men? This was a life or death situation, and they were playing stupid games. Although it would have given her immense satisfaction at that moment to go back and knock Carlos flying with his own moto, saving Angeli was more important. Juno hunkered over the handlebars and aimed for the road.

"It's okay, Juno," said Angeli's voice beside her. It sounded remarkably strong coming from someone who'd been so close to expiring just seconds earlier. "It's over. Turn this thing around."

Bewildered, Juno glanced at her passenger. Angeli was sitting up in the sidecar, fully conscious and smiling. "I don't understand," she stammered. "You had broken ribs, internal bleeding."

"You had to think I did," Angeli told her, "so your reaction would be authentic. The truth is, I was never actually in danger."

So her injuries hadn't been real? It had all been a pretense? A con? Blinking back tears, Juno returned the moto to the center of the plaza. The three men came to stand around her. Incredibly, they were applauding, as though her fear and desperation had been some kind of performance put on for their entertainment. How could they do this to her? How *dare* they?

"Well done, *chica*," declared Carlos.

"I'm so glad I was able to amuse you," she said, cracking each word at him like a whip as she visualized herself chasing him down and squashing him under the moto's wheels.

"This was not a practical joke, Juno. It was a test, ordered up by Forrand to make sure you were ready for what lies ahead," said Angeli. "And you've passed it with flying colors."

If they thought this would mollify her, they were wrong. "So, Forrand is a cold-hearted son of a bitch too?" she demanded sharply.

Angeli and Carlos exchanged worried looks.

"Okay, we understand why you're angry—" she said.

"You can't begin to understand me," Juno informed her, with difficulty keeping all emotion out of her voice as she dismounted from the moto. "But you will, especially when Ronny and I leave here without you tomorrow. I trusted you, Angeli. I won't make that mistake again. And I refuse to travel with people I don't trust."

"Can I at least give you a lift—?" Carlos offered.

She silenced him with an icy stare and began walking back to Isabela's house in the dark.

CHAPTER 5

"I knew something like this would happen." Mrs. Bakshi placed a cup of mint tea in front of her young guest before sitting down across the table from her. "When Angeli told me your age, I had a bad feeling right away. And yesterday, when you said how much you detested being controlled and lied to, that only confirmed it."

Juno felt a laggard tear trickle down her cheek and wiped it off with the back of her hand. Then she leaned forward and blew gently across the top of the steaming beverage to help it cool. "Was that why you were so mad at Carlos?"

"I warned him not to push you too soon. I told him you needed a few more days to settle in, but he insisted that you could take it. After all, what would a schoolteacher possibly know about young people?" Smiling, Isabela continued, "Well, it turns out that he was right. You not only took it, you also threw it right back at them. Do you know where Carlos and Angeli are right now?"

"I don't know and I don't care," she declared emphatically. "I hate both of them."

"They followed you here, *chica*, and they are sitting on the front porch at this moment, afraid to come inside."

Surprised, Juno blurted, "They're afraid of *me*?"

"They're not sure what you might do the next time you see them. When you unleashed your rage, you took away any power they had over you. These tears you've shed all over my kitchen table are nothing to be ashamed of. They are tears of anger, and anger is where we women get our power."

Funny — Juno didn't feel like a grown woman right now, let alone one with power. She recalled stamping her way across the fields in the dark, muttering vengeful threats under her breath, then standing for long minutes working up the courage to knock on Isabela's front door. She'd had no idea what to expect when it opened. But at the sight of Mrs. Bakshi's outstretched arms and broad smile of relief, something inside Juno had given way; and she'd fallen, weeping, into that welcoming embrace.

"Power doesn't work the same way for men," Isabela told her. "That is why they don't understand us. For a man, power is something he earns by conquest — by defeating a rival or overcoming an obstacle. He sets an expectation of victory for himself, and then he achieves it. And that makes him feel that he's in control of his world."

"And for a woman?"

"A woman's power lies in being unpredictable. Shrugging off the expectations of others and making our own independent choices — that is what makes us feel in control of *our* world. And if you *feel* in control, then you *are* in control."

"So, I can overcome obstacles and achieve a position of power but still not feel in control?"

"Unfortunately, yes, but only if you continue to play by men's rules once you've gained your high status. One day you will decide that you've had enough of their silly competitions and challenges — and their ridiculous expectations — and you will experience anger. Not the hot kind of anger that makes you throw something across a room or yell at someone for being careless. The emotion I am talking about is a deep, icy cold rage that lives in here," said Isabela, clapping a hand firmly to her midriff. "It is invisible to others. You are the only one who knows it exists. This inner wrath will give you the strength and courage to make unpredictable choices, and those choices will put you in control of the power that you have earned."

"It sounds as if you want me to be angry all the time."

"Not all the time, *chica*, just when it counts."

Juno smiled involuntarily, remembering how uncomfortable Carlos had looked as he stood on the threshold of Isabela's classroom, prevented from crossing it by a single frosty glare.

"Having power means having choices, but you, not your anger, must be the one making them," Mrs. Bakshi continued. "You must have felt betrayed when you realized that Angeli was only pretending to be hurt, and that Carlos was being stubborn and uncooperative just to see how you would react. But before you decide whether or not to forgive them, you need to learn why they did it."

"I know why they did it," said Juno. "They were following Forrand's orders."

"Then you need to learn why he gave those orders. People in power cannot make uninformed decisions — not if they wish to remain in power. Talk to Angeli. I advise this for two reasons: first, because she has known Forrand for a much longer time than you have and can help you to understand him; and second, because you will need her help to survive the next twelve months."

— «» —

Angeli slept in Isabela's living room that night. Juno noticed the rumpled bedclothes spread over the sofa cushions as she was leaving the house to get breakfast the following day. The walk to the dining hall in the fresh morning air gave her time to consider her situation and come to a decision. She might not trust Angeli, but she did trust Mrs. Bakshi's judgment, enough to listen, at least, to what Angeli had to say. Whether to believe it, of course, was an entirely different choice to make.

Juno paused in the entrance of the dining hall and surveyed the room. She found Angeli sitting alone and bleary-eyed at Carlos's table, propping herself up on her elbows. The older girl had evidently not slept well. That made two of them, thought Juno as she walked over and took the chair across from her. Angeli glanced up briefly, then returned her gaze to the table top.

Juno let the silence stretch between them, waiting for some kind of reaction to her presence. An apology would be preferable, she'd decided, but an acknowledgment would suffice.

Angeli didn't speak or even make eye contact until after the food had arrived. Wordlessly the two girls filled their plates from the serving dishes. Then she said, in a voice weighted down with resignation, "Ronny will drive you back to New Chicago whenever you're ready to leave."

"Who says I'm going back to New Chicago?" Juno demanded. "I passed Forrand's test — you said so yourself. He's given me a longcar, a driver, and a year's worth of fuel, and he's ordered me to expand my horizons. So, I plan to do some exploring."

That got Angeli's attention.

"Do you have an itinerary?" she asked with studied casualness.

"Actually, I was thinking I'd play it by ear. I'd like to stay in Veggieville for a while longer, tour the facilities, talk to the workers, then head to Breadbasket and see what's over there. And if Carlos wasn't lying about those three families, they can come along."

"I see." Three mouthfuls later, Angeli dropped her fork onto her plate and said, "Juno, I'm sorry. Not for testing you, but for the way we went about it. You seemed mature beyond your years, but we should have— *I* should have remembered how fragile a thing trust can be when you're just sixteen years old."

Juno continued chewing thoughtfully. Now the byplay in Forrand's office earlier was beginning to make sense — the hard looks that had passed between him and Angeli, and the way her expression had set when Olivia Townsend had entered the room.

"How old were you when you were tested?" she asked.

Angeli gazed at her across the table. "Just about your age."

"Did you pass?"

"I did." A smile spread slowly across the older girl's face. "And I was so furious at being conned that I kicked the driver off the MPV, drove it all the way back to New Chicago by myself, stomped into Forrand's office, and told him what he could do with his stupid test, in exact anatomical detail. If I'd let myself cool off first, I probably wouldn't have done it. But it seemed like a good idea at the time."

"How did he react?"

"He laughed. Then he offered me a job. I took it."

"Have you forgiven him?"

The smile faded. "Yes, now that I understand why he feels the need to test us. Do I trust him? Yes and no. Trust is like a teacup. If it breaks, you can glue it back together. It may look the same as it did before, but you'll never drink out of it again. Each time you pick it up, your eye will be drawn to a tiny crack on its surface and you'll remember it lying in pieces on the floor. I trust Dennis Forrand as much as I need to. One day I hope you'll feel the same way about me."

"You said he tests *us*?"

A pause, then, "Candidates. People who may be able to work with him and eventually step into his shoes. Powerful men like Forrand don't raise families — they groom successors and entrust them with legacies. I met the initial requirement and passed the test, but I was too headstrong and impulsive — actually, 'loose cannon' was the phrase he used — to be considered for the position of protégée."

"So instead, he put you in charge of testing and guiding other candidates?" To Juno, that sounded more like a punishment than a job.

Angeli grinned. "Not right away. First I had to spend a year on my own in the industrial zones, developing a network of contacts and learning survival skills. Urban-born Eligibles have no idea what life is like for the Ineligibles out here. You thought Carlos was being hard-hearted? There are crew chiefs and gang leaders all over the zones who make the bastard he was pretending to be look like a saint. Some bullied their way to power, while others took a back route, sniffing out and exploiting the weaknesses of others. That's why candidates have to be tested, Juno, to make sure they've got what it takes to survive the rest of the road trip."

"And I passed the test?" she said uncertainly.

"You took point when you saw that I was too weak to continue leading, and you were willing to break the law to save my life. And when Carlos and his men challenged you, you stood up to them and then charged right through them. That is exactly the way to deal with the rotten apples who have grabbed power in the industrial zones."

"I only did that because I was desperate. It's not the way I was raised to be, and it's not what I want to be known as."

"But it's what you're made of deep down, what you can become if the circumstances demand it. That's what the test reveals, to you as well as to me, and that's why it's necessary to push candidates to their limits. We both need to know we can rely on each other as well as on ourselves if we get into a tight spot once we leave Veggieville. That is," she added, settling back in her chair, "if you decide you want me to come along for the rest of the trip."

Juno wasn't ready to answer that question yet. She shrugged it off and changed the subject. "Tell me about Veggieville. It's not really like the other settlements, is it?"

"It has its own character," said Angeli. "If you're finished eating, let's go for a walk. There's something you need to see. And something important I need to tell you."

The dining hall was less than half full by now, and servers had begun clearing tables. *Getting ready to feed the children*, thought Juno as she and Angeli stepped outside, into the busy ebb and flow of field and greenhouse hands hurrying to catch their rides to work. Angeli paused briefly, then struck out in the direction of the schoolhouse, with just a momentary glance over her shoulder to confirm that Juno was following her. As they crossed the first open field, however, the older girl changed direction and slowed her pace, letting Juno catch up to her. They were now headed for the row housing where the workers lived.

"Forrand would burst a blood vessel if he heard me telling you this, but I think you have a right to know," said Angeli as they strolled. "The initial requirement for candidates that I mentioned earlier...? You have to be related to him."

Related? The word gave Juno pause. The current Supreme Adjudicator was the most disliked and powerful man in Americas. She'd known that even before she'd sought him out. Desperate times, desperate measures. However, it was one thing to strike a deal with the devil, quite another to find herself hanging from a branch of his family tree.

"So ... just how distantly *am* I related to him?" she asked, doing her best to sound only marginally interested. "Is he a cousin four times removed or something?"

"Much closer than that, actually." Angeli shot her a sideways look before continuing, "You're his granddaughter."

Momentarily speechless, Juno nearly tripped over her own feet.

"His granddaughter? Are you sure?" she finally managed to stammer.

"Beyond a doubt. Are you wishing I hadn't told you?"

"Would it matter if I said yes?"

"Not to me, but it should matter to you, and it definitely will to Forrand. Ignorance is not bliss, Juno. Where he plans to send you, it's a fatal flaw. In the halls of power, lack of information will end your career and ruin your reputation. It can even shorten your life. So, never shrink away from learning the truth.

"Dennis Forrand is entered in the database as being single and childless," Angeli went on, "but he sowed a lot of seed when he was younger. He's kept track of every child he fathered, and of their children as well. We're his legacy."

"And he's my grandfather," Juno repeated, trying the words on as though for size. They were an imperfect fit. This particular truth was going to take some getting used to, on every level. "Wait a minute," she said, coming to a halt. "If we're both related to him, that means we're related to each other. So, what are you to me?"

"It's complicated. Let's just say that we're cousins and leave it at that."

Angeli had continued walking. Rushing to catch up again, Juno asked, "And you have just one name?"

"Yes. Like you, I had to choose a new identity. I told him I wanted to be Angeli Forrand. When he flatly refused to let me use his last name, I worked myself into a temper and informed him that it would be Forrand or nothing. Something else that seemed like a good idea at the time. Anyway, I'm in the database as Angeli A. Angeli."

"What does the 'A' stand for?"

She made a wry face. "Guess. You were half-right about him, Juno. He isn't cold-hearted, but he can be a real son of a bitch at times."

"Is that why you decided to tell me he's my grandfather?"

"No. But it's a well-documented fact that loose cannons have a lot of trouble following orders unless there's a damned good reason for them. And we're here."

Juno looked up and saw a whole regiment of boxlike structures standing in formation directly in front of her. The previous day at dusk, she and Angeli had skirted the perimeter of the workers' housing, concerned only with fading into the shadows it cast. Today, Juno was seeing the actual buildings. There had to be hundreds of them, lined up in facing rows to create at least ten streets, all straight and unpaved and running parallel to one another. Metal numbers shone on each of the doors. And just like the ones on Isabela's street, each door was a different color than the ones on either side.

Juno had grown up in a neighborhood very similar to this, surrounded by tidy rows of identical, well-maintained homes. There were no PVs here, of course, and no gates with guards to keep outsiders where they belonged, but... "This is the enclave," she murmured.

"Take a closer look at the backyards," said Angeli.

They had backyards?

Juno peered down the long space between the backs of the houses on two adjoining streets and was astounded. Behind each house was a small plot of land containing a garden, and it appeared that no two of them were identical. Some were all colorful blossoms, while others had none. Most were a combination of flowers, dwarf shrubs, and vegetables, selected and arranged by whoever lived in the house. Unpredictable choices made by workers who were constantly being told — by the Council, by the Relocation Authority, and by crew chiefs and overseers like Carlos — that they had no power.

"Take a good long look," Angeli advised her. "Engrave this on your memory, Juno. This is what happens when people are treated like people instead of like interchangeable cogs in a great big machine. They take pride in their homes. They grow things that they enjoy, that make them feel happy."

"Things like babies," said Carlos's voice behind them. "This way, ladies."

They followed him to a bright blue door bearing the number 511, then waited while he knocked on it and announced himself to whoever might be inside. There was no answer. He reached into his pocket and pulled out a collection of keys on a metal ring, something else Juno had heard about but never actually seen.

"I can't discourage people from falling in love," he said, still facing the door as he flipped rapidly through the keys, isolated the one he was looking for, and shoved it into the lock. "Isabela would probably kill me if I even tried. After all, she and Vikram found each other in Veggieville." He twisted the key and swung the door open. "But there's a byproduct of lovemaking that always seems to take young people by surprise."

With that, Carlos pocketed his keys once more and entered the house, waving to Juno and Angeli to join him.

They were standing in a narrow beige hallway with plaincoated walls. Juno counted three doorways on the first floor, belonging to a washroom, a living room, and a shared bedroom respectively. A banistered wooden staircase led to a second floor landing. Everything was clean and tidy. The two single beds she could see from the hall were neatly made. The floor was polished and free of clutter. In one corner of the living room sat a lidless packing crate filled with toys.

"There's a barracks like this one on each street. This is where we billet children who are without parents," Carlos explained.

"They're orphans?" said Juno.

"No," he said sadly, "their parents are living, but not in this district. When the transfer order comes, workers have no choice but to move. If they've had children since arriving here, the transportation and moving costs may be much higher than they were before — and Ineligibles have to pay the full amount out of their credit accounts. Too often, their credit isn't sufficient to move the whole family at once, so a son or daughter old enough to require a separate seat on the MPV may be left here, to be sent for later when enough has been saved at the next posting to cover the transportation fee. The problem is, that depletes the account of the parents at the next posting, leaving them in even worse straits if they're transferred again before they've had a chance to build up enough credit to move their whole family. And you see how it goes.

"Realizing how well school-aged children are cared for in Veggieville, most parents in that situation simply leave one or two behind for us to finish raising. In a way, it's flattering; but it's also problematic having so many extra mouths to feed. Our resources are stretched pretty thin right now."

"How many of the students—?" Juno began.

"Between forty and fifty, evenly distributed among the four classes," replied Carlos. "If their parents were Eligible, the moving costs wouldn't be an issue. We tried applying to the Relocation Authority for some relief for Ineligible families being transferred, but were told to quit whining and be grateful for what we've got."

"Is there someone you can complain to? Someone higher up?" she persisted.

"I'm afraid not," he told her. "And in any case, drawing attention to Veggieville would not be a good idea. We don't want anyone on the Council looking too closely at the way we do things here. It would undermine all of Dennis Forrand's good work."

Confused, Juno stared a question at Angeli.

"Forrand feels the same way as we do about the Relocation Authority," she explained. "That's why he set up Veggieville in the first place, as a small act of rebellion against the powers that be. As soon as he was high enough up the government ladder, he hand-picked Carlos and Isabela to run things, expedited permits so proper housing could be built for the workers, quietly established a medical supply channel to keep the infirmary stocked... Basically, he turned a barebones settlement into a town with decent living conditions, then stepped aside and let the Calveras handle the on-site details. As long as the Agricultural District continues to meet its quotas and the workers' standard of living appears to be roughly the same as what's available elsewhere in the Food Production Zone, Veggieville will continue to sit in the Council's blind spot."

Juno looked around her and made a decision. If this was part of Dennis Forrand's legacy, then she definitely wanted to share in it.

— «» —

"It stinks of dead fish in here," Angeli reported, her nose wrinkling with disgust as she wiped down the back of a seat with a damp cloth.

"Well, I wasn't going to let them throw their catch into the luggage compartment. There's next to no ventilation down there," came Juno's voice from the rear of the MPV. "It'll be okay. We'll just keep the windows open for as long as possible and hope someone in the Waste Management Zone has invented a super-strength air freshener that we can trade for."

"We?" Angeli straightened up and turned in the aisle to face her. "So you've decided I can come with you after all?"

Surfacing with the tattered remains of a food wrapper that one of the students had dropped on the floor during the field trip, Juno stepped into the aisle as well and replied stiffly, "I believe your knowledge could come in useful, so yes. But there are going to be rules. This is my road trip. I decide where and when we travel."

"Fair enough, as long as we don't run out of fuel," she warned. "Synthetics are hard to come by out here."

Juno shrugged. "Ronny can keep track and let us know when it's time to head back to New Chicago. In the meanwhile, we're not just going to observe or sight-see — we're going to help people as we go. And we're going to have fun doing it."

"Forrand did say you should get as much enjoyment out of the trip as you could," Angeli agreed, her blue eyes beginning to twinkle.

"What's in Breadbasket, anyway?"

"Besides the hospital? It's a transfer point on the edge of the grain fields, so there's not much. All the elevators and flour mills and such are deeper inside the district. But they've planted hop and have built themselves a fair-sized brewery."

"A brewery," Juno echoed thoughtfully. "That could be interesting."

CHAPTER 6

One year to the day after they'd left Dennis Forrand's office in New Chicago, Juno and Angeli strolled into his ante-room, happily chatting.

Mrs. Delgado welcomed them with a broad smile and punched her intercomm.

"They're back, Mister Supreme Adjudicator," she informed him as she waved them past her desk.

Forrand watched them come through the door. They'd been good for each other, he mused, noting Angeli's relaxed demeanor and Juno's confident poise. Angeli would always be a rebel, of course, and secrecy went against her grain; so it was a safe bet that Juno now knew they were both related to him. However, if Juno Vargas turned out to be everything he had hoped for, it wouldn't really matter.

Composing his features, he pulled a printout from his desk drawer and indicated the guest chairs where they were to sit, Angeli at his left side, Juno directly opposite him.

"So, Juno Vargas," he began, "tell me in ten words or less what you've managed to learn in the past year."

Counting on her fingers, Juno replied, "I've learned how to fix what's wrong with this world."

His gaze darted to Angeli's face before settling once more on Juno's. "I'm impressed. And just how do you propose to repair our broken planet?"

"By getting rid of the Relocation Authority," she declared, with the blithe conviction that only a seventeen-year-old fresh off a year of adventuring on her own could possess. "It may once have served a purpose. Now all it does is create misery. It needs to go."

"Reshaping a government is no easy task," he pointed out. "Men much older and more experienced than you are have tried it and failed. What makes you think you can do better?"

"Because power works differently for women than it does for men."

"I see you took my instructions to heart," he said approvingly. "In fact, you took *all* of my instructions to heart. You've been a busy girl, Juno Vargas. When Ronny parked the MPV this morning, the reservoir held about five minutes' worth of fuel. Let me just replay some of the highlights of the past year." Opening the printout, he began to read. "According to my sources, you filled the MPV with children from the Veggieville school and took them on a fishing trip to the Gulf of Mexico."

"It was the nearest large body of water," she explained. "They'd never seen the ocean, and the Atlantic and Pacific were too far away."

"You also brokered a trade deal between Voltaica and Breadbasket, energy for beer. That was extremely enterprising of you. Then you went to Stinko and kidnapped a shift boss's pet snake, holding it for ransom...?"

"That was me," said Angeli. "The shift boss's son took a shine to Juno. His attentions were quite persistent. When he got physical, she rebuffed him, and as a result, his daddy locked her up in the town jail. I needed leverage to negotiate her release. Apparently, that snake meant more to Daddy than his son did."

"She rebuffed him," he echoed skeptically. "With what? A two-by-four?"

Angeli looked shocked. "Of course not! Wood is a scarce and precious commodity in Stinko. She discouraged his amorous assault with a length of aluminum pipe."

"Uh-huh," he said, repressing a smile. "And — the *pièce de résistance* — you got yourself run out of Steeltown for attempting to organize a labor strike."

"That crew chief was a thug," Juno told him hotly. "He was charging the workers rent for the use of their Council-mandated safety equipment and extorting credit from them in exchange for protection from his gang. Then he was loaning their own credit back to them at interest so they could afford to move when their transfer orders came."

"And you thought it would be a good idea for a sixteen-year-old girl to take on this criminal and his cronies."

"No," she replied, "I thought it would be a good idea for the workers to express some anger and put him in his place. All I did was stir things up a little."

"No, Juno. All you did was temporarily nudge the balance of power. Even if the strike had been successful and the crew chief deposed, the moment you left he would have called in reinforcements and taken back everything he'd lost, and more. The workers would have been worse off than they'd been before you arrived. They realized that — it's why they refused to cooperate with you. Quite frankly, young lady, I'd say you were lucky to get out of there alive."

"I had Ronny and Angeli watching my back, along with about a dozen muscular steel wranglers. They weren't going to let anything happen to me."

"You trusted these men?"

"As much as I needed to," she informed him coolly. "Everywhere we went, I helped people, or tried to. Everywhere we stopped, I made at least one friend. I can't offer what you do — a fresh start with a new identity. But in nearly every industrial zone between here and all three southern coasts, there are people who now owe me favors."

"And you figure that makes you ready to begin gathering real power?"

"Don't you?"

He leaned back in his chair. His gaze riveted on Juno's determined features, he said, "Angeli, you've done your job well. Now give us the room, please."

Wordlessly she got up and left. As the door slid closed behind her, Forrand continued, "The answer to your question is, it depends on how much you're willing to give up."

"I've already walked away from my name, my past, and my family. What else is there for me to lose?"

"Your privacy, for one thing. Anyone who begins climbing the ladder of power comes under close scrutiny from every direction. Those above you will be watching your progress, alert to anything that might threaten their own position. Those below you will be waiting patiently for you to misstep so they can pull you down. And your peers will be constantly looking for ways to latch onto your coattails. Think back to our first conversation about this. I told you that power comes at a price, and that it will always be higher than you expect. I also told you that killing off Olivia Townsend would be the easy part of the payment. Consider carefully, Juno, because once I put you on that ladder there will be no turning back. You'll have no privacy, no real friends, and very little personal life. And you can forget about having children."

"You mean I can forget about acknowledging them," she cut in tartly.

"Angeli told you?" he said, scowling for effect.

"She didn't have to. I'm Eligible, remember? I figured it out."

"My point is, any emotional relationships that you form must remain secret, and that's a lot harder to achieve than you think. I know this from experience, Juno. The safest thing is to avoid them completely."

"Is that why you failed to bring down the Relocation Authority? Someone found out about one of your emotional attachments and used it against you?"

"No, it's something else I learned the hard way," he said with a sigh. "Political power comes with its own restrictions. The higher you go, the more hemmed in you are by constitutional law, and the more closely your actions are monitored to ensure you stay within bounds. I'm at the top of the political hierarchy in Americas right now, with everyone and their brother-in-law gunning for my job. I chair the Regional High Council, hold a seat on the Earth High Council, and am on the executive board of the Earth Relocation Authority." He paused to let this last part sink in, nodding affirmation when her eyes widened with astonishment. "You heard right, angel. When I was younger, I honestly believed that the way to change something as large as a government agency was to get inside it and pull some strings. So, I set my sights on a seat on the board and worked my way up the ladder. Now here I am, trapped in the big machine, with less power to act than I had years ago when I was the Chief Adjudicator for New Chicago."

"But you can still pull strings."

"Yes, as long as I'm careful not to pull too hard, or on too many at once."

Remembering what Angeli had said about Veggieville, Juno added thoughtfully, "You can give preferential treatment to people as long as you don't get caught. If you do, your ability to help them is cut off, leaving them worse off than they were before you got involved. That's why you had to let Drew lose his Eligibility when he broke the law. You couldn't risk drawing attention to everything else you were doing for us. And that's why you're looking for a protégée, isn't it? You need somebody on the outside, pulling strings that you can't touch without giving yourself away." She inhaled sharply as the realization hit her. "Because you're still determined to dismantle the Relocation Authority!"

"Smart girl. Now you have an important decision to make, Juno."

"I've made it. I'm in," she declared.

"This kind of change doesn't happen overnight," he warned her. "You've got years of study and preparation ahead of you. You'll have to claw your way up that ladder — and stop, before you fall into the same trap as I'm in. You'll have to stay focused on the goal at all times without letting anyone find out what it is. You can't let yourself be distracted from it by emotional issues, either. So, no dating. Are you absolutely certain you want to do this?"

She rose from her chair and leaned across his desk. "Do you want my help or not? I'm only asking because you seem bent on talking me out of it."

He gave her a smile. "I do. Welcome to the shooting gallery. Before we get down to business, do you have any questions?"

"I'm sure you've taken care of all the details, Mister Supreme Adjudicator. But I do have one request. I want to be kept up to date about my parents and my brother. You've said I can't contact them," she continued, "and I won't. But I know you've been tracking them. Now I want to track them too."

"Tell me, is this the deal-breaker?"

She shrugged. "Not really. Eventually I would find a way to access the information on my own. But it would make our working relationship much smoother if you agreed to share it with me now."

"All right, then. We have a deal. Do you trust me, Juno?"

"As much as I need to."

"Very wise. How much do you know about your namesake, Adam Vargas?"

"I know that the Reorganization was his idea. He redrew the political map of the Earth, beginning around 2180 C.E."

"He did much more than that," said Forrand. "In the 'dark age' following the pandemic of 2172, Adam Vargas came out of nowhere and gained control of the Earth High Council. He was able to cut through the chaos, carving the planet into political unions and dividing each political union into its various districts. Then he funneled every available resource into finding and colonizing other planets. At the same time, he expanded the powers of the Relocation Authority, giving it a mandate to screen and classify the entire Human population into two categories: space-going and planet-bound."

"Eligible and Ineligible."

"Exactly. Adam Vargas didn't create the Relocation Authority. It was already there. He just turned it into a very large, very cruel machine. And you and I are going to lead the movement that will force the dismantling of that machine. We'll need to keep a certain amount of distance between us in case someone gets lucky and hits the target on my back. If the Reformation hasn't begun before I die, I'll make sure you have what you require to continue working toward it, that's a promise. And, quite appropriately, a second Vargas will bring down what the first Vargas put in place nearly two hundred years ago."

PART II

THE BETRAYALS OF BARRY NOVAK
EARTH, 2399 C.E.

Barry Novak (b. 2355 – d. unknown) was one of the leaders of the Reformation Movement that seized power on Earth following the Battle of Daisy Hub in 2402 C.E. Little is known of his early life, although available records indicate that he played an active role in the establishment and running of the black ops organization known as the Earth Intelligence Service. He was a registered passenger on the arrow-class vessel, *Liberty*, captained by Gael Dedrick, that disappeared while en route to Earth's meeting with the Galactic High Council in 2417 C.E.

— *Sic Transit Terra, An Unauthorized Planetary History*
(2673 C.E.)

CHAPTER 7

"**So, Townsend pulled** it off?" Barry Novak commented, easing himself into the chair closest to Melville Ridout's desk. The Chief of Security for New Chicago had put on some weight since their last face-to-face meeting, Novak couldn't help noticing. District Council officials obviously ate well.

Ridout pulled an ice-packed wine bottle and four stemmed glasses from a drawer, then arranged them carefully in the middle of his antique desk blotter. "Don't sound so surprised," he chided his visitor. "We chose the right man and trained him well. I've already sent the gatecast confirming his appointment to the post of station manager on Daisy Hub. The Space Installation Authority isn't happy about it, but it's a done deal."

"What about the murder investigation he was supposed to be conducting?"

"Closed, and the records have been sealed indefinitely. Officially, the death has been ruled accidental."

A shame, mused Novak. Townsend's predecessor had been a good station manager. It wouldn't have taken much to turn him into an asset. But Madame Vargas had ignored their advice — as she usually did — and ordered the hit anyway.

"Are you making any progress in the Patel matter?" Ridout asked.

"We know who didn't kill him, and that's something, I guess," Novak replied carefully. "But it's going to take a lot more digging to get to the bottom of this."

"Well, I have complete confidence in you and your team — which, if I may remind you, we also chose and trained well."

Novak smiled thinly in response. As Chief Operations Officer of the Earth Intelligence Service, he commanded every agent in the field; but his team had always been — would always be — the original Warrior Kings crew, and "we" hadn't even existed when he'd become their leader.

He looked up as a third person strolled through the Chief of Security's doorway.

"You're right on time, Doctor," Ridout greeted him. "We're celebrating."

Nayo Naguchi, officially reborn fifteen years earlier as Doctor Randall Chin but happily answering to both names, settled himself into the indicated guest chair. The scientist was whip-thin, with ancient eyes set in an ageless face. ("Make me look inscrutable," he'd reportedly instructed the plastic surgeon while picking his new identity.)

"So I hear," Naguchi remarked. "I also hear that my old nemesis Nestor Quan has resurfaced."

"On Riviera Hub," said Novak. Meeting and holding Ridout's gaze, he added, "I've issued standing orders to all operatives to terminate him on sight. He won't be a problem much longer."

Ridout raised both eyebrows, then dropped them into a scowl and shook his head. Novak nodded his own in reply. She'd told them she wanted Quan captured and interrogated. Too bad.

Ignoring the byplay, Naguchi smiled faintly and said, "Good. It took Marion a long time to accept my death. I'd hate to have to rise from my grave to deal with this."

"Speaking of rising from graves, how is the erstwhile Captain Bonelli doing?" Ridout inquired. He probably thought he was diverting the conversation; but for Barry Novak it always ended up in the same place.

Bonelli and Novak had grown up together on the streets of New Chicago. Street justice was simple — pay it back with interest. Quan had attempted to murder Bonelli. In fact, as far as the population database was concerned, he'd succeeded. Therefore, Quan had to die. Dennis Forrand had known and accepted Novak's priorities when recruiting him, and the two men had worked well together, building a secret organization that had operated smoothly for more than twenty Earth years. True, things had begun sliding sideways lately. But that would be corrected soon.

"Bonelli is recovering nicely," said Naguchi. "Marion did an exemplary job of putting him back together. Of course, I expected no less from my star student."

A rustling sound in the anteroom drew everyone's attention to the doorway, and a moment later the fourth and final member of their group stepped into Ridout's office.

The other three sprang to their feet.

"Madame Chief Adjudicator, we're honored that you could join us," said Ridout.

Juno Vargas gave them a regal nod of acknowledgment before taking the seat that Novak had vacated for her. "I'm always glad to help celebrate the successful conclusion of a long-term project like Daisy Hub," she responded. "How soon before they can be activated?"

"Based on the reports, we estimate one Earth year before we can begin giving them level one assignments," Novak told her. "They'll need another year after that to properly consolidate their own defense systems."

"So," she said thoughtfully, "in another two years we can begin setting things in motion here on Earth. The Reformation is right on schedule, gentlemen. That *is* something to drink to."

At her signal, Ridout busied himself uncorking the wine.

Novak's wristcomm buzzed. He had remained standing in anticipation of this call. Now he moved toward the door, waving off Ridout's offer of a glass of rosé. Feeling the pressure of Madame Vargas's cool gray stare, Novak pinned a disarming smile on his face and said with a shrug, "Some of us do have businesses to run, and mine doesn't close up at six. My apologies, but this could be a client emergency." He almost added a reminder that his clientele included every member of the New Chicago Security Council, but thought better of it.

Novak stepped into the anteroom. He waited for the conversation to resume behind him, then turned on his earpiece. "Go ahead."

The taut, tremulous voice on the other side of the connection belonged to the evening receptionist at SecuriTech's storefront office. "There's a man here who says you're expecting him. He says his name is Trager."

"Give him a java and ask him to sit. Then page DeWitt. He'll know what to do. I'll be there as soon as I can."

Weighing his options, Novak decided to return and have the glass of wine. DeWitt had been instructed earlier about this particular visitor. Trager would be safe in the clean room with him for the extra fifteen minutes, and there was no point in raising Madame Vargas's hackles — or her suspicions — any higher than they already were.

Novak harbored no illusions on that score. They'd been butting heads ever since Forrand had made her the EIS's Chief Intelligence Officer, so she'd come to expect a certain amount of pushback from him. However, the woman was not a fool. Forrand had purposely put Novak and Vargas in positions of equal power, trusting that the balance of yin and yang working together would be enough to keep the organization on course once its founder was gone. He obviously hadn't considered the possibility that Juno Vargas might have an agenda of her own. From the moment she had unveiled her grand plan, she had to know that Novak would be preparing countermeasures. The best he could hope for was to keep her guessing about their specifics.

— «» —

The streets were dark and the receptionist had already gone home by the time Novak strode past her desk at SecuriTech Systems Inc. He pushed through a set of glass doors and marched briskly along a wainscoted corridor decorated to look like part of the old hotel that had once occupied this site: diamond-patterned carpeting on the floor, walnut boards and white stucco sharing the walls, and round-domed light bulbs in sconces mounted two meters apart all up and down the hall.

The antique appearance was just for show. In fact, SecuriTech dealt in cutting-edge surveillance and encryption technology, installed first and foremost on its own premises. Every door locked and unlocked using a combination of voice and thumbprint recognition. Every room was outfitted with concealed securecams recording everything that happened within it.

Every room but one — the clean room.

Novak stepped through the door marked "Maintenance" and into a closet lined with open metal shelving stocked with tools and janitorial supplies. The shelf unit against the back wall was a holographic projection. He thrust his arm into it up to the elbow, found and pressed a concealed contact plate, then heard the subdued hum of a sliding panel. Seconds later he was in a place that only the original twelve Warrior Kings and a trusted handful of their associates even knew about.

The clean room at SecuriTech was a medium-sized office suite with some very special features. In addition to having a hidden entrance, it did not appear on any official building plans. It also contained no monitoring or surveillance devices of any kind, was equipped with state of the art "rogue technology" independent of the planet-wide InfoComm network, and was one of the three safest places in New Chicago to hold a clandestine meeting. This was where Novak found Zane 'Man Mountain' DeWitt standing over the individual who had earlier introduced himself to the receptionist as Trager.

Novak froze and stared in disbelief. Their visitor was sitting upright in one of the swivel chairs, his big hands clamped tightly over the ends of its arms as though bracing to launch him out of it. He was also covered with blood — his own. Trager looked as though someone had been using his head for knife-throwing practice. His face was etched with cuts, some of them deep and still oozing. His pale blond hair was spiked and matted with darkly drying blood from at least half a dozen scalp wounds. And someone with gory fingers had slapped an improvised patch over his right eye. Just imagining what it might be covering was enough to pull the taste of bile up the back of Novak's throat. He gazed an accusing question at DeWitt.

"It wasn't me, boss," the other man replied. "He walked in looking like that. Nearly gave Ellie a heart attack. We've already disposed of his transportation, and Sam is doctoring the surveillance vids. I was just about to get the first aid kit and fix him up."

Disconcertingly, Trager smiled and leaned back in his seat. "This looks worse than it is. I had to sever my connections to the intellinet before attempting to contact you," he explained in a matter-of-fact voice. "It's a precaution in case we're captured, so the enemy can't backtrace the link to our headquarters. I'm afraid I frightened your receptionist. My apologies. But if I hadn't disengaged from the net, they would have tracked me down and terminated me before I could give you this."

He reached into his pocket, then turned his fist over and opened his bloodied fingers. Still trying to process the fact that all of Trager's wounds — including the missing eye — were self-inflicted, Novak stared for a moment at the datawafer sitting in the palm of the other man's hand.

"What is this?" he inquired.

"It's what Bruni Patel was trying to bring you when they caught up to him. What I promised him I would deliver if he couldn't."

Things began clicking into place in Novak's mind. "So you're Stragori, like Bruni."

It wasn't a question, and Trager gave no response. Novak took the offered datawafer and placed it on the desk behind him. Then he continued, purposely putting an edge on his voice:

"When we spoke earlier you told me you had information about his murder that could only be shared in a private meeting. Well, this is as private as it gets around here, so you'd better start sharing. Who exactly are 'they' and why did they target Patel?"

Trager's mouth twisted as though he were trying to swallow something distasteful. "A majority faction of our government would rather the Humans of Earth remain ignorant of certain historical events involving our two planets," he said. "Bruni felt differently and I agreed with him. A friend helped him gain access to the necessary documentation. Bruni copied it, intending to bring it to you. Unfortunately, the data theft was discovered more quickly than expected. The Directorate held a hearing in his absence. The friend confessed to being an accomplice and Bruni was branded as a traitor. And on our world, as on yours, the penalty for treason is death."

"Just a minute!" Novak commanded. "Are you telling me that the Stragori Directorate ordered Patel's assassination? And it was carried out on Terran soil?"

After a moment's hesitation, Trager replied calmly, "Yes."

"By whom?"

"Unknown. All I can say with certainty is that any Stragori who kills a fugitive offplanet is required to bring back the body — or some essential part of it — as proof of termination before a reward can be claimed."

Novak had seen Bruni's corpse when it was brought in — and immediately wished he hadn't. His friend's face had been brutally stabbed and slashed, his eye sockets emptied. In fact, his wounds — all inflicted *postmortem* — had appeared very similar to the ones now visible on Trager's head. That might explain a lot.

But it couldn't explain everything — not to Novak's satisfaction, at least. He always listened to his gut, and right now it was telling him that they'd barely scratched the surface of this alien's story.

"Patel was killed months ago," Novak pointed out. "Why did you wait so long to contact me?"

Trager shrugged uncomfortably and averted his gaze. "I was recalled to Stragon before we could put our plan into action. Then I had to persuade a friend in the Directorate to send me back here. It took time."

Despite his many wounds and alarming blood loss, he was showing no signs of physical weakness. Impressive. And useful. Trager had defied his government and couldn't possibly go back home. Juno Vargas had already made it painfully clear where she stood on the subject of adding aliens who looked just like Humans to the EIS payroll. So, Novak wouldn't recruit this particular Stragori into Earth Intelligence. He would simply help him disappear. Trager would be given a new identity and sent as far away from

Earth as possible, where he could also serve as one more countermeasure to Vargas's Reformation.

Before they moved him anywhere, he would need at least one regenerative healing treatment, Novak decided. And a change of clothing. His shirt and jacket were dark with the blood they had been drinking. Were all Stragori this tough? he wondered. And if they were...

"Why didn't Bruni do what you did? Sever all connections with the intellinet, I mean, so they couldn't track him."

"We were differently optimized. Even if they'd taught him how to do it, removing his implants would have killed him."

Whereas the man sitting in front of Novak seemed capable of cheerfully surviving anything short of a direct missile hit. Blood loss wouldn't knock him out, and he was trained to foil the enemy if he were captured.

A perfect soldier.

Forcing himself to breathe normally, Novak leaned over the alien and said in a raspy voice, "You obviously know a lot about us, Trager, including the fact that we can help you stay alive. You wouldn't have come here otherwise. But there's a price for that service, and you need to begin paying it now. Tell me: Are there other Stragori on Earth optimized the same way as you are? And if there are, what the hell are they doing here?"

The visitor's features contracted slightly, then relaxed as he made his decision. "We aren't here to make war on your people, Novak. We're here to protect our own. It has been clear since we first arrived on this world that not all Humans are ready to welcome an alien presence. In fact, many Humans have openly expressed hatred of us. So, every one of our observers has a military shadow ordered not to make contact unless there is a clear and direct threat to the subject's safety. And I— I was assigned to watch over Bruni Patel."

Biting back the first comment that leaped into his mouth, Novak remarked instead, "To watch over him without his knowledge? And yet, you assisted his efforts to bring us this information."

Trager's gaze dropped to his lap. "It wasn't supposed to happen, but it did," he murmured sadly.

In that instant, Novak understood. "You broke protocol and revealed yourself to him, didn't you? Over time you probably became good friends. Then your superiors learned that Bruni was in possession of the data on that wafer and—"

"—and I was ordered to terminate him, and I refused," Trager supplied, lifting his remaining, pain-filled eye to Novak's face. "You're right. Bruni Patel and I became friends, and then we became kin. On our world, that is a sacred bond. Kin do not harm kin."

At last they were getting to the bottom of things! Trager had been recalled, most likely to answer for his mutinous conduct, and was consequently unable to protect Bruni from being killed. Guilt-ridden, he was willing to risk his own death to ensure that Patel's would not be in vain. Now it all made sense.

"There is a place where you'll be safe," Novak told him. "We'll need some time to build you a new identity. And of course," he added, indicating the datawafer, "we'll want to check this out."

Trager dipped his head in acknowledgment. "You'll need the decryption key."

"Which is...?"

"Bruni's genome. He said you would be familiar with the technology." Trager reached into a different pocket and extracted a small bundle. He unwrapped it on his lap, revealing a sealed vial containing about a spoonful of dark red liquid.

A Human datawafer and a bit of alien blood.

Novak took the vial and placed it carefully on the desktop. Then he turned questioning eyes toward the man in the chair.

"It was Bruni's backup plan," Trager explained. "I found it concealed with the datawafer when I returned from Stragon."

Novak thought hard. His crew of Warrior Kings were wizards when it came to circuitry and microprocessors using polarized light. They could hack into any kind of software. They had developed the programming for the tactile transmitter that every EIS agent carried. But the kind of technology now sitting on the clean room desk was far beyond their skills.

In fact, Novak knew of only one person on the planet who might be able to crack the alien encryption code. Good thing he was local.

— ⟨⟩ —

With growing frustration, Barry Novak stared at the blocks of text shown side by side on the wall-mounted light screen in Nayo Naguchi's laboratory. Sitting above EIS Operations Headquarters, this was Nayo's personal clean room, installed on the top floor of what outwardly appeared to be an abandoned mid-rise office building in the heart of Warrior Kings territory — the Zone.

Naguchi had long ago outstripped his peers in the field of genetic research. He was the one responsible for figuring out how to key the tactile transmitters to each agent's DNA. He had discovered a reproducible mutation that enabled him to extend the life spans of the animals in his lab by a factor of four, and counting. And he had clearly perfected the use of genetic patterns to encrypt sensitive information, because it had taken him less than an hour to unlock the contents of the datawafer Novak had brought him.

Unfortunately, it appeared there were multiple levels of encryption, and magnifying the text to fill most of Naguchi's laboratory wall didn't make it any easier to decipher. The file on the datawafer contained three documents in three different languages, none of which Novak could identify. The one on the far right of the screen used symbols that looked vaguely like trees with strangely broken branches. They may have been letters of an alphabet, but since he had no idea how to sound them out, the message they contained was incomprehensible. Bruni Patel had died and Trager had risked the same fate in order to bring him this information, so it was obviously important. Right now, however, it was nothing but gobbledygook.

"Good — you're still here." Soundlessly, Naguchi crossed the room and slid onto the tall four-legged stool beside

Novak's, facing the screen on the wall. "Trager is cleaned up and settled in for the night. He's had regen treatment for that damaged eye socket, and Danziger assures me he has an ocular prosthetic in stock that should fit the cavity perfectly. He's painting an iris onto it as we speak. And you and I need to talk. I found something disturbing in the blood sample you gave me."

"Well, it did come from an alien."

"That's not what the test results are telling me."

Frowning, Novak finally turned his attention away from the screen. "What are you talking about? Trager told me the blood was Bruni Patel's, and Trager and Patel are both Stragori."

Naguchi's normally serene face was furrowed with concern. "I mapped a drop from the vial, and then some of Trager's blood from a piece of gauze used while administering first aid," he explained. "They contain identical anomalous enzymes, but both samples register genetically as Human."

A chill trickled down Novak's back, like an icy finger gently tracing the length of his spine. Patel had been an alien gathering information about Human society when Dennis Forrand had hired him all those years ago. Forrand had been hypercautious back then. He would have checked Patel out thoroughly. He certainly wouldn't have missed something like this.

"Are you sure you didn't make a mistake, Nayo?"

"Yes. Are you sure *you're* not making one?"

"Could this be just an elaborate hoax, you mean?" It was possible. With Patel dead, they had only Trager's word for any of this story.

"The thought did cross my mind," said Naguchi. "I'm also thinking it might be a diversionary tactic to get you busily chasing your tail while Madame Vargas coordinates her offensive. Think about this, Barry. We both know that she doesn't completely trust you — she has her own people in the field gathering intel about EIS operations. And experience has shown that she won't hesitate to sacrifice a pawn if she thinks it will gain her an advantage."

It was hard to imagine Trager being anyone's pawn. Nonetheless...

Novak considered the strange languages on the screen and the expertise that would have been required to create and encrypt the documents. He reminded himself of Trager's optimized and definitely not Human soldierly abilities. Then he listened to what his gut had to say on the subject, giving it the final word.

"I'm pretty sure this didn't come from her, Nayo. She may be ruthless but she knows what you're capable of, and that would rule out using Human blood as the decryption key. Especially if the goal is to keep me distracted for as long as possible."

"Not necessarily," said Naguchi, gesturing toward the light screen. "How distracted do you think you'll be while trying to make sense out of *this*?" A sideways glance became a double take. "Now, this is interesting. The symbols in the third document appear to be runic. That was an ancient Earth alphabet. I wonder..."

Naguchi spun on his stool and entered an instruction into the computer. The third document winked out and reappeared, its message written in Anglo letters this time. To Novak, it was still unpronounceable nonsense. However, Naguchi's lips were curving into a satisfied smile.

"You've got something?"

"I believe this is Galactic Standard."

"I thought Gally was spoken only, not written."

"Normally, yes," Naguchi explained. "It's the *lingua franca* of space travel, making it possible for all the alien races to communicate verbally with one another. As I understand it, the decision was made not to create a unique alphabet for Galactic Standard, but rather to let each race use its own letters and symbols for recording purposes."

Novak scowled at the screen. He hadn't spoken Gally in years and would need at least a week of somno to get his fluency back. Even so, he should have been able to recognize a word here and there. Nope. *Nada.* He shot Naguchi a dubious look.

"This document was transliterated using the letters of a dead language," the other man continued patiently. "It's a primitive method of encryption. When I was a schoolboy we used to encode secret messages to one another the same way, using the ancient Greek alphabet. The thing about runic symbols is that not all the sounds correspond exactly to Anglo, and some are missing. You have to read a passage aloud to get the sense of it."

"So, what does it say?"

"Give me a second." Naguchi's lips moved silently as he read the text on the screen. Finally he replied, "These appear to be observations relating to some sort of experiment."

"According to Trager, it involves our two planets and is worth risking death for."

Naguchi returned Novak's dubious look. "Well, I have to tell you, it's pretty mundane stuff. This Gally may have a strong accent, but I'm a scientist, and these are definitely lab notes. It says here that a control group was assembled consisting of sample populations from five different areas. They were all housed together in a fenced compound. But the various subgroups didn't get along with one another and were unhappy being penned up. They made several attempts to escape. Finally, the entire control group had to be — had to be—" The last words came out as a whisper.

"Had to be what?" Novak prompted him. "Dispersed? Killed?"

"Neither. Barry, did Trager tell you where this originally came from?"

"No, just that Bruni Patel had copied it illegally and was killed by the Stragori while trying to bring it to us. Nayo," he persisted, "what does it say happened to the control group?"

Naguchi inhaled deeply before responding. "They were relocated to another world."

The silence that fell then had an almost physical presence. Novak felt trapped inside it, a helpless witness to an inescapable conclusion.

...certain historical events involving our two planets...

...and Trager's genome was registering as Human.

Novak struggled to keep his voice steady. "Does the document include the coordinates of the other world? Is it Earth?"

"It doesn't specify. Maybe that information is contained

in one of the other two texts."

"We don't dare reveal the existence of these until we've had them translated and we know precisely what they say. If the tabs even caught a whiff of them—!"

Hoax or not, the contents of the third document alone would be enough to trigger world-wide xenophobia.

"Never mind the tabs. What if Madame Vargas found out we had them and were keeping them to ourselves?" Naguchi warned.

Or what if the Stragori find out we have their stolen file?

As the implications of this thought sank in, Novak's stomach tipped over. Somebody — in all likelihood an alien somebody — had experimented on Humans, either on Earth or elsewhere. He wasn't sure which would be worse, finding out that the Humans of Earth were the control group or learning that they weren't. In any case, if the Stragori had already killed to prevent this knowledge from falling into Human hands, they probably wouldn't think twice about killing again to keep it quiet.

Bruni Patel had been optimized. That meant he'd been connected to the Stragori intellinet the whole time he was working for the EIS. Forrand must have known, because he'd restricted Patel to low-level courier runs and had given him no access to anything that could compromise the organization. But he'd made Barry Novak Patel's handler, and the two men had forged a relationship over the years.

The Stragori had to be aware of this. By ripping out his implants, Trager might have shaken off his pursuers for a while; however, it wouldn't take them long to connect the dots and figure out what he'd done and where he'd probably ended up.

There was no time to spare. Trager would have to be moved off-world as soon and as stealthily as possible. And Novak would need to make several copies of the datawafer and conceal them in the care of people he trusted. People Madame Vargas didn't know and Patel had never come in contact with. People who had never heard of the Earth Intelligence Service.

There remained a slender chance that this was all a con,

but Novak was betting that it wasn't. The Stragori were right about one thing: the Humans of Earth weren't yet ready to know about this part of their past. One day they would be. When that day came, they had the right to know the truth. That was, after all, what the EIS was supposed to be about — uncovering and safeguarding the truth. That was what the Kings had originally signed on for and, Vargas's political ambitions notwithstanding, as far as Novak was concerned it was still their primary purpose.

"…imperative that we get the rest of the data translated as soon as possible," Naguchi was saying.

"Do you have someone in mind? Someone we can trust to keep it secret?"

"There's a brilliant xenolinguist at the university in Clearmeadow Enclave — Doctor Susan Rosenberg. Top of her field and I'd trust her with my life. She's currently working on some special government project, so it won't be easy to get to her; but since time is of the essence, I'd like to give it a try."

— ⟨⟩ —

Novak and Naguchi had been up all night and half of the following day. It had taken Novak twelve hours to create a new identity for Trager from scratch, one that cross-referenced with Earth's database and couldn't be traced back to the EIS or SecuriTech. Naguchi had spent the same length of time creating a strand of RNA that would eventually contain all the information from the datawafer. In another 48 hours, the Stragori soldier named Trager would wink out just as the document on the screen had done, reappearing as Max Karlov, an Eligible Human with a fondness for brawling. The data-laden retrovirus would be ensconced inside the body of a black hooded rat named Akiko. And the two of them would then be quietly transported to a place where, with luck, nobody would think to look for either of them — Daisy Hub.

"Max will be a fine addition to the Hub's crew," Naguchi remarked, peering over Novak's shoulder at the display on his light screen.

Novak's lips quirked in a brief smile. "Yeah, he'll blend

right in. It'll be the perfect cover for his mission."

"You're giving him a covert assignment? We're already pushing the envelope by smuggling him and Akiko aboard the Hub. Are you sure this is wise, Barry?"

Privately, Novak didn't think anything they'd been doing lately could be called wise; but about this one thing, at least, he felt confident. "He'll be carrying a message for Drew Townsend. After it's delivered, Townsend's safety will be his personal responsibility. That was Patel's first job for the EIS, by the way. He wasn't officially an agent at the time, but Forrand hired him to guide the kid along while he was in detention and make sure he came to no harm. Now that we've seen how far Trager is willing to go to complete Patel's work..."

"You're anticipating trouble on Daisy Hub?" Naguchi murmured.

Novak turned and met the other man's thoughtful gaze. "You heard Madame Vargas at that meeting yesterday — she's planning a *putsch*. A *coup d'état*. That was never part of Forrand's agenda when he established the EIS, and it isn't what you and I signed on for. When she makes her move, we'll make ours. The EIS will split down the middle, and Townsend will have to choose a side. Before that happens, he needs to know everything we've found out about Vargas and about the people under his command. And he needs to know about the Warrior Kings. And then, if he jumps the way I think he will, trust me, he'll be glad to have a super-soldier watching his back."

CHAPTER 8

One week later, bribes had been generously distributed and Karlov and Akiko were safely stowed aboard a long-range freighter making stops at colonies and hubs in three different sectors of Earth space. Novak and Naguchi turned their attention to the next phase of the operation.

Clearmeadow University was housed in a building at least three hundred years old. Its walls were assembled out of rough-hewn blocks of gray stone and pierced at intervals by narrow arched windows. Its main entrance was impressive, a massive concrete stairway fronting a pair of heavy wooden doors with wrought iron fittings. At the foot of the stairs sat two large bronze statues, one to each side. The one on the left was of a man wearing a classical-style draped tunic and looking wonderingly over his shoulder. The one on the right depicted a woman in modern dress with her hands on her hips, gazing with determination at the sky.

Study the past, conquer the future, thought Naguchi. If only it were that simple.

First he had to find a way through the present, which took the form of several armed guards in tailored blue uniforms, stationed at the building's front door. They were part of an elite unit commanded by the Earth High Council, carefully chosen and rigorously trained to protect state secrets at any cost. Apparently, that was what Susan's current project was.

That she would be difficult to get to was an understatement, Naguchi now realized. The men outside were just a forewarning of the security surrounding her temporary office in the restricted area of the building. Every stairwell and corridor leading to her workspace would be both surveilled and watchdogged, and probably guarded as well for good measure. And classes had evidently been suspended, meaning that there would be no movement of students to provide cover for anyone trying to slip inside the building unnoticed.

Novak had been right to talk him out of taking the direct approach. Now Naguchi was wondering whether he should have come here at all. Subterfuge was not his forte. He swallowed hard, fighting the urge to simply turn around and walk away. Then he noticed that one of the guards at the door had begun watching him.

What to do? The longer he stood there looking indecisive, the more likely he was to be approached and challenged. He knew his creds would stand up to scrutiny — Novak had forged them personally, and his work was impeccable — but the scientist had had similar details of blue-uniformed security officers assigned to him in the past. Randall Chin's face and biowafer wouldn't count for much if this suddenly attentive, obviously armed guard were to recognize Naguchi's voice. Just considering the possibility was enough to raise beads of perspiration across his forehead.

"Doctor Chin?" A large, muscled man was striding across the lawn toward him, wearing the tan shirt and trousers and brown shoulder patch of an enclave patrolman. As the man drew nearer, Naguchi recognized Zane DeWitt's face under the peaked cap. "You're expected, sir. Please follow me to the quadrangle."

"Thank you," said Naguchi, feeling buoyed by a powerful wave of relief. As he fell into step behind DeWitt, a sidelong glance confirmed that the guard at the door had turned his attention elsewhere.

Located around the side of the building, the quadrangle was a large paved courtyard surrounded on three sides by the stone walls of the university and on the fourth by a fence made of tall, sharply-pointed iron posts. There was only one sentry on duty here. DeWitt had clearly spent some time chatting him up earlier, for he waved to them as they approached, and then stood aside to let them pass through the gate.

Always cautious since his faked death, Naguchi paused on the threshold to scan the area. It had been thoroughly secured. There was only one way out, and he was standing in it. The double doors opening onto the quad from the main building had once had handles on their outer surfaces. Now the handles were gone, leaving a matched pair of featureless black metal slabs set into the unyielding gray stone. No doubt there were eyes already trained on him from the upper floor windows. Weapons as well. Just thinking about that made his legs want to run away, but he was committed at this point and overruled them. Susan was waiting for him. Forcing down the lump in his throat, he entered the quadrangle.

It was lined on all four sides by long, inward-facing wooden benches, separated from one another by raised flower beds brimming with pink and white blossoms. On the bench farthest from the gate, her gaze resting expectantly on Naguchi's altered features, sat a woman with short auburn hair and a fair, freckle-splashed complexion. As he approached, she invited him with a gesture to sit down beside her.

"Talk to me," she commanded him, staring stolidly ahead. "Let me hear your voice."

He sighed and leaned back against the bench. "It's me, Susan."

"I knew it," she muttered and turned to face him, a storm brewing in her eyes. "You're the first outside visitor I've been permitted since they picked me for this damned assignment. When they told me my outraged lover was demanding proof that I was still alive, something told me it had to be you. I never quite swallowed that story about you dying in a laboratory explosion."

Her voice remained low, but it sizzled with intensity, reminding him once more why he had first been attracted to her.

"How have you been, Susan?"

The storm began blowing in. It was, he reflected sadly, no more than he deserved.

"How have I been? I've been cooped up here for the past three months, micromanaged half to death by a government agency demanding that I figuratively spin straw into gold and becoming more frustrated by the day. That's how I've been, *Randall*, and you've got one hell of a nerve showing up here after fifteen years of silence, pretending to care."

"I understand your anger—"

"You could at least have *told* me you were breaking up with me before you went into hiding. I would have cursed you out and cried for a while, and then I'd have gotten on with my life. But this—! This was just cruel."

"You're right. You deserved better. But I was never trying to leave you, Susan. I was keeping you safe. When I broke that contract with EuroGenics, they came after me, and I don't mean in the adjudication halls. They already had most of my work, but it wasn't enough. They wanted everything. I went off-world for nearly five years, hoping they'd lose interest. No such luck. When I returned, one of their enforcers met me at the airfield. He threatened to ruin you if I didn't cooperate. I knew I had to do something drastic to put an end to the situation. Fortunately, I had friends by then with the wherewithal to help me. I never meant to hurt you, I swear it. But the only way to shake off those thugs and ensure that you wouldn't be harmed was to make everybody — including you — think I was dead."

Stubbornly facing forward once more, she gave him a long sideways look. "You expect me to believe that?"

"No, but that doesn't mean it's not true. I've never stopped loving you. In fact, I've been following your career."

She took a deep breath, let it out slowly, and pretended to count the blossoms in the nearest flower bed. He recognized the tactic. She was giving herself time to think, to decide how to feel. To pick the sharpest words in her arsenal to throw at him. After a moment, her choices made, Susan Rosenberg straightened her shoulders, stared into his face, and said in a surprisingly soft voice, "You're not here for old times' sake or because you suddenly felt the need to mend fences, are you, Nayo? You need a favor.

"I don't care whose face you're wearing. I know you. I know that you're a fearless scientist and a gifted educator; but you've never been a soldier, and you're certainly not a spy. Only a desperate man would challenge the wall of security the Council has thrown up around me, so I'm guessing that you're neck-deep in trouble and I'm your last hope. How am I doing so far?"

Her expression was unreadable. It planted a sudden uneasy feeling in the pit of his stomach. "Not my last hope," he protested. "My first and only choice. This isn't just for me, so if you're thinking of saying no to punish me—"

"I'm saying no because there's nothing I can do for you," she said, her gaze filling with reproach. "I wish I could help you, truly. But you have to understand, I have minimal privacy in my home, and at work I'm under constant surveillance. This meeting is an exception, made under duress. After today, they'll probably keep me incommunicado again until I've completed the current assignment. And quite honestly, the last thing I need right now is another impossible task on my plate."

The pleading he heard in her voice brought a lump to his throat. Once upon a time, he would have done anything she asked. He would even have gone away forever if it would make her happy. But not today. Today the stakes were far too high. And she *had* said she wanted to help.

Steeling himself, he assured her, "We can do this, Susan. The task is not impossible, just not my area of expertise. And I've already set up a way for us to communicate without anyone else knowing about it. Do you still have my old playback device, the one that isn't linked to the InfoComm system?"

She frowned uncertainly. "You're in luck. It's one of your few belongings that I didn't recycle or give away. Do you need it?"

"No, but you will," he said, leaning in closer and lowering his voice as he palmed the datawafer in his pocket. "What I'm about to give you is keyed to your DNA. The data on the wafer will decrypt at your touch and re-encrypt if anyone else handles it. Encrypted, it sounds like a staticky recording of a Trash Bin concert. Take it home with you tonight and read the file it contains, using the playback device. Make sure you're somewhere private, and disable the vox. Use the keypad only. Under no circumstances show the file to anyone else. Don't even bring it *near* an InfoComm unit. Follow the instructions on the datawafer when you're ready to contact me again. And, Susan...?" he added, taking her hand in both of his and slipping her the wafer in the process. "I don't blame you for being angry with me. I'm just grateful that you're someone I can trust with this."

She gave him a wary look. "Nayo, what the hell are you dragging me into?"

"We're going to change the world," he promised her.

"Again? Oh, for heaven's sake," she muttered, pulling him closer and planting a kiss on his lips that he could feel right down to his ankles. "We're supposed to be lovers stealing time for a tryst," she whispered while nibbling on his ear, "and people are watching."

As he wrapped his arms tightly around her, savoring once more the delightful curves of her body and the intoxicating fragrance of her hair, Naguchi realized just how much he had missed her. Judging from the cover story Novak had provided for him, he must have realized it as well.

When DeWitt finally opened the gate to escort Doctor Chin past the slyly grinning sentry and off the campus, the scientist felt a drop of nervous perspiration slither down the side of his neck. Susan was right. Cloak and dagger was definitely not his style.

— «» —

Three days later, a pale, plump woman sailed through SecuriTech's front door, followed by a broad-shouldered man in a business suit who remained close by, watching her carefully.

"I'm here about a special order," she told the receptionist. "I commconnected earlier and was told I should come in and pick it up. The name is Rosenberg."

The woman smiled at her and pressed an intercomm button. "Mr. Novak handles those himself. He'll be here in just a moment."

Darting a glance over her shoulder, Susan saw her "shadow" pull a compupad out of his pocket. Checking out this Novak fellow, no doubt.

"It's *Susan* Rosenberg, right?" The man who had materialized to the left of the receptionist's desk stood medium height, with sharp features and neatly trimmed dark blond hair. He was holding a small box marked with a series of numbers. "I apologize for the delay. Since the manufacturer released the upgrade, our supplier in Indo-Asia is having trouble keeping up with the demand for parts. If you'll give me your compupad, I can replace the component right now."

"Of course."

She reached into her pocket for the device. Before she could hand it over, however, her escort leaped forward and snatched it away.

"And what exactly does this new component do?" he demanded.

The smile on Novak's face didn't even flicker. "It's a third-generation reliable transtator. It stabilizes the image on the compupad screen. Unifies it, prevents it from pixelating when signal strength stutters. Keeps horizontal lines straight as a page scrolls up."

"And she ordered this upgrade herself?"

"Yes, three months ago. Normally these things take three weeks, but—"

"Funny that you didn't mention this when we were doing your Security interview," commented the man, his gimlet eye now trained on the rapidly reddening face of Dr. Susan Rosenberg.

It was a flush of anger. "You told me to answer every one of the two hundred questions that you asked, and that was what I did," she pointed out in a voice that could have cut glass. "If you wanted to know about every little piece of technology in my possession, including my battery-powered toothbrush and my personal compupad — which I keep in a drawer in my living room and never bring to work — then you should have asked me. I've already paid for this upgrade and, trust me, it wasn't cheap. Now, give the man my compupad so he can install it."

"Not until I've reviewed every file on this device."

"It's called 'personal' for a reason," she informed him stiffly.

"You can change your password when I'm done, Doctor. Right now I need to verify that there's nothing classified on here."

"Fine. But I'll be entering the password," she told him, snatching back her compupad and unlocking it before thrusting it once more into his hand.

A minute later he was satisfied. "I had to do that, you understand."

"Unfortunately, I do. Working on this project has given me tremendous insight into systemic paranoia," she hissed at him, her expression darkening again. "In fact, it's been contagious. So *you* should understand that I'll be programming my InfoComm unit to alert me if even a single sentence of any of my personal messages turns up anywhere else on the system. If it does, I'll be reporting this shameful violation of my privacy, first to the Data Management Department and then to your superiors. And after that, I've no doubt, you'll be lucky to end up cleaning out drains in a waste management facility."

The guard turned to the man beside the counter. "Can she—?"

"Program her unit? Yes, any user can. There's even a way to have the system generate an automatic message to the local Security Council if there's a breach of any kind."

His confidence visibly shaken, the guard handed over the compupad and watched as Novak expertly took it apart and, smiling inwardly, made the switch.

Susan Rosenberg was tough and smart. Nayo had chosen their translator well. And once Novak finished installing her keystroke-activated encryption module, she would be able to update them regularly on her progress.

CHAPTER 9

Nayo, you wonderful Rumpelstiltskin, do you know what you've given me? Have you any idea what this document is?

Susan's first encrypted message arrived on the computer in Naguchi's lab in the Zone, one week and four days after her visit to SecuriTech. Her excitement fairly leaped off the screen. Reading the words, he could almost visualize her dancing around the room with delight as she keyed them in.

He activated the encrypter at his end before beginning his response: *I've figured out what the third page says. It's transliterated Gally, using the runic alphabet of ancient Earth.*

Ten minutes later, her reply arrived: *Then you know what they all say. This is a Rosetta Stone, Nayo. A single text recorded in three different languages. And one of them was also used to create the document I'm currently translating. It was found by an archaeological team on a dig in Indo-Asia. It's very old, and there are always significant differences between past and present versions of living languages, but I'm almost certain the first sample of text in your file — most likely the original, given its scientific content — is ancient Thryggian. The second one is written in a variation of a language I've seen on documents from the Central Archives and the Galactic Great Council. Its first sentence is identical in meaning to the opening sentences of the other two texts.*

If he hadn't been sitting down, Naguchi would have fallen over. As it was, he had to work for his next breath. The lab report had been written by Thryggians? The same Thryggians who had stepped forward so helpfully when Earth's colonies were being devastated by the Angel of Death plague? The same Thryggians whom fellow researcher Sylvie Deneuve had publicly praised for aiding the development of a broad-spectrum vaccine against the virus, thus saving potentially millions of Human lives? *Those* Thryggians? Was it possible that they had visited Earth many centuries earlier? That they had also experimented on Humans, either there or on Stragon?

If so, it was a truth worth killing to protect. There could be no unlearning something like this, no turning away and pretending never to have realized it. And if a government decided to suppress it, anyone with first-hand knowledge of the original document was in mortal danger.

For several minutes as his thoughts raced, he couldn't reply to her message; but eventually he was able to compose himself sufficiently to say: *Please confirm that the first language is Thryggian. Was the Earth-found document part of a lab report also?*

She responded quickly: *Yes and yes. I still have a long way to go with that translation, but thanks to your wonderful file I am far enough along to say for certain that the Earth document is about some sort of scientific experiment.*

He dreaded asking the question but keyed it in anyway: *Any mention in there of a control group?*

This time she made him wait several minutes for the answer: *Yes, in the Rosetta Stone file you gave me. Not sure whether to share this. Are you sitting down? Nayo, the Thryggian word for control group is "stragori".*

— «» —

"So they're the real Humans and we're — what? Mutations?"

Novak stood in the middle of the clean room, his spine rigid and his voice razor-sharp. Frowning, Naguchi looked for his compupad and found it leaning crookedly against the back of the chair where Novak had hurled it after reading Susan's messages. The most recent one, less than an hour old, was still on the screen. Naguchi blanked it and tucked the 'pad safely into his pocket.

"We're victims, Barry," he finally said. "Or rather, the descendants of victims. Our distant ancestors were subjected against their will to scientific experimentation by aliens. As a race, we've suspected something like this for a very long time. Now we have the proof."

"And a fat lot of good it does us," spat Novak. His expression darkening, he glanced around the room as though looking for something else to throw. For just a second Naguchi debated whether to take cover. Then, as quickly as the storm had blown up, it subsided.

Exhaling the final gust, Novak sank down onto the nearest chair, gesturing to Naguchi to do the same. "Whichever way we move with this, it's going to be wrong. Best case scenario, we present the information to the Earth High Council, who decide, like the Stragori, to suppress it and silence everyone who knows about it. Worst case scenario, it goes out over the InfoCommNet, sparking a xenophobic witch hunt the likes of which I don't even want to imagine. We're juggling hot potatoes, Nayo," he added wearily, digging the heel of his hand into his right eye, "and I don't know how much longer I can keep them all in the air."

"It would be easier if we knew what those experiments were about," Naguchi remarked. "From what I've seen so far — and admittedly, it was only a cursory analysis — there's almost no difference between us and the Stragori, other than their having some extra blood elements and a more advanced level of technology. Unfortunately, blood can only reveal so much. If I'd been thinking straight, I would have obtained some additional specimens from Trager before you sent him off." He paused for a moment. "Not to sound like a ghoul, but you wouldn't happen to know where Bruni Patel's body ended up, would you?"

Novak tried on a smile. "Sorry, Nayo. We had it for less than a day before it was stolen, probably by agents of the Stragori government. If there were some foolproof way to recognize a Stragori on sight, I might consider sending DeWitt and Croft to 'borrow' one of them so you could take a few more samples. However, there isn't," he concluded with a helpless shrug.

"I appreciate the thought," Naguchi reassured him. "You know, I always wondered, when I saw the vidclips of that first contact with the Stragori on Mars, what were the odds of an alien race in this arm of the galaxy evolving to look just like us? Someone should have been suspicious from the start."

"A lot of someones *were* suspicious, but they were even more fearful. That's why each observer comes with protection, and why we have fringe groups ranting on the InfoCommNet about the alien spies among us. And to be honest, with no one on either side taking steps to allay those fears, I don't see the situation getting better any time soon. By the way, Nayo, would you tell me please, what the hell is a rumple-whatever?"

Naguchi swallowed his next comment. Novak was so skilled, confident, and obviously intelligent that it was easy to forget he'd acquired most of his education on the streets.

"Rumpelstiltskin is a character from a very old European folk tale. In the story, a woman is locked in a tower and ordered on pain of death to spin straw into gold. Rumpelstiltskin magically appears before her and makes it possible for her to complete her task. That's what I've done for Susan. Our Stragori file is exactly what she needs to finish translating the ancient document she's been working on for the Earth High Council."

"Great! Another hot potato," Novak grumped. "A Thryggian lab report, found on Earth and in government hands. If it says what we suspect it will, you and I both know what's going to happen when she turns over her translation to the Council. They'll bury it and then bury *her*. Does she have any family on Earth?"

"No, just — just off-world." *Just me*, he'd been about to say, before remembering how their relationship had ended. "Are you thinking of extracting her?"

His expression pained, Novak replied, "I wish we could, but it would only make the situation worse. She's in mid-translation, working from one of who knows how many copies of that document, and the High Council is well aware of it. Her files are probably being uploaded to a secure server at the end of each day. And I'll bet you anything that she's not the only translator they've got on this assignment."

"She's barely started," Naguchi corrected him quietly. "Barry, she's the foremost xenolinguist on the planet, and she was getting nowhere until I gave her that datawafer. Now she's the only one who'll actually be able to complete the translation, and I'm wishing I hadn't done it."

"She's barely started?" Novak echoed. He pursed his lips thoughtfully. "Then maybe something *can* be done."

Naguchi stared a question at him.

"Send her a message ordering her to hide the datawafer and not look at it again. She'll also need to completely destroy any notes she's made relating even marginally to the contents of the Stragori file."

"And that accomplishes what, exactly?" Naguchi wanted to know. "Susan has already made her breakthrough, and she has an excellent visual memory."

"I know. But since your visit to her a couple of weeks ago immediately preceded that breakthrough, questions are bound to come up. It's not the High Council I'm concerned about — it's Madame Vargas. We need to give ourselves and Susan deniability and ensure that nothing can be traced back to me or forward to Trager or Daisy Hub.

"Next — and for someone like her this is probably the hardest part — as she continues to work on the rest of the document, Dr. Rosenberg is going to have to make some errors. Nothing blatant or embarrassing, just a minor mistranslation here and there. She needs to blunt or obscure the meaning of the most dangerous parts of the text. Do you think she can do that?"

"She's brilliant — I know she can. But how will she know which parts to alter?"

"You're going to tell her. Make a list of words and phrases that mustn't appear in the finished translation and send them to her. If you're right and none of the other translators have been making any progress at all, then Dr. Rosenberg's work will be accepted as authoritative, the High Council and Madame Vargas will remain in the dark, and you and I will be in the clear. If not, your lady friend can always say she was suffering from mental fatigue. After all, she's been spinning their straw for months now, right?"

Novak's wristcomm buzzed, startling both men. DeWitt was on the other end of the call. "She's lookin' for you, boss. Wants to have a meeting this afternoon at three sharp."

"She" could only be one person. Naguchi felt the blood leave his face. "How did she find out?" he whispered urgently.

"She didn't," said Novak. "This has to be something else."

— ⟨⟩ —

Following the reported death of Dennis Forrand in 2387 C.E., his protégée Juno Vargas had ended up with many of his worldly goods. Chief among them was the mansion in Millbrook Enclave, a collection of exclusive properties owned — not rented — by influential Eligibles on the west side of the canal. Novak was quite familiar with the neighborhood, having attended regular meetings with Forrand in the clean room installed in the Supreme Adjudicator's basement.

This afternoon, as his PV rolled to a stop before the broad veranda, the mansion's front entrance was opened by a smiling dark-haired woman in a blue and white maid's uniform. She watched him climb out of his car, then stepped aside to admit him into the foyer.

"Mister Novak, welcome," she said. "Madame Vargas is expecting you."

"Thanks, Estrella, I know the way," he told her, and headed directly for the basement door.

The front rooms of the Forrand — now Vargas — home were like a museum: spacious, richly furnished, and full of polished surfaces, sparkling chandeliers, and original paintings, tastefully arranged. In the great room, the dining room, the drawing room, the library, and the foyer were all the trappings of wealth that one would expect to find in the living quarters of a powerful individual.

To Novak they were nothing more than familiar scenery lining the path to his destination. In truth, it had been decades since anyone had actually lived in these rooms. Dennis Forrand had dutifully preserved them out of respect for his late father; but he had personally preferred to occupy the more modestly appointed three-bedroom apartment at the back of the house, where he and his sisters had grown up. Juno Vargas had chosen to continue the practice, presumably out of respect for the late Supreme Adjudicator himself. Just off the hallway leading to the "children's quarters" was the plain-looking door that opened onto a flight of carpeted wooden stairs going down to the basement.

This was where Novak found the recently promoted Madame Chief Adjudicator — in the clean room, presiding over a silver tea tray holding a pot of jasmine blend (her favorite) and two delicate porcelain cups. She had replaced Forrand's desk and swivel office chairs with a pair of midnight blue loveseats, three lighter blue padded armchairs, and a glass-topped wrought iron coffee table. As he sat down across from her, they acknowledged each other with identical perfunctory nods.

"Juno."

"Barry. So glad you could come. The tea is ready. Shall I pour?"

"Please do."

The mask never slipped. As she busied herself with the teapot, he marveled at the sculpted perfection of her hair, the careful arrangement of her features, even the precise efficiency of her movements. Juno Vargas was more than a persona — it was a suit of armor, flawlessly constructed. But what about the flesh and blood woman it was meant to protect? Was there any Olivia Townsend left in there at all?

She slid the tray closer to him, inviting him with a gesture to pick up his cup. "I have some good news for you, Barry. Nestor Quan has been apprehended."

Novak had spent most of his life concealing his emotions. Today those years of practice paid off. The tea in his cup barely swayed as he brought its rim to his lips and took a thoughtful sip.

"Really? Who caught him? One of ours?"

"No. It was Space Installation Security, four days ago. He was seen waiting to board a transport on Shakespeare Hub, and the local Ranger detachment served the arrest warrant — with prejudice. I've exercised some influence to ensure that he is brought back here to be tried. That should keep him alive long enough for you to interrogate him."

"Someone tried to kill him? What a shame."

She gave him a reproachful look. "Do you think I'm not aware of your shoot-first order? I know why you issued it, and, believe me, I sympathize. Nobody should get away with the attempted murder of one of our operatives. But I need Quan interrogated first."

"To find out what, exactly?"

"I want to know who he's really working for, because it's not EuroGenics. I made a commcall to their current CEO. Other than admitting that Quan was the one who offered to sell them his and Naguchi's patents years ago, she denies the existence of any connection between her company and Nestor Quan."

"He got caught so they're disavowing all knowledge of his mission. This surprises you?"

"He boarded Zulu carrying fake identification and beat its commanding officer nearly to death to prevent his cover from being blown," she reminded him. "I want to know why Quan was there and who sent him. So humor me, Barry. Put your most persuasive interrogator on this assignment and use whatever methods you have to, but get me names. After that, you can do whatever you want with Nestor Quan. Just make sure I have deniability, and don't leave a mess."

— «» —

Two weeks later, an unmarked Security transport vehicle disappeared from the traffic grid while carrying an arrestee from O'Hare Airfield in New Chicago to the Dearborn Detention Center. A massive search was launched, but it was already too late. In the below-ground parking area of the Warrior Kings' headquarters in the Zone, four armed men had taken up positions around the rear doors of a black and gray van, their trigger fingers itching.

Zane DeWitt stepped forward and swung the doors wide, uttering a syllable of surprise when he realized what he was looking at.

Somebody had gone to great lengths to make this passenger as uncomfortable as possible. DeWitt had never seen anyone so thoroughly shackled. Nestor Quan sat on the hard floor of the van, embroiled in sturdy metal chains and struggling to raise a hand high enough to shield his eyes from the sudden light. His face bore the marks of several savage beatings, one quite recent. It was hard to believe that this pathetic-looking little scrag had nearly killed Steve Bonelli with his bare hands. But appearances could be deceiving, as DeWitt well knew.

"Take no chances with this man," he instructed the other three Kings. "I want eyes and weapons on him at all times."

"I assure you, I'll be no problem," said Quan.

"Damn straight, you won't." DeWitt signaled to one of the men, who immediately climbed inside the van and began examining the prisoner's chains.

"He's tethered to a bolt in the floor," the chain checker called out. "Throw me those cutters."

Quan cleared his throat and pointed out, "It will be much easier for you to move me if I can walk. If you'll just remove the leg restraints as well?"

A smile crept onto DeWitt's face. "Nope. Once you're out of there, we plan to roll you along the ground. More fun that way."

"And can I assume because you're letting me see your faces that you also plan to kill me?"

DeWitt pretended to think about it. "I would call that a reasonable assumption," he replied.

"Oh, dear," said Quan. "I seem to have made a lot of people extremely angry."

DeWitt signaled once more and the man in the van pulled a hypodermic injector out of his pocket. There was a brief hiss, a soft gasp, and a flat metallic chord as "the ninja" slumped in his chains.

CHAPTER 10

"Barry Novak! You're just the person I was hoping to speak with."

Hearing these hearty words emerge from Nestor Quan's bruised mouth sent a chill through Novak's entire body. Reminding himself to breathe, he resumed walking into the interrogation room and settled into the chair across from the one to which Quan was now securely fastened.

Stripped of his bulky chains, the prisoner sat upright with his arms and legs immobilized against the bent-pipe frame by thick leather cuffs with sturdy buckle closures. A matching leather collar prevented his head from moving more than a couple of centimeters away from the padded steel headrest. There was no way he could release himself from these bonds. They were designed to tighten if he struggled against them. Quan was helpless. He was also disconcertingly relaxed, and smiling.

Novak's gut rarely steered him wrong. Right now it was warning him not to take his eyes off this man.

"Tell me, Quan," he inquired softly, "how exactly do you know my name?"

Quan's smile broadened, further distorting his battered features. "You're not the only one with a network of operatives. We've known about the Earth Intelligence Service for some time. That's why I'm here talking to you instead of begging for a meeting with your planetary government."

"You're here because you got caught trying to board a transport departing Shakespeare Hub."

"Think about what I'm capable of, Mister Novak. If I'd wanted to evade capture on Shakespeare Hub, don't you think I would have done so?"

"You want me to believe that you allowed the Rangers to beat you to a pulp on the off-chance that somebody would take pity on you and bring you to Earth to be tried? After what you'd done to Bonelli?"

"No. I had to let myself be arrested by the Rangers *because* of what I'd done to your man Bonelli. I needed to return to Earth in one piece for this meeting, and my chances of arriving here alive were much better if I surrendered myself to Security. Issuing orders to all your agents to kill me on sight? That wasn't very sportsmanlike, I must say."

Incredulity drew Novak slowly to his feet. "Not very *sportsmanlike*? You think this is some sort of *game*?" In two furious strides he was standing behind Quan's back. From there it would have been a simple matter to turn that collar around his neck into a noose and choke the life out of him. Tommy Novotny would have considered it a debt repaid. But Novak's curiosity had been aroused. So instead, he leaned over Quan's right shoulder and hissed into his ear, "You're a sociopathic menace, Quan. Every breath you take puts people in danger. Give me one reason for not ending you here and now."

The prisoner continued gazing serenely frontward. "I have the crucial piece of the puzzle you're working on. If you kill me now, you might never solve it."

It was probably just a delaying tactic. Nonetheless, Novak forced himself to stroll casually back to his chair and sit down. "I'm working on a number of puzzles right now. Which one are you talking about?"

"Please don't play coy with me, Mister Novak. We know your organization recently came into possession of a highly sensitive piece of information about Earth's ancient past."

Bringing all his training to bear, Novak kept his expression impassive and took a slow, deep breath to steady his voice before speaking again.

"By 'we', I gather you're referring to *your* organization."

Quan tried to nod in reply but was brought up short by his collar.

"Who do you work for?" Novak demanded.

Silence.

"Who gives you your orders, Quan? What's the name of your organization? How do you know about this sensitive information that we're supposed to have?"

More silence. Novak studied him for a moment. The prisoner's demeanor remained calm and infuriatingly unconcerned. If he'd been conditioned to resist interrogation, they could badger him, ridicule him, bully or threaten him for hours on end without getting a rise or making a dent. And considering how much physical punishment he'd already endured with no apparent loss of resolve, torturing him was unlikely to gain them anything useful. The Forrand fortune had been made in pharmaceuticals, so the EIS had an array of substances at their disposal, extremely effective for wiping memories, inducing hallucinations, even counterfeiting death. Although quite useful in the field, none of them could properly be called a "truth drug". Still, maybe the threat of one would be enough to crack Nestor Quan's composure.

Novak leaned in and said in a lowered voice, "Right now, we're just having a conversation. But there's a data extraction specialist waiting outside the door, with a whole kit full of tools he can't wait to try out on you. It's not only about pain, you know. He's developed drugs that can turn the Human brain inside out. He can scramble your synapses, wipe your cortex, plant you permanently in the middle of your worst nightmare. So, sooner or later you're going to tell me what I want to know. The question is, how much of Nestor Quan is going to be left at that point?"

Cold dark eyes locked with Novak's as the voice of someone far more confident than himself replied, "No, the question is, when are you going to ask me the right question?"

— «» —

"He knows way too much," growled Novak, glaring at the light screen in the observation room. "About Human nature and about the EIS. And about me," he reflected aloud.

"He knew enough to call your bluff, anyway," DeWitt pointed out. "So, who do you want to send in with the briefcase of surgical tools to rattle his nerves? Mendez does a great mad scientist impression."

Novak was in no mood for joking. His gut had been right about this interrogation. It had been an hour-long verbal siege, revealing not so much as a chink in the prisoner's defenses. An exercise in futility. To every one of his questions, Quan had replied with a melodramatic sigh, "Not the right one." Finally, Novak had given "the ninja" a knockout injection before stalking across the hall for a change of scenery.

"Or," DeWitt suggested quietly, "we could make him disappear and fabricate something to tell Madame Vargas. How would she know the difference?"

After a moment, Novak shook his head. That he'd even considered the idea was a measure of the frustration he was feeling. But it was one thing to keep secrets from Juno Vargas, quite another to lie to her face. They'd both promised Dennis Forrand that they would share power equally and be honest with each other after he was gone. When everything came to a head — as it inevitably would, given the direction she was taking — Novak wanted the moral advantage of having stuck to that promise.

He turned to glance at the monitor again, then looked around the room, suddenly realizing that someone was missing. "Where's Chin?" he demanded.

"He went a little nuts shortly after you began the interview. Jumped off his chair muttering something about 'your planetary government', then ran out of the room."

Novak frowned. *Your* planetary government? Was that what Quan had said? "Replay the feed for me, De— What the—?"

"I think we found Chin, boss," said DeWitt, pointing at the live image on the screen.

A man wearing a surgical mask had entered the interrogation room, carrying a cloth-covered tray. As they watched, he pulled the right sleeve of Quan's jacket out of the leather cuff on his wrist, removed a vial's worth of blood from his forearm, then carefully placed a stickyplast over the puncture wound before tugging the sleeve back down to cover it.

"Do we care whether the prisoner knows what just happened?"

"No," said Novak, "but *I* would sure as hell like to know. Tell Chin I want to talk to him, right now."

Chin had evidently been expecting the summons. The second DeWitt opened the door to the hallway, the scientist stepped inside the observation room. He was grinning behind his surgical mask.

Smugness wasn't normally Naguchi's style; however, given the history between him and Quan, the urge to gloat was probably irresistible. Novak gave him a long look. "Are you volunteering to torture the prisoner, Doctor?"

"Not at all. I've just returned from confirming a theory in my laboratory. Now I can proceed with a closer analysis of his blood."

"Confirming what theory?"

"Mr. DeWitt and his colleagues were less than gentle with Quan when they brought him in. This on top of a vigorous beating by several Rangers that should have rendered him comatose but didn't. When you began questioning him and he said 'your planetary government' — *your*, not *our* — something clicked into place at the back of my mind. Remember Trager? I didn't need a large sample to perform a definitive test, just a smear or two of blood from the towels used to clean Quan up when he arrived."

"And you're absolutely certain of the result?"

"Absolutely. The enzymes are identical. Bruni Patel, Trager, and Nestor Quan — they're all Stragori."

— «» —

Two hours later, Novak was sitting in the interrogation room watching Nestor Quan regain consciousness. He came to with a shudder, making a reflexive effort to stretch before the cuffs and collar stopped him. When his gaze alighted on Novak's face, Barry could swear he saw disappointment in the prisoner's dark eyes.

"No, it wasn't all a dream," he assured him. "While you were sleeping, however, we made a couple of interesting discoveries."

Quan smirked. "You have a learning curve. How encouraging."

"We now know that you're Stragori."

"Good for you. And what was the second discovery?"

"We've scanned you top to bottom, and you have no implants. No scarring, either, to indicate you ever did."

Somehow, the prisoner managed to tilt his head expectantly. "And what do you suppose that means?"

"You're not a soldier, and you're not an observer. And yet, you lived on Earth for decades. Doing what, Quan? What brought you to our fair planet?"

"Not the right question," he replied. "Too bad."

"Maybe you're an assassin," mused Novak. "Your government would want total deniability, so they would make sure you weren't connected to the intellinet. You could be trained in killing techniques without being optimized. And if a soldier refused to terminate the observer he was shadowing, you could swoop in and do the job instead. How about it, Quan — did you kill Bruni Patel?"

He swiveled his head slowly side to side. "Not the right one. Not even close."

"Because if you did," Novak went on doggedly, "that would explain how you know about the sensitive data that recently came into our possession."

Barry's earpiece tingled. He activated it and heard Naguchi's voice instructing him, "Ask him about our work together. And EuroGenics."

Before faking his death, Naguchi had been renowned for his groundbreaking work in genetics, but some of those breakthroughs had been made in partnership with Nestor Quan. Quan couldn't have been doing it on behalf of the Stragori government, not without a connection to the intellinet. So who could have sent him to Earth to cultivate one of the most brilliant scientific minds on the planet? It had to be an organization with deep pockets and a network of operatives. Perhaps a large corporation?

That made sense, actually. It explained the enforcers who had strong-armed Naguchi into thumbprinting the contract to sell his patents, and the thug who had met him at the airfield when he returned from Daisy Hub. They would have put pressure on Quan as well, when they realized Naguchi had reneged on the agreement. After the lab explosion that supposedly killed Naguchi and destroyed all his notes and records, Quan must have been desperate. And desperate men did desperate things.

"Don't tell me you've run out of questions, Mister Novak," Quan admonished him.

"I haven't. I'm just tired of playing this game. You're toying with us, teasing us with information that you claim to have but refusing to talk. Well, you'd better start giving me some straight answers, because I am fast losing patience with you, and when I run out of patience, that's when you run out of time."

Quan made an impatient sound of his own. "It isn't enough just to ask questions. They have to be the right ones. Scientists appreciate the importance of asking the right question, Mister Novak. That's how we classify and organize the answers that surround us in such abundance. For example, the two of us sitting in this room constitutes an answer. But before it can be fully comprehended, one must ask the right question."

"And that is...?"

"Which of us is the prisoner, and which of us is free? If I believe that my being here puts me beyond the reach of an implacable enemy, then regardless of the way you treat me, I've achieved freedom. And if you feel your future depends on getting information from me that someone else requires, then you are in fact the prisoner. You see how the complexion of the situation can change, depending on the question being asked? How easily it could be misunderstood by someone not asking the correct one?

"Throw off your shackles, Mister Novak. Ask me what you *really* want to know."

"All right. But can we trust anything that you say?"

Quan threw him a reproving look. "Regardless of my intentions, the answer would be yes. Come on, you can do better than that."

"What was your real reason for letting yourself be captured on Shakespeare Hub?"

"As I said earlier, I have information that you need in order to solve the puzzle, and I wanted you to have it.

Not your government. Not even your organization. You, personally."

"Why me?"

"Because you're the only Human Bruni Patel was willing to trust with the file he stole from the Directorate's archives."

"You're aware that he was murdered by Stragori agents before he could deliver it?"

"What makes you think his death was the work of our government?"

"When his body was found, all the implants had been ripped out. Only a Stragori would have known to do that."

An unreadable expression slithered across the prisoner's face. "Mister Novak, if this had been an official assassination, there would have been no body left for you to find. Our operatives are trained to clean up their messes. So, the killer may have been Stragori, but it's highly unlikely that this individual was acting under orders from the Directorate."

"You betrayed and destroyed Nayo Naguchi and viciously attacked one of my agents. Now suddenly you're being helpful. What's going on, Quan? Have you developed a soft spot in your heart for Humanity after all your years of living among us?"

"Really, now, do I strike you as someone who has a sentimental bone in his body? Here is the answer to your question: My government has made a decision with which I disagree, and I've decided to show them the error of their ways by sabotaging their plans for your world. Whatever they think is going to happen, they'll be wrong. And I'll be vindicated."

"And what do we get out of this, exactly?"

"The truth, Mister Novak. Whether or not Humanity is ready to handle it, at long last someone on your planet with both the means and the will to act on it is going to know the truth."

— «» —

When Naguchi returned to his lab, he found a message from Susan Rosenberg on his computer: *I've destroyed my notes as you instructed, but I'm not seeing any of your trigger words so far in the document I'm translating, Nayo. Seems pretty harmless to me — something about preparing animals to be used for experimentation — but then, I'm not a biologist.*

CHAPTER 11

"You said your government had made a decision, Quan. What was it?"

They'd been at this for quite a while. Stifling a yawn, Novak realized that he had no idea whether it was dark or light outside. Weariness was creeping into his muscles, sending chills rippling across his back and down his legs. He debated with himself which would be wiser: to succumb to his fatigue and take a break, or to fortify himself with java and keep going. Quan, on the other hand, remained maddeningly fresh and alert, apparently deaf to his own diurnal rhythm. Maybe he didn't have any. Maybe the days on Stragon were fifty hours long, or the Stragori version of Humanity had evolved beyond the need for sleep.

"Am I keeping you awake, Mister Novak?"

He gave himself a hard mental shake and replied evenly, "No, Quan, I'm keeping *you* awake so you can answer my question. What was the Directorate's decision?"

As he expected, Quan's response to this was silence. However, it was a thoughtful silence, not a defiant one, so he continued, "We've translated the document in the file you mentioned earlier. We've deduced that Humans and Stragori are the same race. We also know that your government would rather keep that explosive little fact a secret."

"All true," said Quan. "Knowing the truth about our origins, the Directorate had a choice to make. They could either acknowledge our shared history and reunite with our distant cousins of Earth, becoming a single race of Humans once more…"

"…or?"

"Or not. They chose not."

Novak was dumbfounded. "Why would they do that? Stragori isn't a name you chose for yourselves — it's a Thryggian word meaning 'control group'. It's a constant reminder of the crime that was perpetrated against our race in more primitive times."

"As far as the Directorate is concerned, Humans are still living in primitive times."

"Yes. We're a young race with a lot to learn and the other races try to have as little as possible to do with us. Believe me, we're painfully aware of that."

"Not just a young race. Compared to the rest of us, you're literally a race of youngsters. And as for the crime you refer to, you have no idea of its magnitude."

Novak had left his earpiece on. "Barry," said Naguchi from the observation room. There was an unaccustomed urgency in his voice. "I've got a hunch. Ask him his age."

"What?"

"Just do it. Please!"

Returning his gaze to Quan's bruised and swollen face, Novak asked, "How old are you, anyway?"

"That little mouse in your ear is very clever," remarked the prisoner with a knowing smile. "Reminds me of someone I used to work with. Make sure he gets an extra piece of cheese for dinner."

"Answer the question, Quan."

"Very well. Measured in Earth years, my age is one hundred and seventy-two."

— «» —

"Why do I have the feeling that he's enjoying this?" muttered Novak.

Sitting in the swivel chair to his right, Naguchi swung it a quarter-turn toward him and replied, "Because he is."

It was six o'clock in the morning and they were alone together in the observation room, gazing at the light screen. Mendez had brought the prisoner a cup of water and was holding it to his mouth so he could drink. But Mendez was slow to tip the cup and Quan's head movements were severely restricted by his collar, forcing him to lap up the water with his tongue, like an animal. Watching the scene pulled up memories for Novak.

As Rex Regum, he had ordered and supervised demeaning punishments like this for transgressors in the Zone, and even for new members of the Warrior Kings, to impress on them where they stood in the hierarchy. He'd put an end to "nest raiding" by castrating the rapists who had invaded his territory and leaving them outside it for Security to find. Tommy Novotny had given the Kings a strict code of honor and forced them all to observe it. Now Barry Novak was in charge, juggling "hot potatoes" and living by a much more complicated set of rules.

The part of him that was Tommy Novotny was enjoying the sight of an enemy brought low, but Barry knew that Quan couldn't be kept shackled indefinitely. EIS agents were routinely instructed to either turn or terminate an adversary. As Chief of Operations, Novak would have to do the same.

"You worked with him for years and know him better than I do, Nayo. Can he be trusted?"

Naguchi moved his shoulders as though physically attempting to shrug off the question. When that apparently failed, he replied, "You give me too much credit, Barry. We were partners for nearly twenty years, spent eight to ten hours together almost every day of that time, and all I managed to learn about him — the hard way — was that Nestor Quan is a consummate pragmatist with no sense of loyalty. The only thing he can be depended on to do is whatever happens to be in his own best interests at the time. If you're asking whether I believe his story about helping us in order to gain a personal victory over his government, all I can tell you is that it sounds typical of him. Make no mistake, this man is nobody's friend, and he never does anything out of the goodness of his heart."

"What about his claim to be one hundred and seventy-two years old? You said you had a hunch, so you must have been expecting it."

"Not a hunch, exactly — a hypothesis. Susan's most recent update mentioned preparing subjects to be used for experimentation, and that got me thinking. We use rodents in our laboratories, partly because they're prolific breeders, making them a plentiful commodity, but also because their short life spans enable us to see the results of our experiments more quickly. So I asked myself, what if the preparation mentioned in that document included shortening the Human life span to make us better lab animals?

"To test my hypothesis, I revisited some of the blood tests I'd done on our Stragori friends and cultured a few additional samples from Quan for good measure. The cultures are still immature, but based on what I've observed so far, I believe he may be telling the truth.

"The telomeres in the nuclei of Stragori cells appear to be unaffected by replication. If so, that means something else must be regulating their aging process. It may be those extra enzymes in their blood, or something else I've yet to discover; and it wouldn't necessarily be on the same clock as ours. All I can tell you for certain right now is this: since Quan and I first met, thirty-five Earth years ago, I've aged thirty-five years — and he doesn't look a day older than he did the first time I laid eyes on him."

Novak returned his attention to the light screen and was startled to find Nestor Quan staring directly into the securecam. As though sensing that eye contact had been made, the prisoner fidgeted in his chair for a moment, then said, "Now that we've established my intentions, do you suppose these restraints could come off? I've been sitting here for hours."

Naguchi was watching Novak expectantly. "It's your call, Barry," he said, "but I would exercise caution."

Turn him or terminate him. The words rang in his mind as Novak crossed the hall and re-entered the interrogation room.

"I see you found the surveillance eye," he remarked, dropping once more into the seat facing Quan. "Convince me that you're an ally and not a threat and I'll let you stretch your legs."

"And how do you suggest I do that?"

Novak leaned back in his chair and pinned a pleasant smile on his face. "It's simple. Just tell me everything that your government is determined to keep secret from us."

"You've evidently taken my earlier advice to heart." Still immobilized by the collar, he managed to tilt his head slightly in approval. "Very well. I'll tell you what I can. Where would you like me to begin?"

"Start with the decision made by your government that you are so intent on undermining. You said they want nothing to do with us, and yet they have plans for our world. What sort of plans?"

"To preclude your making a claim to the Galactic Great Council for the reunification of the Human race, the Directorate has been actively working to prevent you from learning the truth about our shared past."

"That's old news," said Novak. "The man who brought us the file after Patel was killed told us about the Directorate's decision to suppress what was in it."

Quan's eyebrows went up. "Did he also tell you that the Directorate had set up corporations on your world for the sole purpose of aborting any scientific or technological advancements that might lead you to uncover the truth on your own?"

Novak stared wordlessly at him for a moment as the ramifications of this barreled through his thoughts. In his ear, Naguchi's harsh whisper expressed enough astonishment and outrage for both of them. "Those *bastards!*"

"That's why EuroGenics was so determined to own Naguchi's patents?" Novak said grimly when he could speak again.

"Among many others. When it was discovered that he'd absconded with his most important work, I was ordered to find and bring back the missing experiment, using whatever methods were necessary."

"But it was your work too," Novak pointed out. "Naguchi shared credit with you on papers, and both your names appeared on most of those patents. You were helping him to make those breakthroughs. That couldn't have sat well with your superiors."

"It was only technically my work. I secured funding for the laboratory and designed and ran some experiments. The concepts and theories, however — the heart and soul of his research — that was all Naguchi. But you're correct, Mister Novak. When my superiors learned that I had actually been facilitating his progress, they were beyond listening to reason. By then, of course, I had already decided that the Directorate was making a huge mistake by holding Humanity back, and that I would gain great satisfaction from rubbing their noses in it. Not surprisingly, my final official assignment came in the form of an ultimatum: succeed or die."

Novak nearly smiled. Clearly, the "implacable enemy" Quan had referred to earlier was far from hypothetical.

"Well, according to my sources, you left Daisy Hub empty-handed, so you didn't succeed; and here you are, still alive — for now. A double loss for the Directorate — how disappointing."

"That is not entirely true," said Quan. "And it's one of the reasons I wanted to ensure that I fell into your hands as quickly as possible. Shortly after my arrival on Platform Zulu I discovered a tracking device tucked into the seam of my jacket. Evidently, my superiors did not trust me to carry out their orders."

Novak let out a snort of laughter. "What a surprise."

"I destroyed the device immediately; however, the damage was already done. The Directorate now knows where to find the rest of Naguchi's work. I may have come away empty-handed, but the next operative they send will assuredly not. In fact, that individual is probably already on the station, tasked with completing my mission."

For about three seconds, it was a sobering thought. Then Novak declared, "It's not that easy to sneak aboard Daisy Hub, as you should know from experience."

"True," he conceded, "but there is more than one way to infiltrate an enemy camp. This man you spoke about who brought you the file after Bruni Patel was killed — would you indulge me by describing him, please?"

A nameless unease crept over Novak then, like a nagging feeling that he'd forgotten to do something important. "He was tall and muscular, with blond hair and blue eyes. Well, one blue eye — he'd ripped out all his implants to sever his connection to the intellinet. He came to us torn up and bloodied, quite a mess. Asked us to help him disappear."

"So he was a soldier, and he no doubt claimed to have a close connection with Bruni Patel, whom you knew quite well and whose loss you were still mourning. And because of the gift he'd brought you, ostensibly on poor dead Bruni's behalf, you accepted his story as truth and agreed to help him."

Novak's gut already knew the answer, but he asked the question anyway. "What are you trying not to say, Quan? You think this man could have been sent by the Directorate as your replacement?"

"Oh, I'm certain he was. Bruni belonged to the moderate faction, and he was a pacifist. He wanted nothing to do with soldiers, wouldn't even accept a military shadow on Earth, and his superiors humored him. If they'd insisted, he might still be alive — in a cell on Stragon, awaiting execution for plotting treason, perhaps, but alive. So, this lying impostor who brought you the file — dare I guess where you sent him?"

His stomach now curling into an icy knot, Novak rose from his chair and stalked silently out of the room.

— ‹› —

First the Thryggians had screwed them up, and now the Stragori were screwing them over.

"You can't take anything he says at face value, Barry," Naguchi reminded him. "He'll twist things to make you believe what he wants. He's done it before."

Novak rubbed his eyes with a thumb and forefinger. "I don't think he's lying this time, Nayo. Not about all of it, anyway. Too many things are starting to add up. Bruni Patel, for example. Dennis Forrand would never have hired him, not even for low-level courier work, if there had been a 'shadow' in the picture. And if the Directorate knew through the intellinet that he was moonlighting for us and they wanted to take him out quietly, they had the means to do it. As his handler, I might have suspected foul play, but without a body to prove it, and knowing that he was an alien, I would eventually have been forced to assume that he'd been unexpectedly recalled to Stragon. No muss, no fuss, no questions. Instead, Patel was murdered — we still don't know how — and his body with all its implants ripped out was left on the Kings' doorstep for anyone to find."

"As a message?" mused Naguchi. "We know where you live and you can expect a visit?"

"I suspect it was more than that. Think about it, Nayo. When did we even become aware of the file on that datawafer?"

The other man's eyes widened slightly as comprehension dawned. "When Trager brought it to you, along with what seemed a rational explanation for Patel's death. It answered most of our unanswered questions…"

"…making us want to believe it. And once we'd swallowed that much of the story, the rest went down without any difficulty," Novak concluded ruefully. "We're not dealing with aliens, Nayo. They're as Human as we are, and they knew exactly how to play us. Bruni was a pawn. His death gave Trager access to me, and I was his pipeline to Daisy Hub. Damn! We need to alert Townsend right away."

"Actually," said Naguchi hesitantly, "he probably already knows that Karlov is not to be trusted."

Halfway out of his chair, Novak halted and dropped back down, his expression stern. "You'd better explain that, Doctor Chin."

"I had Danziger darken the iris of the prosthetic eye by a couple of shades. Nothing dramatic, just something that would strike the crew as being not quite right about Karlov and put them on their guard. If those people are still as smart as they were when I was station manager, they'll already have begun unraveling his cover story by the time your warning arrives."

Novak leaned back into his chair, slack-jawed. "Wow. And I thought Quan took unconscionable risks. This was the last thing I expected from you, Nayo."

"In retrospect, I realize I probably shouldn't have done it, but—"

"Damn straight, you shouldn't have! Blowing the cover of an operative on a mission is a betrayal punishable by death. What if Trager had turned out to be on the level?"

"Look, I'm sorry, but from the moment I met him, I could sense that there was something wrong about him. When I tried to warn you, you brushed me off. I knew that the way you planned to send him to the Hub, smuggled aboard a freighter with a rat for a traveling companion, was bound to raise eyebrows at the other end anyway, so I changed one little thing to reinforce that reaction. That's all I did. I was sure that if his story checked out down here, then he would pass all their tests out there, with no harm done. On the other hand—"

"Better safe than sorry. I get it. But dammit, Nayo, we've been friends for more than eighteen years, trusting each other with secrets that could blow up like bombs, and you still felt the need to go to Danziger behind my back?"

"Would you have approved my plan if I'd suggested it?"

"Dunno," he growled. "You never gave me the chance." After a pause that hung in the air between them like a wall, Novak finally added, "Maybe I would have, if I'd had time to think about it. If we— If *I* hadn't been in such a rush to hide the file and get Trager offplanet before the Stragori arrived." He threw Naguchi a sideways look. "They still haven't come after him, you know. I've been hoping it's because he actually managed to throw them off his scent, but— I should have paid attention to your instincts, Nayo. I'm sorry."

"As you should be," said Naguchi drily. "And while we're on the subject, something else has been nagging at me. If the Directorate's purpose is to keep us in the dark about our ancient past, then why hand us the document in that file? If the messenger is a liar, mightn't that mean the message he's carrying is false as well?"

"Are you talking about Trager, or about Quan?"

"About both. At least one of them is conning us, and as your physician I'm prescribing a healthy dose of skepticism."

"Point taken, Doctor." Striding to the door, Novak cracked it open and called out to his second in command, standing guard in the hallway. "DeWitt, take Quan some food and free up his hands so he can eat it himself."

"Just his hands, boss?"

"Yes, and make certain he can't reach the buckle on his collar. I have a few more questions for him to answer, and one of them is the deal breaker."

— «» —

"Is there something about that file of sensitive information that we should know, Quan?"

Novak's voice had an impatient edge to it, and with reason. Quan had taken his time eating, turning his meal of a tomato sandwich, a cup of yogurt, and a mug of java into an hour-long theatrical performance for the benefit of whoever might be watching him on the monitor.

Now, sitting with his arms crossed over his chest and wearing a smile that fairly begged to meet up with a right hook, Quan replied, "Are you belatedly wondering whether it is authentic? If not, you should be."

"And if you were to give me a truthful answer to that question, what would it be?"

"You would learn that the document in that file is a true copy of the original, which was purportedly stolen from Earth many of your centuries ago and is now kept in the Stragori government archives. Although its provenance has never been verified, it provides an irrefutable explanation for the commonalities shared by our two races, as anyone who has drawn the unwanted attention of the Thryggians will attest."

"And yet your government — the same Directorate that is actively working to prevent us from finding out about our ancient past, according to you — has contrived to put this information into our hands. Why?"

"Think about what you've done with that information, Mister Novak, and in particular what you are *not* able to do with it, because I assure you, the Directorate considered it carefully. In the absence of a person you trusted who could introduce and vouch for him, their agent presented you with an artifact that they knew you could verify as being genuinely ancient but would be forced to keep secret, and thus could never use against them. In this, as in many other of the Directorate's assumptions regarding Humanity," he added, the maddening smile spreading to encompass his gleaming dark eyes, "I intend to prove them disastrously wrong."

Tommy Novotny was finding that prospect extremely attractive. With an effort, Barry Novak dragged him back to the interrogation at hand.

"One more question: You said something earlier about us being a race of youngsters. What did you mean by that?"

"I meant what I said. In the eyes of every other spacegoing race in the galaxy, Humans are children."

"Why?" Novak demanded. "Because we don't live as long as they do? That makes no—" The words died in his throat as he suddenly realized that it did make perfect sense, if the other races knew what the Stragori really were.

Quan had been watching for his reaction. "Am I to gather from the expression on your face that you've had an epiphany, Mister Novak?" he said pleasantly.

"It's because we don't live as long as *you* do, isn't it? What's the average life span of a Stragori?"

"Two hundred and fifty Earth years, give or take a decade."

Novak had to force his lungs to accept his next breath. When he could once more trust his voice, he repeated, "Two hundred and fifty? That's twice as long as ours."

"Now it is. You've made strides in medical research, managing to increase your ability to cling to life by about fifty percent. It's a laudable achievement, to be sure. But your physical aging process still begins prematurely."

"And we can thank the Thryggians for that?" said Novak.

Quan hesitated a moment, then dipped his chin slightly.

"You're a scientist, Quan. Has anyone on Stragon been investigating ways to remedy our situation?"

"Can you be fixed, you mean? Reset to factory specifications? Of course, you can. Does anyone on Stragon have the will and the resources to dedicate to such a project? No. The original mutations were engineered gradually, over hundreds of your years. To change you back would take numerous generations of a prescribed breeding program, and would entail considerable risk to all involved."

"Good luck getting everyone on the planet to agree to *that*," Naguchi's voice whispered in his ear.

Nonetheless, Novak pressed on. "If we could gather the resources ourselves, and demonstrated the will, would it be a risk worth our taking?"

Quan gave this some thought before replying. "At the moment, no. In the future, possibly. Once the Directorate has been neutralized, we might even be willing to help you."

"Neutralized?" For Novak, this word had dangerous implications. He swallowed hard before continuing, "Neutralized how, Quan? What exactly is your grand plan to show your government the error of its ways?"

"The ninja" smiled. "One step at a time, Mister Novak. First, we must forge an alliance, you and I. And then, perhaps you'll permit me to leave this chair."

CHAPTER 12

Nayo, the deeper I get into this document the more disturbing it becomes. I figured out early on that when the Thryggians said "animals" they really meant Humans. Now my brain makes the substitution automatically. Just knowing what our distant ancestors went through while they were being "prepared to be experimented on" makes me feel sick to my stomach. I'm unable to sleep at night. I keep waking up from nightmares about aliens coming into my bedroom to cut tissue samples out of my body. This assignment can't end soon enough. I wish you could ride in on your white charger and rescue me.

— ‹›› —

Randall Chin's face was the portrait of incredulity. "Are you serious?" he demanded. "You're going to give Quan what he wants?" He glanced reflexively toward the monitor screen. The display hadn't changed. The interrogation room was as empty as it had been ten minutes earlier, after Mendez and Croft had unbuckled the prisoner from his chair and escorted him out the door.

"That isn't my decision alone to make," Novak pointed out. "However, we've finally hammered out a deal that I think she might be willing to go along with. And as long as giving him what he wants gets us what *we* want, then it's what I'll be recommending to Madame Vargas."

"Tell me you're not thinking of providing him with a new identity."

Novak threw him a reproachful look. "Give me some credit, Nayo. He's an escaped murderer taking sanctuary in our custody, and half the Security forces on Earth are looking for him. The face he's currently wearing is as good as a leash. And on a leash is exactly where we want him to be."

Before Naguchi could say another word, Novak strode past him into the hallway and beckoned to the waiting DeWitt to join them. "Put extra surveillance on our guest and make sure he doesn't talk to anyone until I get back," he instructed. "And try not to have too much fun while you're doing it."

'Man Mountain' grinned. "You've got it, boss," he said to their backs as Novak and Dr. Chin headed for the elevator. The vehicle parking area was seven floors down.

Despite its outward appearance of decrepitude, the old office building in the Zone was a fortress — reinforced, renovated, and equipped with rogue technology of every kind. The elevators in the lobby had been disabled and the first three floors made to look abandoned in order to discourage exploration by the curious or adventuresome.

Only Novak's crew and a handful of EIS operatives were permitted access to the Kings' secret headquarters. It was reached via a private elevator whose thumbprint-locking entrances, like the door to the clean room at SecuriTech, were concealed inside closets and disguised by holographic images on each floor. At a glance, the ones below ground each appeared to be nothing more than a span of blank wall in a shadowy corner. (It could be quite disconcerting to see someone suddenly emerge from one of those walls. The day Mendez had leaped out at him, roaring like a wild animal, Naguchi had nearly had a heart attack.)

"Barry, think of all the negatives. Given everything he's pulled on us so far, you'll never be able to trust him," Naguchi fretted as the two men stepped into the elevator car. "And even if you're able to make the partnership work in the EIS's favor, it exponentially increases the risk of Vargas finding out about Trager and the Stragori file."

Novak pressed P2. "She's our Chief Intelligence Officer, Nayo. With all of her contacts in the field, I'd be surprised if she didn't already know more than we would like. She's invited me to have tea with her in about an hour, probably to grill me about what Quan has or hasn't revealed under inter-rogation. I'm going to tell her who he used to work for. Then I'll tell her who he'd *like* to work for and see what she says."

Naguchi was at a loss for words. Not until the car bumped to a stop and the elevator's inner door slid aside on the sub-basement level was he able to speak again. "You know how she feels about having aliens on the payroll. If she finds out that he's Stragori—!"

Wearing a lopsided grin, Novak pressed his thumb to the lock and shoved the outer door open. "Last time I checked, captured hostile sources didn't draw a salary. Wish me luck."

— ‹›› —

The tea on the silver tray was green this time, with enough orange flavoring added to aromatize the room. It wasn't a variety she personally liked. Presumably, it meant Novak wasn't a favorite of hers either right now.

"Shall I pour?" she inquired with porcelain politeness.

"Please do."

Instead of turning the tray toward him, she made him reach across it to pick up his cup. He studied her face, searching for some hint of emotion, and found nothing — not a twitch of tension, not a crease of concern. Novak could still feel Tommy Novotny stirring inside him every time he formed a thought or made a decision. Looking at Juno Vargas, it was hard to believe that this stiff, painted doll had ever been a bold and volatile teen named Olivia Townsend.

She sat back in her seat, blew gently across the surface of her tea, and took a tentative sip. Then, leveling cool gray eyes at her guest, she remarked, "I received some interesting information this morning."

Here we go, he thought. Aloud, he said only, "Oh?"

"It seems that the ancient document found in that archaeological dig six months ago in Indo-Asia has finally been translated. Apparently, it was written in an ancient alien tongue. The xenolinguist hired by the Americas High Council had a terrible time with it. She struggled for months to pull any meaning out of the text. Then, suddenly, she had a revelation and was able to finish the job in jig time. Quite a lucky break, wouldn't you say?"

"Very lucky," he agreed.

She gave him a reproving look before carefully setting her teacup back down on the tray. "Come on, Barry.

We both know luck had very little to do with it, and so does the Supreme Adjudicator. She has a file on Doctor Susan Rosenberg, revealing a long and intimate history with our good friend Nayo Naguchi before he died. On-site Security has also reported to her that the translator had a visit from a Doctor Randall Chin shortly before her dramatic breakthrough. Randy should get out of the Zone a little more often — Security's efforts to locate him for questioning have so far been unsuccessful, and red flags are going up as we speak. Doctor Rosenberg's mental stability has come into question as well. Her behavior lately has been described as 'erratic', even 'paranoid'. All of this casts serious doubt on the veracity of the translation, as you can well imagine.

"Don't worry — the High Council still doesn't know that Naguchi is alive, or that Naguchi and Chin are the same person, so for the moment you and I and the EIS are all safe. Unfortunately, I can't say the same for Doctor Rosenberg and her elusive lover.

"I was with the Supreme Adjudicator when the finished work was delivered to her, and I can tell you that she was suspicious even before she looked at it. After reading it she was considering laying charges. I believe she was expecting something a lot more important and enlightening than a detailed description of how to torture a rabbit. I have her ear and can control some of the damage at my end, but I need to know the truth. Did Rosenberg falsify the translated document?"

Novak had feared something like this might happen. Fortunately, he'd also prepared for it. Firmly placing his cup on the coffee table, he replied, "No, she didn't. There must have been other translators assigned to this project. I'm sure any one of them can double-check her work and verify its authenticity."

Vargas stared at him for a moment. "What exactly did Naguchi give her, Barry?" she asked softly.

"Doctor Chin worked alongside a team of Thryggian scientists to trace the contagion vector of the Angel of Death plague back in the late 80s. In the process, he may have — ah — *acquired* some of the originals of the translated documents that were given out at meetings."

"Say no more," she ordered him. "I'm going to need deniability. Now tell me, in your opinion, is Doctor Rosenberg the sort of person who could become extremely upset at the thought of helpless animals being dissected alive?"

"I think she could become seriously sleep-deprived from having recurring nightmares about it," he confirmed, adding silently, *and I probably won't be sleeping too well either from now on, knowing what the Thryggians are capable of.*

He retrieved his cup and sipped from it. The tea was cold and tasted bitter.

"That's what I thought. All right, Barry, leave this with me. However, once everything is smoothed over, you and I will need to have a long talk about that document, as well as the ones that Naguchi acquired and then withheld from us."

Novak replaced his cup on the tray. If she was using the royal 'we', this might not be the best time to discuss—

"Nestor Quan," she announced, charging through his thoughts. "You've had him for well over a week. What, if anything, have you managed to learn so far?"

"I interrogated the prisoner, as per your orders—"

"Oh, please! Since when do you do anything 'as per my orders'?"

The cool stare had become positively frosty. He took a deep breath and pressed ahead. "You wanted to know who he was working for at the time he boarded Platform Zulu? It was the Stragori government."

Madame Vargas leaned back against the loveseat cushion, frowning thoughtfully. "And has he told you what his mission was?"

"Not yet, but I'm certain he will."

"And you feel this way because…?"

"Let's just say that now that his former employers want him dead, he's reconsidered his career options."

"The Directorate wants Quan dead? Why?"

He paused, carefully picking his words. "He's failed one too many times, and he knows too much about the Stragori.

And he's willing to put all of his knowledge at our disposal, in exchange for protection from them."

Her expression darkened. "Of course he is! Doling it out by the teaspoonful, no doubt, to remain useful to us for as long as possible. And to keep us busy verifying each piece of his dubious data. Get rid of him, Barry," she snapped. "He's a Stragori plant. Once he's revealed what he was doing for them aboard Zulu and Daisy Hub, give him a stiff dose of Warrior King justice. In the meanwhile, I have repairs to make to the reputation of a certain xenolinguist. And if Randy Chin knows what's good for him, he'll pay her a social visit as soon as possible. That woman needs a hug, and he's the only one who can give it to her. Now, shoo!"

Barry Novak returned to the Zone with mixed feelings. On the one hand, he'd managed the translation of the ancient document to a relatively safe conclusion. Nobody's cover had been blown, and the existence of the Stragori file was still a secret. On the other hand, his hard-negotiated deal with Nestor Quan was apparently a non-starter.

Or was it?

True, Madame Vargas had summarily ordered him to execute the prisoner. But she had also acknowledged that Novak never followed her orders.

It appeared that Olivia Townsend wasn't completely gone after all.

A smile spread across his face, and for the next twenty minutes, at least, all was right with Tommy Novotny's world.

PART III

THE EPIPHANIES OF DREW TOWNSEND
DAISY HUB, 2399 C.E.

Daisy Hub (brought online 2368 C.E.) was an inspection and resupply station on the outermost edge of Earth space (Sector 5). Initially proposed and funded to be a long-term experiment in independent deep space living, it soon became an orbiting gulag where Earth's government could send Eligible dissidents and boat rockers. **Observation Platform Zulu**, home to the local Ranger detachment, was consequently installed in shared orbit with Daisy Hub in 2381 C.E. There have been allegations that Earth Intelligence was in fact behind the selection of the "troublemakers" who formed the Hub's crew, although no proof was ever found to support such a claim. Daisy Hub was the site of Earth's first interstellar battle in 2402 C.E. Although both the Hub and Zulu sustained considerable damage in the conflict, they remained in use until their decommissioning in 2422 C.E., per the terms of the Reunification Agreement of 2420 C.E.

— *Sic Transit Terra, An Unauthorized Planetary History (2673 C.E.)*

CHAPTER 13

It was quiet on Daisy Hub. Evening shift had just begun, and most of the crew were either relaxing or taking classes. Assistant Manager of Station Operations Ruby 'Mom' McNeil was on the short-hopper landing deck, teaching half a dozen techs how to fly the Corvou-built shuttlecraft she'd named *Devil Bug*. Cargo Inspector Lu Xensiu was on K Deck, turning another dozen or so crew members into ninjas. Data and Communications Specialist Lydia Garfield sat at her console in AdComm — the administration and communications center of the station — keeping a remote eye on the ship inspection underway on A Deck. And behind his desk on the other side of AdComm, in a workspace defined by banks of old-fashioned metal filing cabinets and a disreputable-looking square of blue carpet, Manager of Station Operations Drew Townsend was staring at row after row of text on his InfoComm screen and stifling yawn after yawn.

Lydia's voice calling to him across the deck was a welcome interruption.

"Drew, Gavin Holchuk found a couple of unregistered passengers in the cargo hold of the *Arcturus*. One of them insisted on speaking with you, so he's being escorted here from Med Services once the Doc is done with him."

Townsend leaned back in his chair with a sigh, rubbing his eyes with the thumb and forefinger of one hand.

They were plague refugees, most likely.

Daisy Hub was Earth's farthest-flung space station. Sharing an orbit with Ranger Platform Zulu, it ran circles around a gas giant located just inside the border of Sector 5. Two years earlier, a mutated strain of Angel of Death had broken out in the sector, and shortly afterward, Holchuk and his team of cargo inspectors had begun finding stowaways on outbound ships. The Hub's crew had so far been lucky — none of the quarantine breakers had actually been infected. But Townsend knew from experience how quickly that kind of luck could change.

"And the other passenger?"

"The Doc wants to keep her, at least for a while."

That didn't sound good. "Did you see her on the monitors?" he demanded. "How did she look? Did she seem healthy?"

"Actually, she was adorable. She'll make a great playmate for Yoko."

Startled by the sudden nearness of Lydia's voice, Townsend glanced up and found her standing at the end of his improvised room divider, wearing a mischievous expression on her face.

"She's an animal," he said as his fatigued brain finally made the connection. "A pet?"

"A black and white rat in a cage. The Doc is running tests on her as we speak, but she looked pretty lively to me. Unlike someone else I've been observing. You've been at this for hours, Drew. Are you sure there's nothing I can do to help?"

He was sure. He'd been reviewing twenty standard years' worth of reports logged by the previous station managers to determine the extent of Earth Intelligence's involvement in Daisy Hub's affairs. This was not a job he could delegate without the crew finding out about his own involvement with the EIS; and he wasn't certain that any of them — including himself — were ready yet for that to be revealed. In fact, they might never be.

As he was opening his mouth to reply, the tube car door to the right of his desk slid aside and two large men stepped onto the deck. One of them was Orvy Hagman, the station's dock foreman and stern-faced Head of Security. The other fellow reminded Townsend of the street toughs he'd often had to deal with when he was a field investigator with District Security in New Chicago. This man was Eligible — a prerequisite for space travel — but clearly no stranger to violence. His face was etched with scars and appeared to have recently been shoved through a pane of glass. And his lips were fixed in a faint, improbable grin.

Drew and Lydia exchanged a bemused look.

"I'll be at my station if you need anything," she told him, and retreated to sit watchfully at her console on the other side of C Deck.

"Mr. Townsend, this is Max Karlov," said Hagman, his voice even gruffer than usual. He nudged the visitor forward with one hand and dropped a datawafer onto the middle of Drew's desktop with the other. "According to his biowafer there, he's from Earth, and he's been posted to the Hub."

Oh, really? Townsend reached for the wafer. As his fingers closed around it, he felt it gently vibrate against his palm.

Mental alarms began to shrill.

This wasn't just a biowafer — it was EIS technology, keyed to Drew's DNA. So, Earth Intelligence had smuggled another operative out to the Hub, carrying extremely confidential information for its station manager. Wonderful. As if Townsend didn't have enough secrets to keep from his crew. Even worse, he had purposely made his reports to the EIS cryptic, since the last thing he wanted them finding out was that Daisy Hub had entered into an independent alliance with an alien race, effectively seceding from Earth.

Obfuscating to the EIS had been much easier when they were a couple of hundred light years away. Now that Karlov was here, Townsend had a feeling that his life was about to become orders of magnitude more complicated.

"I have an important message for you," Karlov told him. "I was instructed to deliver it to you privately."

In addition to what was on the datawafer? Townsend glanced across the deck and saw Lydia slowly shaking her head. Hagman didn't look too pleased either. But if Earth Intelligence had resorted to sending him a live courier, especially if he arrived by unconventional means and looked as though he'd had to fight his way onto the ship that had brought him here, the message had to be top secret and extremely sensitive. He couldn't refuse delivery of it, regardless of what his instincts were telling him.

"Lydia, take a java break. Hagman, go with her. I'll let you know when we're done here."

Reluctantly they headed for the tube car. When the door had closed behind them, Townsend stared into the face of the new arrival and demanded, "What's the message?"

Karlov leaned forward, beckoning to him to do the same. Then he stage-whispered, "You have friends back on Earth, Mr. Townsend, and they are concerned for your safety. There is information that you need to know embedded on that wafer. Your DNA has decrypted it. Anyone else's will re-encrypt it. The playback device that accompanied you to this place is rogue technology. Take it somewhere private and use it to read the wafer. Then you'll understand why I'm here and what you must do next."

— «» —

"They've found out, haven't they? Earth High Council has learned about our alliance with the Nandrians. That's probably why they sent him out here — to throw a wrench into things. His eyes don't match. Did you notice? One of them is darker than the other. It's probably a visual recording device. I hate this. We're sitting ducks. We can't ask Trokerk to defend us without starting an interstellar war. And now the secret's out and everything is going to hell."

Lydia and Hagman had bypassed the caf and gone directly to Med Services on H Deck. Still running tests on the black and white rat, Doc Ktumba had ordered them to wait in the triage area, where Lydia had immediately begun pacing back and forth and venting to no one in particular.

Hagman watched her fret for a while, then said mildly, "So, Earth Council decides to infiltrate and sabotage us, and instead of simply posting their agent to Daisy Hub through the usual channels, they smuggle him onto an outbound freighter, with an artificial eye and an animal, no less? I don't think they're that stupid, Lydia. Unless they think we're that stupid."

She swiped a stray lock of blond hair off her face. "Then who is he and why is he here?"

Hearing the edge of concern on her voice, Hagman remarked with a knowing smile, "You're worried about Townsend."

"Of course, I am!" She rounded indignantly on him. "Aren't you? We just left him all alone with that Max Karlov character. If that's even his real name."

Before Hagman could respond to this, the Trauma room door hummed open and the Doc stepped through it. Marion Ktumba was a large, dark-skinned woman with naturally stern features. At this moment, however, her expression was quite pensive.

"Well?" Lydia prodded.

"I just did a preliminary genetic analysis of our new rodent arrival. She and Yoko are definitely siblings, possibly even from the same litter."

Hagman gave her a dubious look. "That would make them about the same age."

"I know. And there's something else they have in common — each of them is infected with a retrovirus. It appears to me as though someone has either duplicated Nayo Naguchi's work or ended up with one of Naguchi's long-lived rats."

"And sent her here? That makes no sense," said Lydia. "I mean, the European gene broker that took over Naguchi's patents must know by now that we have Yoko. So, what are the odds of a second stolen Überrat turning up here for safekeeping?"

"Unless it isn't stolen and wasn't sent here for safekeeping." On the tail of her thought, Hagman had had one of his own. "Doc, the man who brought this animal aboard the Hub claimed to be carrying an important message for Townsend. Is it possible the rat could be part of it?"

Doc Ktumba paused, visibly debating with herself and then arriving at a conclusion. "Clear out, both of you," she commanded. "I've got work to do."

— «» —

From the age of five, Drew Townsend had had a recurring nightmare about coming home from school to discover that his family had moved away, leaving no forwarding address, not even a trail of bread crumbs for him to follow. When he was twelve, that nightmare came true. One evening there was a funny aftertaste to his milk. The next day he woke up with a headache, all alone in an empty house, and another family was waiting impatiently for him to pack up his few personal possessions and leave so that they could move in.

When he'd lost his Eligibility, his parents had been deeply disappointed. It wasn't the first time he'd let them down, so he figured they would get over it. Olivia had tried to warn him how serious this was, but he'd paid her no mind. He simply refused to believe that the people who loved him could turn their backs on him, even under extreme duress.

But they did, that day when he was twelve.

Years later, after learning how heartless the Relocation Authority could be, Drew was finally able to find a measure of consolation for himself, and forgiveness for his parents and sister. They hadn't really wanted to abandon him. The Relocation Authority had coerced them. The Relocation Authority was the villain of the piece.

Except when it wasn't. If the datawafer Karlov had brought him was credible — and that was a very large *if* — Olivia hadn't died out in space all those years ago, despite what the population database said. Instead, she had *chosen* to be dead to him, and to consider him dead to her as well. And then she had changed her name and gone on living her life on Earth, climbing the ladder of influence under the tutelage of the most powerful man she could find. Eventually, she had even stepped into his shoes. Olivia was the boss now of not only the Earth Intelligence Service but also the Urban District of New Chicago. Whatever she wanted got done, and nothing was done without her approval. But it still wasn't enough for her.

According to the datawafer, Olivia was planning to take over the world. In two years at most, Daisy Hub would become the lit fuse for a planetary *coup d'état*. Earth's government would fall and the EIS would move in to fill the power vacuum, with Olivia Townsend — or rather, Juno Vargas — at the helm. As for the station's crew, well, what were pawns for except to be sacrificed?

There had been a lot more information on the datawafer. That everyone on the Hub had been purposely placed there by the EIS, he already knew, thanks to Steve Bonelli. That at least one member of his crew was taking orders directly from someone at the EIS and wasn't actually under his command at all, he'd suspected for a while. The rest was almost too much to process, but it all boiled down to this:

First by the Kings and then by Bruni Patel, Drew's life from the age of twelve had apparently been shaped and directed to suit the purposes of one man — Olivia's highly-placed mentor, since deceased. And now, with curious timing and for some undisclosed reason, someone with EIS connections had chosen to reveal this to him. More curious still was the way the data had arrived, raising all sorts of red flags on the Hub, as though the sender wanted Townsend to distrust it. So maybe there was more to this message than just the data on the wafer. Maybe Karlov and the rat needed to be decrypted as well.

Or maybe the whole thing was a con, like Nestor Quan's bogus assignment to command the Ranger detachment on Zulu. Either way, Drew reminded himself savagely, any attempt to manipulate him by playing the family card was doomed to fail. Tommy Novotny and six years on the streets had taught him well. Drew Townsend *had* no family, not anymore. His parents had abandoned him. Olivia was dead to him. Bruni Patel had been brutally murdered. The only people he cared about now were his fellow residents on Daisy Hub. And Juno Vargas, if she existed, and if she saw him and his crew as nothing but future collateral damage, could count herself damned lucky to be two hundred light years away from him right now.

Two hours after sequestering himself in his quarters with the playback device, Townsend returned to AdComm, his jaw so tightly clenched that it was aching. Despite his determination not to let anything on the datawafer get to him, just a quick read-through of its contents had given him a powerful urge to put his fist through a wall. Meanwhile, the mantra Bruni Patel had taught him played and replayed on a loop in his mind: *Never trust appearances. Get all the facts. Then and only then, take action.*

It sounded like a plan.

As Drew exited the tube car and settled in behind his desk, Ruby and Lydia shared a meaningful look.

Ruby was nicknamed 'Mom' for a reason. Not only was she old enough to be the mother of nearly everyone else on the Hub, she also tended to take a maternal interest in their lives. Now she approached Townsend, stopping at the edge of the blue carpet to ask, "Is there anything you'd like to talk about, Chief?"

"Where's Max Karlov?"

"Hagman parked him in the caf, where I'm told he's been drinking cup after cup of Jensen's famous sludge. He likes it — says it's robust," she replied, then tried again. "What's going on, Drew, and how can I help?"

"You can get O'Malley up here. Then you and Lydia can give us the room."

She nodded wordlessly and spun away.

A couple of minutes later, Robert O'Malley — the Hub's resident hacker and official caretaker of Yoko, the Überrat — dropped into the chair facing Townsend's. Ruby and Lydia stepped into the tube car, looking concerned as the car door slid shut in front of them.

Although in his thirties, the ratkeeper had the face and demeanor of someone half his age, making it hard not to think of him as a kid. Right now, the kid was wearing a cocky expression. "What can I do for you, boss?"

"The database you copied from Earth onto our local net goes back to the last pandemic, correct?"

"It goes back a lot earlier than that, but it's complete and up to date from 2320 C.E. to the present."

"Can you tell whether a record has been altered?"

"Altered how, exactly?"

"For example, a name added to a ship's passenger list once the ship has departed."

"Hard to say. Adding a name is the easiest fudge in the book, but depending on who makes the change and when, it can be the most difficult one to detect. The system is set up for retroactive entries so that children born on distant colonies and unregistered passengers on deep-space transports can be made official whenever the data reaches Earth. Did you have a particular ship in mind?"

"The *Gloria Terrae*, carrying settlers and supplies bound for a colony in the Draconis system. The transport never even made it to deep space. It lost atmosphere and crashed in the asteroid belt in 2374."

O'Malley let out a low whistle. "Yeah, there would have been a full investigation of that one. All evidence should have been immediately frozen in the system, meaning anyone changing data after the fact would have left a trail. It's doable, boss. Give me a name and I'll try to find out whether the information was planted."

"One condition — you have to keep this strictly to yourself."

O'Malley leaned forward, wide-eyed and attentive. "Understood."

"Olivia Townsend. Five of the bodies were never recovered. One of them was supposedly hers."

"Townsend," O'Malley echoed. "She was your relative?"

"My sister. And that's all you need to know."

The ratkeeper grinned and sat back in his chair. "Whatever you say, boss."

"And there's something else. You can't talk about this either. It's been niggling at the back of my mind for a while and I just want to know for sure."

O'Malley's expression became quizzical. "About...?"

"Harry Mintz."

"Mintz. As in, Teri's ex-husband?"

"She once told me that Harry Mintz has big, important friends, and that he pulled strings to get her detoured to Daisy Hub because he wanted to ruin her singing career. It sounded strange to me then. It makes even less sense to me now. I think there's more to this story, and I want to know what it is."

"Shouldn't be a problem, boss. I'll start looking into it right away."

A moment after O'Malley had pressed the call button for a tube car, a second door opened and Ruby stepped out.

She marched up to Townsend's desk and asked, "So, what now?"

"You said Karlov is in the caf. Is he alone?"

"Last time I checked, Hagman was with him. He was still smiling after a dozen cups of Jensen's brew. Either his stomach is lined with titanium or he's going to be in Med Services later on with enough heartburn to propel a shuttle to Zulu. Lu and Singh have set up a betting pool and are requesting that you delay spacing Karlov until we have the results."

There wasn't even a twitch of mischief on her face.

"You're serious," said Townsend, his voice rising in disbelief. "Why would I space our newest crew member? Why would they even think that?"

"Well, let's see," she began, counting on her fingers. "There's the alliance with the Nandrians, the cloaking field, the shipments of lemon juice that keep arriving here, Yoko the Überrat and her clone…"

A memory flashed across Drew's mind then, something Bonelli had said the first time they'd met on Zulu: *Why worry about hypothetical threats to security? If a real one arose, I'd say we're equipped to handle it ourselves.*

Yes, they were. Someone in his crew had already disposed of one "outside influence" and wouldn't hesitate to act again if the need arose, or if a kill order were received from Earth. Just thinking about that last possibility made Drew restless. Somewhere a clock might be ticking down. He needed answers and he needed them now.

"If anyone is looking for me, I'll be in the caf," he told her, and got to his feet.

Arms crossed, Ruby watched him head toward the tube car. "You know, eventually you're going to have to talk to me," she informed his retreating back.

"Yes, Mom," he replied wearily.

— «» —

The newest crew member was sitting alone at a round table in one corner of the caf. After more than twelve cups of java, the man was caffeinated up to his eyeballs, one of which was visibly a replacement part. A hastily prepared replacement part, Townsend amended, noting as he took the chair across from Karlov's that the artificial iris was shades of blue darker than the organic one. Interesting. And troubling. Someone had been in a hurry to get this man offplanet with the rat and the bioencrypted datawafer in his possession;

and despite the use of EIS technology to create the wafer, it was almost certainly not an EIS-sanctioned operation.

For starters, if Earth Intelligence had wanted Townsend to have this information, they wouldn't have bothered with a courier. They would have simply transmitted the encrypted data to him via established secure channels. But if for some reason they *had* chosen to send it by courier, they would have used their considerable resources to ensure that this individual attracted no undue attention. Among other things, that meant making damned certain both his eyes were the same color, no matter how short the notice. So, the question was: Who did Drew know on Earth with access to EIS encrypting technology who might have sent him a questionable datawafer, a large one-eyed man, and a rat?

It sounded like the opening line of a joke.

"I have a few questions to ask you," said Townsend, keeping his voice conversational.

"So ask."

Karlov was tall and muscular, with a hardness around his mouth and a vaguely menacing air. Even when relaxed and smiling, he was evidently someone not to be trifled with. The last time Townsend had sat across a table from someone who looked like this, they'd been in a precinct interrogation room and the other man had been in shackles after his arrest for mass murder. Security officers tended to categorize people, and the relationship between the cop and the killer in that room had been well defined. Knowing whom he was dealing with, Drew had also been able to gauge how much danger was present. Now he was on Daisy Hub, where nobody fit neatly into a category and the jeopardy level had already shot off the scale. But the detective inside him still clamored to know: Was Max Karlov an ally, or was he a threat?

There was no point in prolonging matters by beating around the bush. Townsend slammed his hand down on the table and declared, "Okay, let's begin by ditching the cover story. You said when you arrived here that you'd been posted to the station. We both know that isn't true. Who sent you, and what are your actual orders?"

Karlov reacted twice. His features were schooled, but Townsend was practiced at spotting tells, and Karlov's were in his eyes — or rather, in his one good eye. Drew saw surprise, followed closely by acceptance. A conscious decision to cooperate? He certainly hoped so.

"My orders. To bring the rat and the datawafer to Daisy Hub. To deliver the message I was given for you, word for word. After that, to do whatever job you assign me to the best of my ability while making sure you come to no harm."

"You've been ordered to protect me? From what, exactly?"

"From anyone who might wish to hurt you. The order was nonspecific."

Townsend leaned forward and said tightly, "And who gave you this assignment, Karlov? Who gave you the wafer and told you what to say to me when you arrived here?"

The other man paused for a moment, then leaned across the table as well. "I promised never to speak his name. But he instructed me that if you asked this question, I should remind you of the first time the two of you met. You were crying, and he told you to cry harder and get it all out of your system because tears were a sign of weakness on the streets. He told you that if you wanted to survive, you must never cry in front of anyone else again."

Rex Regum. For one breathless instant Drew was twelve years old again, small and alone and choking on fear as the gang leader's hand gripped the collar of his jacket, propelling him into the worst six years of his life. Each time the memory resurfaced, it ricocheted like shrapnel inside his head. Today it was a painful reminder of the fact that, regardless of the name he was using or how he chose to portray himself to others, Tommy Novotny had never been Drew's friend.

According to the datawafer, Tommy was reformed — made brand new and given command of all the EIS field operations, including the mission on Daisy Hub. However, as Drew knew only too well, once a King, always a King. For Rex Regum the Kings had always come first. Whatever motives he might pretend to have for sending Max Karlov to the Hub (assuming that Karlov was telling the truth and Tommy was actually the one behind this), what he was really doing was putting a King's welfare above everything else, and letting Drew know that if push came to shove, he had better be prepared to do the same.

A swelling tide of anger reached Townsend's throat, hardening his voice. "So that's it? All I'm supposed to do is put you to work, and all you have to do is watch my back?"

"And complete whatever tasks you assign me. Isn't that enough?"

"To persuade me to add you to the crew manifest? I'm afraid not. There's more to this than you're telling me, and I can't trust you if you're holding back. And if I can't trust you, nobody else on the station will either. You think *I'm* in danger? Some of the crew are convinced that my next order will be to shove you out an airlock. A couple of them might not even wait for me to give it."

Karlov's chuckle sounded like a death rattle. "They're welcome to try. But I took this assignment in exchange for my life and I'm going to carry it out, with or without your cooperation. What is important is that you remain safe. Agree to that and I'll tell you whatever you want to know."

Townsend breathed an impatient syllable. Rex Regum had no idea what had been going on out here. Daisy Hub was no longer just a Terran border station. To the Nandrians, it was a House, equal in importance to one of their own; and should House Daisy Hub fall, the full wrath of the Nandrian race would descend on whoever was responsible. The Nandrians were fierce warriors. According to Holchuk, the last time an allied House had been dishonored, they had destroyed a home world, triggering an interstellar war.

Drew was walking a knife edge, and nobody on Earth could be permitted to know about it. All he was able to say was, "You're wrong. What's important is that Daisy Hub remain safe. The survival of this station takes precedence over the life of any member of its crew, including the manager."

"Then assign me tasks that will help preserve the Hub. I'm quite versatile."

"What if Daisy Hub were attacked by an enemy force? Which of us would you protect then?"

"It wouldn't be my first battle. I would fight at your side and ensure that you survived it."

"But you wouldn't keep me out of the combat zone?"

"Why should I? You're a Warrior King, are you not?"

— 《》 —

It was a lot to take in, and Drew still wasn't sure that any of it was true; but at the end of the interview he and Karlov had shaken hands. Now he just had to find a way to break the news to the crew.

Resisting the urge to return to his quarters for a second, closer reading of the encrypted datawafer, Townsend headed for AdComm instead. Bits of Karlov's story kept repeating on him, like the onions in one of Jensen's casseroles: "...the people who killed Bruni Patel ... they came after me because Bruni and I were kin ... lost my eye in the struggle ... Bruni's contact helped me to escape from Earth on the condition that I carry out this one mission ... this is truth, I swear it on the graves of all my kin."

Kin. King. Cute. And he'd pushed the Bruni Patel button. Leaned on it, in fact. O'Malley was going to be very busy for the next while, checking out Karlov's version of events and verifying selected bits of data from the wafer. And if the big man turned out to be lying?

The spacing threat had been a bluff. Although Townsend had been trained to kill by the EIS and had occasionally had to use lethal force when working for New Chicago Security, he was not a cold-blooded murderer. Nobody would be going out an airlock without a Personal Life Support suit as long as he was in charge. But neither could he turn anyone with knowledge of the EIS over to the Rangers on Zulu. Not yet, anyway. So, if O'Malley's research revealed that Karlov was a threat to the station, then maybe it was time Daisy Hub had a brig.

As Drew stepped out of the tube car on AdComm, he saw Ruby and Lydia with their heads together at the main console. They glanced up at his approach.

"Well?" demanded Ruby.

"Well, what?"

"You know what," Lydia scolded him. "Have you decided what to do about this Max Karlov person?"

Drew eased himself into the chair behind his desk. "Ruby, do you remember telling me when I first arrived that I made your brain itch?"

She raised an eyebrow in response.

"Well, I think I understand now how you must have felt. He tells a good story, and I've agreed to put him to work, but until we're sure about him we'll need to take precautions. I want you to assign him quarters, but I also want him monitored, so get Singh to install a securecam beforehand."

"Will do, Chief."

"Lydia, you're to keep him on your screens and watch him carefully. O'Malley can spell you off. If either of you see him doing anything even remotely suspicious, report it to me immediately."

"Roger dodger, Drew," she said, and snapped him a mock salute.

"I'm going to put him into the detail rotation, just like any other crew member."

"Classes?" Ruby prompted him.

"Why not? He's supposed to be my bodyguard, so martial arts training might be a good place to start him."

"Whoa! Time out!" yelped Lydia, making the classic 'T' signal with her hands. "A bodyguard?"

Drew sighed inwardly. He'd known this wouldn't be easy for anyone to swallow. "Yeah. Apparently, that's why he was sent here. He says his assignment is to keep me out of trouble."

"And who's going to keep *him* out of trouble?" demanded Ruby. "You do realize what's going to happen the next time a Nandrian ship docks at this station? Assuming its Chief Officer doesn't take mortal offence at the very idea of your bringing a protector to the welcoming ritual, all the martial arts classes in the galaxy won't help if this guy manages to insult a Nandrian warrior."

"A short while ago you expected me to space him," he reminded her. "Now you're concerned about his safety?"

"Not his. Yours. Spacing an undesirable is something the Nandrians understand," she pointed out. "They do it all the time. However, letting your subordinate disrupt one of their ceremonies could easily get you killed."

"You're right," he decided. "Karlov's going to need a crash course in Nandrian culture."

"I'll set it up with Gavin Holchuk." Ruby went quiet for a moment. "What do you think, Drew? Was he really sent here to protect you?"

Privately, Townsend doubted it. But his EIS handlers had given him two options for dealing with anyone standing between him and the completion of his mission. He could turn Karlov, or he could terminate him. And there was no question in Drew's mind as to which he would prefer.

"I don't know," he said wearily. "In any case, until his story checks out we'll have to take precautionary measures. Spread the word to the crew to be careful what they say within his hearing, and to report immediately anything questionable that they notice about him. Tell the Doc she has to keep Yoko out of sight until further notice. The cloning operation, too. And first thing next shift, I need to meet with Gouryas. There's something I want him to build."

CHAPTER 14

Lydia stepped out of the tube car on AdComm, looking like the proverbial cat that had just swallowed a canary. "New guy finally has a tummy ache," she announced to the room, adding with a whoop of triumph, "And I won the pool! Five and a half standard days."

Drew turned in his chair and asked Ruby, "How much lemon juice did she just win?"

"Everyone but you and Jensen paid in this time. That's nearly two liters' worth, if my calculations are correct. Good for an extra half hour or so of shopping in the hold of the next Nandrian ship that stops by. And speaking of Nandrians, House Trokerk is leading in the *tekl'hananni* standings again. I don't think you'll need to worry about delivering a first-contact speech next time around."

That was reassuring. Daisy Hub and Trokerk were formalizing an alliance, now that Gavin Holchuk had been adopted into Nagor's Fifth Shield clan. In terms of the Nandrian welcoming ceremony, however, all that meant was that no one would be disemboweled if Drew hesitated or mispronounced while reciting his mandatory speech. His command of Gally was almost perfect now, but he still spoke it with an accent; and the aliens' tendency to take violent offence at the slightest deviation from script had sent him to Med Services on more than one occasion for something to settle his nerves.

With luck, Holchuk would be able to impress on Karlov how important it was that he stand absolutely still and silent during the ritual. Even luckier would be something that kept him away from Deck A altogether. The brig, maybe? Townsend made a mental note to ask Gouryas how those plans were coming along.

"Boss!" O'Malley was standing in front of Drew's desk, his grin even broader than Lydia's. "You were right. Well, not completely right, but right enough." Leaning closer, he intimated in a whisper that carried right across the deck, "She may be alive."

Drew glanced around, saw Ruby and Lydia both studiously ignoring the scene in his workspace, and said with undisguised annoyance, "Meet me in the caf in five minutes, O'Malley, and don't talk to anyone until I get there."

—— ‹›› ——

"Talk to me, O'Malley. Was her name added to the passenger manifest after the crash or not?"

The ratkeeper sat facing Townsend across the small round table, managing to look self-satisfied and exuberant at the same time. "Not. But that doesn't make her death any less bogus."

Drew had little patience right now for guessing games. "You'd better explain," he warned.

O'Malley planted himself more firmly in his chair, adjusting his hips and shoulders like a golfer preparing to tee off. This was one of his tells. The story would be long and recounted in exhaustive detail. Townsend groaned inwardly, but resigned himself to sitting through it. Like the Doc, the ratkeeper was a wealth of information, and there was no predicting where his research might have taken him.

"When I realized the passenger list hadn't been altered, I decided to dig a little deeper. I began by checking out all the names on the manifest. There were forty-two including your sister's. Thirty-seven of them had been added to the population database within a single six-day period. All the entries were made long after each person's supposed date of birth; and some of them were listed as being born on Earth, so there shouldn't have been any delay at all."

"You're saying these were imaginary people?"

"Definitely. Whoever input the information was smart enough to spread out their places of birth, at least. There was also just enough cross-referencing to withstand a superficial inquiry. But it was a rush job, as if there was a deadline involved. So, on a hunch, I looked into the ship.

Transport and mixed-use vessels are pretty thoroughly documented. Every date you can imagine is recorded in the Fleet database." He began counting on his fingers. "Design approval date. Construction start date. Online activation date. Official launch date."

"I get the picture, O'Malley. Now get to the point."

"The *Gloria Terrae* never existed. It was an overlay. Not a bad one, either. Whoever spliced it in was tech-savvy, able to alter the shipyard records, but not well-enough informed to realize that freighters are differently documented than passenger vessels. A couple of important dates were missing."

"You still haven't gotten to the point. Was there a crashed ship or not?"

"There was a crash, all right, but it wasn't the *Gloria Terrae*, and there were no passengers aboard. The ship that collided with that asteroid was an old freighter on a pre-scheduled scuttle run."

"And the date of that run was the deadline?"

"Yep. Someone overwrote the ship's history, keeping all the dates but changing the name and classification of the vessel. Then they replaced the standard scuttle confirmation with the tragic story of a crashed transport, complete with passenger manifest. Pretty clever, when you think about it. Fill an imaginary ship with imaginary passengers — who don't need bodies since nobody will be claiming them — plus the names of five real people who need to disappear, whose bodies are conveniently unrecoverable."

"So she's alive," Drew mused.

"Maybe. Something could have happened to her between then and now, but I can tell you for certain that she did not perish in a transport crash in 2374."

"The other four names. Who were they?"

O'Malley pulled up the information on his compupad and passed it across the table. After a cursory scan, Townsend passed it back. "I don't recognize any of these."

"There's no reason you should. Two of them came from Indo-Asia, one from the League of African Nations, and the fourth from Pacifica. Americas doesn't have a monopoly on sneaky dealings, you know. Every political union on the planet has its 'royal family' and one or two untouchable criminal organizations. And sometimes they're all headed up by the same person, dictatorships being such an efficient way to get things done. I'd be surprised if all the top dogs *hadn't* found a way to work together on something like this."

— «» —

"Drew, we may have a problem."

Townsend glanced up from his light screen and saw Lydia standing at the corner of his blue rug, gnawing anxiously on her lower lip.

He blanked the screen and motioned to her to sit down. "Jensen's sludge has finally claimed a victim?" he ventured, only half-joking. Despite his Cordon Bleu training, the Hub's chef couldn't brew a decent pot of java to save his life.

"No, Karlov has fully recovered. In fact, he's in the SPA room right now with Hagman, white water rafting."

Interesting. Hagman was a cynic and the Hub's resident grouch, making him perfectly suited to hold the position of Head of Security.

"And they're getting along?"

"Yes. They met just eight days ago, but it's as if they've been best friends all their lives. Lately they've been spending most of their off-duty time together. I've never seen Hagman so mellow. I'd swear he's in love."

"So what's the problem?"

"I offered to write Karlov his own SPA wafer and asked him what kind of activities he'd like me to put on it. And…"

When she hesitated, Townsend leaned back in his chair, recalling a conversation he'd had with Ruby on this very topic the day he'd arrived on the station. "What did he request, Lydia?"

"Armed and unarmed single combat, to the death. With Nandrians," she concluded reluctantly.

Drew stared at her, brought up short by the dreadful ramifications of that last word. "He wants to practice killing Nandrians? He didn't happen to tell you why, did he?"

"He said he needed to stay battle-ready. I think he may be some kind of soldier. But why would anyone believe we need a soldier out here, especially one trained to kill Nandrians, unless—"

There was no need for her to finish the thought. "Yeah, that's a problem," he growled. "Tell Gouryas I'm on my way to see him right now."

It appeared they were going to need that brig sooner than expected.

— «» —

Doctor Marion Ktumba stood in her laboratory, her gaze swinging from the screen of her molecular microscope to the hard-copy maps of two retroviruses sitting side by side on her green enameled work table. The RNA was dense with data, much denser than it should have been. The conversion files on her computer occupied nearly a gig of memory, and each of the printouts was a thick sheaf of paper. The first retrovirus had been extracted from the blood of the black and white rat that Karlov had brought aboard the station. The second had been detected much earlier in various samples taken from Yoko, the extremely intelligent white rat that had belonged to Nayo Naguchi when he was alive. The Doc had always assumed that this tightly-curled strand of RNA had something to do with Yoko's longevity — the Überrat was coming up on her twenty-sixth birthday — but now there was a second long-lived rat on the station, carrying a different retrovirus, and Ktumba could feel inner stirrings of both doubt and wondrous excitement.

Before going off-world, Nayo Naguchi had been working on a way to encode information using the base pair sequencing of DNA and ribonucleic acid. It was going to be his next great breakthrough, he'd told her, a foolproof way to transmit data too sensitive or personal to entrust to an electronic device. There was plenty of room on a strand of RNA. Volumes of information could be encrypted and then injected into a messenger's bloodstream. The messenger would literally become the message, and he wouldn't even need to know he was carrying it. Because of the way RNA behaved, the data could also be double-encrypted, with the DNA of another individual providing the initial decryption key.

Like all of Nayo's ideas, it was brilliant. It was a shame he'd died before he could—

Wait.

As though seeing it for the first time, the Doc looked around her at the laboratory that Nayo Naguchi had insisted be built on Daisy Hub before he arrived. It had been state of the art at the time. Clearly, he'd intended to continue his scientific work while managing the station.

Once his tenure as manager was over, the last thing he would want was to have his notes and experiments fall into the hands of a certain European gene broker. And what better way to hide them than by encoding the data as a strand of RNA, concealing it inside the body of the rat that he'd brought aboard the Hub with him, and then leaving the animal behind?

"Oh, Nayo," she murmured, her gaze coming fondly to rest on the two caged animals at the far end of her laboratory work table, "you did it, didn't you?"

— ‹›› —

Townsend stepped out of the tube car on Deck L and into a world of pink. It wasn't just pink, he amended as he stood, slack-jawed, in the middle of a broad work area surrounded by lockers and warehouse shelving, workshops and meeting cubbies, all painted the same startling hue — it was *hot* pink. This was a color he'd never expected to see anywhere on Daisy Hub, let alone on the deck where all the engineers and technicians spent their time. Only the surface beneath his feet had escaped the painter's brush.

"Beautiful, isn't it?" Engineering Specialist Spiro Gouryas stood behind a work table littered with tools and drawings. His arms were crossed over his chest, and a wry expression perched on his swarthy face. "Singh has been figuring out the molecular paintbrush. You told us to give priority to firming up those soft spots the Midnight Muralist created on the Hub's bulkheads. So, he's been looking for ways to reset the refractive index of a plaincoated metal surface without altering its molecular latticework."

Townsend frowned. "You've had no help from the Muralist?"

"Not directly. When you publicly ordered him to report to us for a debriefing, you probably spooked him. He's been leaving us notes, though. Written in longhand, with graphite or something like it, on pieces of paper. We think he's male, judging from the handwriting. In any case, he clearly wants to preserve his anonymity."

"And Singh has picked up where the Muralist left off. Perfect." He repressed a shudder. "How can you even work in here?"

Gouryas shrugged. "I grew up with five sisters. Pink doesn't bother me. But you should have been here a few days ago, when he was going through his orange period. That was a distraction."

"Is he making progress, at least?"

"Appears to be. He can overpaint now without turning anything into transparent acrylic. But I'm guessing you're here to talk about the brig."

Townsend joined him at the work table. "Is it doable?" he asked, gesturing at the scattering of papers that covered its surface.

"Not really. In a pinch, we could convert an airlock or one of the berths on F or G Deck into a temporary holding cell, but there's no way to create additional rooms on any of the decks without affecting the structural integrity of the Hub. Thanks to the Muralist — and Singh," he added, glancing around significantly, "that index is already down to less than 87 percent, so there's no way I'm going to approve drilling holes to set anchors for enclosure bulkheads." He paused, visibly weighing his next words. "There is a brig already built, you know, on Zulu."

Drew had already rejected that option. The Ranger station was currently under the command of Bonelli's trusted second, Lieutenant Rodrigues, but it was an acting position only, until a new commander could be appointed. That was the man Townsend needed to be able to work with, and until he arrived and Drew felt confident about bringing him onside, the Max Karlov problem would have to remain Daisy Hub's responsibility.

Batting aside the engineer's observation, he asked, "What about the stealth shield? Any progress there?"

"Some. Singh has been busy with the paintbrush, but Beale and Oolalong have been going over the manual and—"

"There's a manual?"

"Most of the time we ignore it, but yes, there's always a manual. This one was originally in Nandrian. Nagor translated it for us into Gally, transliterated that into Anglo, then gave it to Holchuk, who gave it to me. We'll let you know when we're ready to present the demonstration."

Townsend's wristcomm buzzed, sending his next thought flying into the ether. "Drew," said Lydia, her voice taut as a bowstring, "you need to go to Med Services. The Doc says it's urgent."

— «» —

Townsend wasted no time getting to Deck H. Doc Ktumba was tall and physically imposing, with an aura of authority that had once made a Nandrian warrior back down. The woman had steel in her, no question. Although it wasn't difficult to annoy her, Drew was hard pressed to imagine a scenario that would faze her. And yet, something must have done just that, or why would she have called for his help? His imagination roiling with dire possibilities, Townsend left the tube car and headed in the direction of the triage room door.

"Over here!"

He turned and saw the Doc standing just outside her lab, impatience stamped on her already formidable features. Funny — she didn't *appear* to be in distress. Then again, this was the Doc, he reminded himself, and she *had* used the word "urgent".

Drew hurried toward her. "What's happened?" he demanded. "What's the emergency?"

"It's not an emergency," she said, throwing him a frown as the door to the laboratory hummed open. "I told Lydia that I needed to talk with you right away so you would be fully informed before making any decisions regarding the disposition of our newest arrivals."

He followed her inside, pausing briefly on the threshold to reacquaint himself with the Doc's private domain. As weighty and inflexible as the Doc herself, at least a dozen gleaming machines lined up along the bulkheads like sentries awaiting commands, their steel-and-plastiplex faces flat and unrevealing. Ruby called the Med Services lab an impressive display of twenty-Earth-year-old scientific technology. Arkady and Sun, the techs primarily responsible for maintaining it, described it in even less flattering terms. All Drew could say was that before coming to Daisy Hub, he had never seen anything like it.

Drew Townsend was no stranger to laboratories. As a field investigator in New Chicago, he had had reason to visit a variety of forensic scientists in their workplaces over the years. He'd even caught the occasional case in which a laboratory was the crime scene. But that had been on Earth, home world of about three billion Ineligibles and routinely the last place the High Council invested its research and development resources. Everyone knew that all the newest and shiniest toys went into space, along with the best and brightest minds, leaving Earth to make do with whatever was left.

That an orbiting detention center like Daisy Hub had been retrofitted to be as well-equipped for medical treatment and research as any off-world hospital of its era — that had been Earth Intelligence's doing. After reading through the first ten standard years' worth of station managers' reports, Townsend was certain of it.

The Doc's brisk voice snapped him back to the moment. "Have a look at these."

She had spread some charts out on a work table directly in front of him. At least, he was assuming that the rows of dark and light bars were charts.

"These are chromosomal maps," she explained. "The configuration on the left is Human, randomly selected from crew records. The one on the right is Karlov's."

"You're telling me he's not Human?"

"That's not what I'm saying at all, Mr. Townsend. At this level of analysis, the two maps are identical. Generally, I have no reason to delve any deeper when examining a new crew member. However, Hagman said something about the black and white rat possibly being part of the message Karlov was carrying. That started me thinking. So I took a closer look, at both their genomes."

"And?"

She reached for another sheaf of printout, then apparently had second thoughts and pushed it away instead. "All right," she began, "you know what makes Yoko special, and why she's on the Hub."

"Yes, of course."

"Nayo gave his rats longevity by activating an enzyme that repairs the telomeres at the ends of the chromosomes, thus inhibiting the aging process at a cellular level. I found the same effect in the nuclei of the black and white rat, who, it turns out, is also Yoko's sibling."

Townsend's brain nearly stalled. "So they're the same age? We have two of Naguchi's immortal rats on the Hub?"

"So it appears. But that's not the most interesting finding," she told him, raising a forefinger and both eyebrows for emphasis. "When I examined Karlov's cell nuclei, his telomeres appeared to be pristine as well. Nayo's next round of experiments would have been conducted on Human test subjects. I believe that's what Karlov is — the next logical step of a longevity experiment."

There was so much wrong with this theory that Drew didn't know where to begin. He struggled for words for a moment, finally managing to remark, "Well. That's— That's quite a leap of logic, Doctor."

"Maybe it is. However, Naguchi died fifteen Earth years ago, and that gives another scientist plenty of time to analyze his work and then expand on it. I have no idea who that person might be, or how and when the black and white rat could have been acquired. I only know what I've seen under the microscope. And I wanted *you* to know that until there is cogent proof to the contrary, I'm going to assume that Karlov is Yoko's Human counterpart, sent to us along with Yoko's sister for safekeeping. You may be the station manager, Mr. Townsend, but according to the regulations governing space installations, you are not the highest authority on Daisy Hub in matters of crew well-being. I am. And I'm taking Max Karlov under my protection until such time as someone gives me a damned good reason not to."

Townsend thought about objecting but realized it would be foolish. The Doc was a force of nature, the proverbial immovable object. Even if he could convince her that he was right and she was wrong, it was bound to be a costly victory.

Privately, he thought the very notion of a soldier like Karlov needing protection was laughable. But she had raised a valid point. They needed to figure out who and what Karlov was, and why he was on the Hub, and they had to do it as soon as possible.

In the corridor outside the lab, Drew thumbed the call button on his wristcomm. "Lydia, I want to meet in AdComm in half an hour with any crew members who have had more than casual contact with Max Karlov since he arrived."

CHAPTER 15

"**Here he is,**" Ruby caroled.

Townsend counted eleven frowning faces turned toward him as he stepped out of the tube car on AdComm. On his instructions, Ruby and Lydia had arranged chairs in a semicircle around his desk in preparation for the meeting, and all but one of them — Hagman's — were occupied. The Head of Security stood off to the side, his legs braced and his arms crossed as though daring anyone to bad-mouth Karlov, his new best friend. Drew sighed inwardly. He should have known this wouldn't be easy.

While still providing the illusion of normalcy, Townsend had done his best to limit Karlov's access to sensitive parts of the Hub. In the past interval, the new crew member had worked shifts on two "safe" details — Tannis Walker's and Fritz Jensen's — and had attended martial arts classes with Lu Xensiu and several briefings with Holchuk. Three of these officers were now present. So was the Doc, scowling at Townsend from her seat in the back corner.

Lydia had taken a chair in the front row, directly facing his own. Once he was seated behind his desk, she leaned forward and said softly, "Drew, Rodrigues is on his way here, ETA in about three hours, and he has information he says he's been ordered to deliver to you in person."

Of course, he had. Life on Daisy Hub these days seemed to be one head-smacking revelation after another. With luck, Rodrigues's message would be something Townsend could share. He was getting tired of keeping secrets from people he cared about.

Drew leaned back in his chair, dragged in a long breath, and announced, "All right, people, I'm assuming that you all know why you've been called here. I want to know what you've observed and what your instincts are telling you about our newest crew member, Max Karlov. The circumstances under which he arrived on the Hub were unorthodox, to put it mildly. To put it bluntly, it appears he was smuggled here, sent by persons unknown and for reasons we can only guess at. For the past while, he's been on a sort of probation with limited access to information. Unfortunately, we cannot afford to let him stay that way. There's too much happening on Daisy Hub right now that must be kept within the family. So, I need your help to decide: Is he in or is he out? Can he be trusted with knowledge of our recent activities?"

"And if the answer is no?" demanded Hagman, his tone even pricklier than usual as he deliberately uncrossed and recrossed his arms over his powerful chest.

"Then we have to find a way to get him off the station, if not now, then at some point in the very near future." Hagman's expression was darkening, and an uneasy murmur had sprung up around him. To forestall an argument, Townsend added quickly, "Who wants to start sharing their impressions of this man?"

"Me." Ruby stood up and turned to face the rest of the group, visibly choosing her words. "I've been suspicious of him from the beginning, and not just because of the way he got here, or the fact that his eyes are two different shades of blue and one of them's a fake. Anyone who's ever had java before coming here has nothing good to say about Jensen's version of it. It's sludge. It's mud-in-a-cup. But Karlov thinks it's delicious. His first day on the Hub he must have drunk twenty cups of it, one after the other. This morning he tossed down three and said it was the best way to start the day."

"So? He likes the taste of old motor lubricant," growled Hagman.

Rounding on him, she snapped back, "And the Nandrians like the taste of lemon juice."

"They're aliens," he pointed out.

"Exactly!" said Ruby, her arms flung wide in a gesture of finality. "There's something not right about Karlov. He looks Human, and he's friendly enough, but my brain has been itching ever since he came aboard. And those are my impressions," she concluded, with emphasis on the last two words, before dropping back into her chair.

"Speaking of Nandrians…" Lydia got to her feet then and repeated her conversation with Karlov about SPA choices. Meanwhile, Townsend could practically hear the wheels turning inside Hagman's head, shredding every argument as it was presented. She was right — he was in love.

"Okay, I can understand a soldier wanting to test himself in virtual combat against the most formidable opponent possible," Lydia conceded. "But what really stuck in my mind was that when I suggested ordinary sports like golf and tennis, he gave me a blank look, as if he'd never heard of them before."

"I got that feeling from him too," chimed in Nora Duvall, Jensen's *sous chef.* "The day after he arrived, he came into the caf on a meal break and seemed to have no idea what any of the menu items were. Granted, Fritz likes to experiment with different food combinations, but a dish is still identifiable when it's served. Stew looks like stew. Pasta looks like pasta. Karlov couldn't tell the difference. It was so strange! He's supposed to be from Earth, and yet I got the impression that he was encountering Terran cooking for the first time in his life."

"Do you suppose he might have been institutionalized or something?" ventured Will DeVries, one of Lu's martial arts students. "Because he struck me as being a good-hearted guy, not stupid by any means, just lacking life experience. As if he'd grown up in a very small and sheltered environment, like an orbiting platform, or…" He hesitated uncomfortably. "Or maybe a hospital."

"Like a mental hospital? Are you saying he's crazy, boy?" Hagman challenged, moving to stand over him as, behind them, Gavin Holchuk and Lu Xensiu began slowly rising from their seats.

Slightly built, DeVries must have realized what would happen if he got to his feet at that moment, but after multiple sessions of ninja training he wasn't about to back down in front of his *sensei,* either. So, he sat stiffly upright in his chair and stared defiance at the larger man. "Daisy Hub is an orbiting detention center," he pointed out. "Does that mean we're all criminals?"

Confronted by calm logic, Hagman seemed to shrink a little. Holchuk and Lu returned to their chairs. Townsend let out the breath he'd been holding. So did everyone else in the room.

"Take my word for it, Max is no fruitcake," Hagman informed them. "We've spent hours together, and he's as sane as I am."

"Careful, Orvy," muttered Nora, just loudly enough for everyone to hear.

"And he's fun to be with," Hagman continued, raising his voice to carry over the wave of laughter her comment had generated. "And he's having fun too. So what if everything's for the first time for him? He's enjoying himself, something the rest of us haven't done much lately. So, here's my impression of Max Karlov: He's like a kid at a thrill park, and he deserves every chance we can give him."

Tannis Walker sprang from her chair then and declared, "Hagman's right about Karlov being like a kid. He was on my waste management detail for five days, and the smile never left his face. I don't remember the last time I saw anyone get that excited about the workings of a water reclamation system."

"First of all, he's not a kid." Holchuk's stern voice cut through the discussion like a razor. "Second, not everything is new to him, or a pleasant surprise." He stood up, and in three long strides the Hub's resident Nandrian expert was standing beside Townsend's desk. "I'm supposed to be teaching him about the aliens' culture so he won't get us in trouble the next time a Nandrian ship docks here. We've had three sessions together, and I can tell you, from a couple of details that he's let slip, that man knows a lot more about Nandrians than he's willing to reveal. If he's even close to being able to defeat a Nandrian warrior in battle, that makes him the most dangerous person on the Hub. Without knowing who sent him and why, I can't see us ever being one hundred percent certain of his loyalties. So, if my gut gets a vote here, it's for moving him the hell off this station, preferably via an airlock."

Angry voices exploded all over the deck:

"Space him? Over my dead—!"

"Who's going to do it, Holchuk? You?"

"Hold on! Drew's already said—"

"This is insane! We can't murder a man just because—"

"We can't just stand by and let—"

Townsend let them blow off steam for about a minute before getting to his feet and hollering, "Enough! You've had your turns to speak. Now, if none of you has anything else to add, it's mine."

Grudgingly, they all fell silent.

"When Karlov arrived, he brought a message for me. Apparently, someone on Earth felt that I needed protection, so they sent him here as my bodyguard. When I questioned him later, he told me he'd accepted the assignment in exchange for his life — his words. What exactly that means, I don't know yet. Am I prepared to accept what he says at face value? Not for one second." Townsend gazed around the room and saw heads bobbing in approval. "There is something … *unusual* about Max Karlov, something he himself may not even be aware of." Townsend shot a warning look at the Doc, who had begun shifting her weight forward as though to stand up. She glared right back at him but, to his relief, remained seated and silent. "In any case, I need to know the whole truth about him — who sent him and why he's really here — before I can decide what to do with him. I was hoping we could arrive at an answer by putting all our pieces together, as we've done before. Apparently, that isn't yet possible. So, I'm afraid the status will have to remain quo where Max Karlov is concerned. That doesn't mean we do nothing."

"You've got a plan, Chief?" said Ruby. The air around his desk began effervescing with curious murmurs.

Townsend paused, turning the details of the con over in his mind one last time. It had sprung from his imagination fully developed as he listened to Karlov being described by the others. It was brilliant. Best of all, nobody in the assembled group could disagree with it, not even Holchuk.

"What do you do when you have a child on your hands and want to keep him safely out of your hair while you work? Think Alison Morgan," he added, addressing Lydia directly.

Her face lit up with comprehension. "You distract him. You keep him busy having fun."

"For whatever reason, it appears that Max Karlov is experiencing Earth's culture for the very first time. He's got a lot of catching up to do, wouldn't you say? Lydia, you're going to program a whole slew of SPA wafers for him, every sport and physical activity you can think of. Whenever he's not otherwise occupied, I want him in that room having fun."

"You've got it, Drew."

"Holchuk, get Teri to introduce Max to the joys of U-Town. The damned thing's addictive. If he's hooked on the activities of a bunch of fictional characters in a virtual community, odds are he won't be paying much attention to what we're doing."

The Chief Cargo Inspector's lips quirked briefly. "That just might work, boss man," he remarked.

"Nora, you and Fritz are going to teach him about all the different Earth cuisines. Emphasis on sweets. I suspect soldiers don't get to eat a lot of those."

"Fun in the kitchen. Gotcha," she declared.

"Doc, the black and white rat is now his pet. Let him care for her."

"What? She's a lab animal," the Doc protested. "I can't just—"

"Fine, then," he cut in. "Don't. But remember that everything is brand new to him. If water reclamation is now a mystery solved, turning litmus paper red might be his next great adventure. Just work with the crew to keep him distracted and away from any sensitive information. Above all, he mustn't find out about our immortal rat or her clone, so stash the daughter somewhere safe and let O'Malley hide Yoko in his quarters."

"Are you certain that's a good idea, Mr. Townsend?" asked the Doc.

She was right to be skeptical. The ratkeeper had already demonstrated his inability to keep secrets.

"No, but it's the best one I've got at the moment. With luck, O'Malley is going to be plenty distracted himself."

—— «» ——

Two hours later, with Operation Fun and Games well under way, Lydia sat at the communications console on AdComm, scanning for Rodrigues's ship. As it came within range, she swiveled her chair and called out, "Ranger short-hopper *Endeavor* is on approach, Drew. Where do you want him to dock?"

He considered for a moment. The Rangers had no idea Karlov was aboard the Hub, and for the time being that was how things had to remain. "Where's Max right now?"

"With Nora. They're making cookies in the shapes of alphabet letters. She said to tell you that she'll be bringing you a plate of them when they've cooled, and that you'll find some of them extremely interesting."

The kitchen was on D Deck, just two levels below AdComm and three south of the short-hopper landing deck, but a safe distance away from the Hub's docking modules. "Okay, assign Rodrigues a portal on A Deck," he told her. "And let him know that I'll be meeting him there."

"Your wish is my command," she responded with a smile in her voice. He heard her open a comm channel and relay his instructions to the pilot of the approaching shuttle.

Rodrigues had said he would be delivering important news. News from the Zoo. How fitting, since life aboard Daisy Hub was rapidly becoming a circus. They even had a carousel to take them in never-ending circles — the Nandrian field generator. Together with its emitter, the alien device squatted gracelessly over a quarter of the shuttle deck, mocking their every attempt to figure it out.

"What the—? Why is he stopping?" exclaimed Lydia. She pushed a button and repeated, "*Endeavor*, you are cleared to dock. Please proceed to module 3."

"I'd love to," came Rodrigues's clipped, dry voice over the comm. "So where the hell is it? And while we're on the subject, where the hell are *you*?"

"Where am *I*? What are you talking about?" she demanded.

"Come on, Lydia. I'm on official business and we're too old to be playing hide and seek. Bring the station back."

Hearing this, Townsend launched himself out of his chair. He covered the distance to her console in four strides. She'd already muted the comm.

"It's the stealth cloak," he said, making no effort to disguise his displeasure. "It has to be. Gouryas was supposed to inform me before they ran any demos. All right, tell Beale and Oolalong and whoever else is on the short-hopper deck to quit messing with the field generator. They're to shut it off immediately. Then put me on with Rodrigues and I'll see if I can talk us out of this."

Several moments later, Lydia turned troubled eyes to Townsend's face and told him, "You're not going to believe this. They're telling me the generator activated by itself. They never touched it. And they've been trying their best, but they can't seem to turn it off."

Of course, they couldn't. This was Daisy Hub, after all, where Murphy's Law was strictly enforced.

He gestured to Lydia to unmute the comm.

"—hell is going on aboard your station, Townsend? Talk to me, dammit!"

"Paul, I'm sorry about this," said Drew in his most conciliatory tone of voice, "but we've been having some problems with our Meniscus field generator. That's why you weren't instructed to park on the short-hopper deck. Are we visible to any of your onboard instruments at all?"

"Not to any of them. You were there and then — *poof!* — you were gone. Am I visible to you?"

Interesting. Townsend glanced a question at Lydia, who was now grinning wickedly. *Tell him no*, she mouthed.

"Sporadically," he decided, and watched her grin reverse into an exaggerated pout. "This glitch with the generator may have compromised other systems on the station. We might be able to talk you in, if you want to take the chance. Or we can have our conversation over the comm and you can return once we've identified and fixed the problem."

There was a heavy pause. "Townsend, if I didn't know better— Damn! This alien technology is going to put us all away. You'll notify me if your generator malfunction is something we need to worry about on Zulu." It wasn't a question. The Rangers had an identical device installed on their own landing deck and would naturally be concerned.

"Of course, I will. Now, what was the news you wanted to tell me?"

"Nestor Quan was arrested three or four intervals ago. He was extradited back to Earth to stand trial, but they lost him somewhere between the airfield and the slammer. The little weasel apparently had friends waiting for him and they set up an ambush on the road that Security would be taking. So, he's at large again. That's the first piece of news. Here's the second: I've been promoted to captain and given command of the detachment on Zulu."

Lydia mimed clapping her hands and leading a cheer. Townsend suppressed a smile.

"Congratulations, Paul," he said. "I'm sure you could have wished for a better posting—"

"Actually, I requested this one. When I come over there for the mandatory new commander's inspection tour tomorrow, you and I are going to sit down for a chat. I'll explain to you why I would actually choose to remain in this godforsaken corner of Earth space, and then I'll give you the message that I was told to deliver to you in person, *in person*. Now, while you're mulling over this conversation, I'll just head back to Zulu and wait to hear *your* good news about the field generator. Rodrigues out."

Lydia's spine had gone rigid. When the comm channel was finally closed, she leaned back wearily in her chair. "Well," she remarked, "that could have gone better."

She was putting it mildly, Townsend thought. And just to make things interesting, the Ranger captain also had something eyes-only to impart. First Karlov, now Rodrigues. Well, he decided, while this latest secret message could wait one more day, the problem with the field generator couldn't.

"We've got until tomorrow to figure this out," he declared. "Inform Gouryas I want him and Singh in front of my desk within the hour, ready to report. Find out when the next *tekl'hananni* scoreboard goes up and whether Trokerk is still leading. And we need to make damned certain that Karlov spends the day in his quarters tomorrow, in case Rodrigues decides to inspect the SPA room while he's here."

"Why would he do that? None of the previous Ranger commanders have given it more than a cursory glance," Lydia pointed out.

"Which is exactly why I'm sure he'll be extra thorough tomorrow. Bonelli ruled the Zoo with intimidation and brute force. Rodrigues is more like us. And now, thanks to that damned generator, he's annoyed and smelling a con." And he was right, Townsend had to admit. There were several cons currently in play, one of them on the Rangers.

As if on cue, the tube car door slid open and Nora Duvall stepped onto the deck, holding a loaded serving platter in her hands. "Cookies, anyone?"

CHAPTER 16

"**Unbelievable.**" **Communications Specialist** Lydia Garfield sat at her console, nibbling at the last of the alphabet cookies and scowling in disgust at the readings on her screen. For the past half hour, Ruby had been flying *Devil Bug* back and forth, approaching and then retreating from the Hub in an effort to duplicate what had happened earlier to the *Endeavor*.

Townsend walked over to stand behind Lydia's chair. "Anything?"

"Nothing. No matter how close she comes or from which direction, the field refuses to activate." She took another bite of her cookie.

It was one of those strange-looking ones that Nora had been so excited about, Drew noticed, the ones shaped like stylized trees with oddly broken branches. The ones Karlov had told her were used to spell out his name. Maybe he'd just been having fun with her. Townsend hoped so. There were already too many things in his life that didn't add up. In any case, the problems posed by Karlov's presence on the Hub paled in comparison with the potential fallout from the flakiness of that damned field generator.

The *tekl'hananni* scoreboard would be going up soon and the first ship full of Nandrian warriors would arrive shortly thereafter, expecting to dock, board, and celebrate, as usual. If Daisy Hub disappeared from their screens as the Nandrians approached, they were certain to interpret it as an insult. And insulting a Nandrian, even if he belonged to a House allied to one's own, was tantamount to suicide. Rodrigues had been speaking figuratively at the time, but he'd been correct. If the techs on Daisy Hub couldn't get a handle on that pile of alien hardware before the Nandrians showed up, it would probably be the death of all of them.

The tube car door slid open then, disgorging onto C Deck the four people who had been front of Townsend's mind for the past hour: Engineers Devanan Singh and Spiro Gouryas, and Field Technicians Vera Beale and Ray Oolalong. They were uncharacteristically subdued. A frown was etched into Gouryas's normally bland features, and Singh's habitual smirk looked frozen onto his face. Drew felt an answering chill deep in his core. It appeared the news was not going to be good.

"Take a seat and give me some answers," Drew ordered them as he returned to the chair behind his desk. Lydia pulled her own chair over to join them. "Karlov?" he asked her.

"U-Town, with Teri. They're binge-meddling. Something about tampering with the jury at Brock's trial."

That part of the plan seemed to be working, at least. Townsend permitted himself a moment of satisfaction. Then he said to the group assembled before him, "So. What's going on with the field generator?"

They spent long seconds passing looks back and forth. Finally, Vera Beale cleared her throat and told him, "Bottom line, we think it's a hardwired factory setting."

"First thing the manual said to do was reset everything to default, and that's what we did," chimed in Oolalong.

"Wait! There's a manual?" Lydia demanded.

"There's always a manual," Singh replied with a shrug. "Usually we ignore it and figure things out empirically."

"Or we ask someone with more experience to explain them to us," added Beale. "But when you're working with alien technology—"

"—following the instructions can still get you in trouble," Gouryas bristled.

Interesting. There had evidently been a difference of opinion down on L Deck, one that still wasn't resolved.

"Walk me through this," said Townsend. "I want to know what went wrong and how you intend to fix it."

"Nothing went wrong, sir. The generator is working to specs," Oolalong informed him mildly.

"That's a matter of opinion," cut in Gouryas again, simmering anger in his voice as he leaned forward to throw dagger-like looks at the young tech.

Townsend had to agree with the senior engineer. The last time the generator had "worked to specs", Drew's predecessor had frozen to death in his own quarters.

"Well, the invisibility shield is being activated when we don't want it activated," he pointed out, in a tone of voice he'd last used to admonish a pair of four-year-old guests at the precinct house for playing hide and seek in the detectives' ward room. "Clearly, the specs don't apply to our current situation, which happens to be something of an emergency. So I would suggest that for the time being, you drop everything else and focus on doing whatever it takes to disconnect that stealth cloak."

The group of four exchanged worried looks.

"That would not be advisable, I'm afraid," said Singh. "Not until we have a better understanding of this technology. We might be disabling who knows what else."

"Or possibly activating something in place of the cloaking field, which could make things much, much worse," added Gouryas.

Worse than being blown up by a salvo from a Nandrian ship? Townsend didn't think so.

"Funny," he mused aloud, "you people had no qualms about fooling with this device earlier on. You even traveled to Zulu and stuck the molecular paintbrush into the Rangers' field generator, just to see what would happen."

"That was then, and we were half an orbit away from the Hub," Singh reminded him. "Whatever we do to *this* generator could have disastrous repercussions for us in the here and now."

"You mean further repercussions, don't you?" Drew pointed out tartly.

The engineer did not respond.

"Part of the problem is that we're not working with the original manual," said Beale. "It's a translation from Nandrian into Gally, and some of the syntax is really convoluted."

Oolalong took instant exception. "That first instruction was crystal clear: Select default for all settings."

Staring pensively at the center of Townsend's desk, Lydia asked, "Does the manual include a description for each of those default settings?"

"Of course it does!" snapped Gouryas. "We went through all that—"

Meanwhile, Beale whipped her compupad out of her pocket and tossed it over for Lydia to catch. "See for yourself."

As his communications specialist began to read, Townsend cleared his throat. "What exactly do the specs say about this invisibility field?"

Prompted by stares from Gouryas and Singh, Oolalong replied, "That it works by altering the refractive index of the molecules forming the station's outer hull, making light bend around us — which we already knew — and that it's triggered by the generator's sensor field, which we apparently activated the second the molecular paintbrush was inserted."

"Activated and then reset to factory specs," Drew repeated thoughtfully. That explained why only Daisy Hub was having this problem. None of the settings had been changed on Zulu's generator. "So, if we could somehow shrink the sensor field down to the size it was before, the problem should be solved."

"Theoretically, yes," said Singh. "And we've no doubt there's a way to accomplish that. However, Ray and Vera haven't found it in the manual, so we're back to trial and error, which means it will take us time to figure it out."

Unfortunately, time was in short supply right now. With growing impatience, Townsend persisted, "And there are no instructions in that manual at all, not even mentioned in a footnote, for disabling the invisibility field?"

"No, that's what we've been telling you," said Oolalong. "It's hardwired to generate at the approach of any vessel that enters its sensing range."

"Not just any vessel," Lydia crowed, holding up the compupad and repeatedly poking at the screen with an index finger. "You tech types should read the foreword occasionally. According to this, the generators that have been installed on Daisy Hub and the Zoo are identical to the ones aboard Nandrian deep space vessels. And Nandrian ships engage in *tekl'hananni*."

She paused, eyebrows arching over a self-satisfied grin. A shiver raced down Townsend's back.

"Lydia," he said sharply, "we need Gavin Holchuk up here right now."

She turned startled eyes to his face, then jumped to do his bidding.

Meanwhile, Vera's expression had brightened considerably. "Of course! In *tekl'hananni*, you would want to conceal yourself from an *opposing* vessel."

"The Nandrians are fierce warriors," Gouryas pointed out. "I can't imagine them hiding from anyone—"

"—except in a situation where being temporarily invisible could provide a strategic advantage, such as while changing location to get a better angle for a shot," put in Oolalong.

"That makes sense," said Gouryas. "And if every Nandrian ship is using one of these generators in battle, that means there has to be an on-off switch somewhere. On the casing?"

"It's more likely to be on the tactical control panel," declared Vera. "It wouldn't be practical for the generator not to be integrated into the rest of the ship's systems."

"But Daisy Hub and Zulu were retrofits," Oolalong reminded them. "Integration might not have been possible."

Townsend breathed a silent sigh. They'd come so close to getting the point, then missed it entirely. Again. Pieces were coming together, forming a picture of life-threatening peril. Why couldn't they see it? And where the hell was Holchuk?

As if conjured by Drew's thoughts, the Chief Cargo Inspector emerged from the nearest tube car and waded into their meeting. He'd evidently been interrupted at some crucial moment — his face wore a "this had better be damned important" expression.

"What's the big emergency, boss man?" he demanded.

Before anyone else could utter a word, Townsend replied, counting off on his fingers, "They've armed the sensor and invisibility fields and don't know how to turn either of them off. The next *tekl'hananni* scoreboard goes up within days. We disappeared before the eyes of the new Ranger commander a couple of hours ago, preventing him from docking and, coincidentally, making our secret defensive strategy not so secret anymore. And it turns out that every Nandrian vessel has one of these field generators aboard, meaning not only will we be invisible to them, but if they should ever decide that we're the enemy, they'll also have the ability to be invisible to us." He turned to Lydia. "Did I miss anything?"

She just gave him a weak smile.

Holchuk looked around him at six strained faces and said, "You do realize that the Nandrians have been testing your problem-solving ability ever since this technology was installed?"

"That was more than a standard year ago. When does it end?" said Gouryas, frustration raising the pitch of his voice.

"More to the point, what happens if we fail?" Vera wanted to know.

Holchuk shrugged. "I can't tell you."

"Why?" sniped Singh. "Because you're a Shield-brother of Nagor son of Nagor, of the House of Trokerk?"

"No," Holchuk replied evenly, "it's because you've passed every part of the test so far with flying colors."

"You honestly have no idea how this is going to shake out?" said Townsend.

Holchuk shrugged again. "It's *tekl'hananni*, boss man. Anything can happen. I've already shown my worthiness as part of the adoption ritual. Now it's your turn."

— «» —

"They wouldn't set us up to fail," said Ruby from her console on AdComm. "It would be dishonorable, like short-changing a trading partner." Her words were meant to be reassuring, but Townsend couldn't help noticing that her voice was less than ringing with confidence.

Staring glumly at his light screen, he slouched behind his desk and thought about the various parts of the Nandrian test that they had already encountered and overcome. The

Midnight Muralist, whose identity still remained a secret, had figured out how to decorate the bulkheads using the various settings on the molecular paintbrush. Gouryas and Singh had then discovered how to use the same device to turn metal into transparent acrylic, enabling them to look inside the field generator. That in turn had allowed them to determine that the paintbrush was meant to fit inside the generator, and putting those components together had led them to the invisibility field, which they were now struggling to control before a deadline passed. According to Holchuk, all these occurrences had been meant to happen, as part of a greater test of Daisy Hub's worthiness. To do what? To be a House? To be an ally?

To be allowed to remain out in space?

"They'll solve the puzzle," said Lydia's voice from the end of his filing cabinet partition. "Every member of this crew is Eligible, which means they're in the top two percent of the Human population for intelligence and perseverance. Just give them a little time."

"Unfortunately, a little time is all we've got."

"Well, Ruby and I have been discussing the Ranger problem, and we think there may be a way for Captain Rodrigues to dock with the Hub when he returns tomorrow. Of course," she cautioned, "it's no more than an educated guess. If we're wrong, or if Rodrigues refuses to go along with it, we're probably fried."

"We need a Plan C," he decided. "Run your idea past me."

Ruby plopped herself down in one of the chairs facing Drew's desk. "We were both wondering about something. In *tekl'hananni,* an enemy vessel is defined as one crewed by members of another House. The sensor field has to be able to differentiate between friend and foe. That means identifying which House owns which ship. But how?"

He thought for a moment. "Each Nandrian vessel must emit a specially coded signal of some kind."

"That was our conclusion as well. If we're correct, the sensor field must be programmed to recognize these coded signals. Our sensor did what it was supposed to do. It activated the invisibility field in response to an approaching ship not of our House, the *Endeavor*, but ignored our own shuttle, *Devil Bug*. The thing is, the sensor field wasn't programmed. Vera and Ray had reset everything to default parameters. So what was the default signal that set off our alarm?"

"It has to be something that Ranger vessels have but *Devil Bug* doesn't," he reasoned aloud. Then the answer struck him, so blindingly obvious that it made him want to slap himself on the forehead. "Guns."

"More specifically, weapons in standby mode," Lydia elaborated, "emitting a weak charge as they remain in contact with the control console of the ship."

"We can test our theory when Captain Rodrigues comes back tomorrow," said Ruby, adding hopefully, "unless you'd rather get it over with today."

They were like kids impatient to spring a practical joke. But Ruby had a point. The sooner they knew whether they'd guessed correctly, the sooner Gouryas and Singh could refocus their efforts and find a real solution to the problem.

"Lydia, send Rodrigues a message."

— «» —

"You want me to *what*?" Rodrigues's voice on the comm rose an octave in indignant disbelief.

Fully expecting his reaction, Townsend didn't even blink. "Shut down your weapons systems entirely. This isn't a trick, Paul. We believe that the field generator is responding to a standby signal emitted by your guns. Shut them down and let's see what happens. What could be the harm? It isn't as though we have the ability to attack you."

The Ranger let out a noisy breath. Drew and Lydia held theirs and shared a long look as they waited tautly for something — anything — to change outside the Hub.

"Son of a bitch," murmured Rodrigues. "It worked."

"*Endeavor*, you are cleared to dock at portal 3," said Lydia with audible relief.

"Will do," came the reply. "Tell your boss we have a lot to discuss and it's mealtime on Zulu right now, so I'm expecting to be fed."

"I hear you. We'll have our meeting in the caf," Drew agreed.

"I want real food, Townsend. None of that leftover pasta Jensen keeps putting in front of my men when they visit."

Her cheeks dimpling, Lydia said, "How about *ratatouille?*"

"And rats to you too, sweetheart," he grumped. "Rodrigues out."

— «» —

Townsend met Rodrigues on A Deck, noting as the newly-promoted captain walked through the portal that the responsibilities of command were apparently already beginning to weigh on him. As Bonelli's second, he'd looked like a recruitment ad for the Rangers — neat and tidy uniform, firm jaw, glint of determination in his eyes. Very appealing. But Ruby's earlier description of Zulu's crew as a bunch of animals had been spot on, and zookeepers didn't stay neat and tidy for long. Rumpled and harassed — those were the words that came to Drew's mind as he stepped forward to greet his guest.

"Let me get this straight. You have a sensor field *and* an invisibility field?" demanded the Ranger.

And impatient, Townsend added. The old Rodrigues would at least have said hello before jumping down his throat.

"Not by choice, believe me, Paul," he said, leading the way to the waiting tube car. "This alien technology is making us all crazy right now. My techs are poring through the manual, but—"

Rodrigues halted in mid-step. "You're serious? There's a manual?"

"It's a poor translation into Gally, but, yes, there's a manual, courtesy of one of the Nandrian Chief Officers." Townsend waved him into the car, then followed him in and pressed the button for D Deck. "So far, it hasn't been much help. My people are sharp, though. They'll figure it out."

"They'd better do it soon," remarked Rodrigues. "I wasn't happy about taking my weapons offline, but I cooperated. If you get a Nandrian ship on approach and make a request like that, I hate to think how they might respond. You need to remember just how vulnerable we are out here. Daisy Hub and Zulu may be constantly in motion, but we're also in orbit. That means a predictable trajectory at a constant speed, making both installations easy to find and target. So, unless you've also got a powerful deflection field up your sleeve, a proximity-triggered invisibility cloak isn't going to be much of a defense, for either of us."

He was right. Briefly, Drew wondered how the EIS would reply if he asked them to arm the station. Because he knew where Rodrigues was heading with this, and the last thing Townsend wanted to do was give the Zulu detachment free access to the Hub. It wasn't even an idea he felt safe about expressing aloud within earshot of any crew members. They would mutiny, and he wouldn't blame them.

Entering the caf, Townsend made eye contact with Jensen, who waved at him and then disappeared into the kitchen. Meanwhile, Rodrigues had selected a table in the far corner, away from the handful of crew who sat conversing over an end-of-shift meal. Three dockworkers and a couple of the general maintenance staff. Drew acknowledged them as he passed by. Then he eased himself into a chair across from the Ranger's and prompted him, "You said you had an important message for me?"

A smile tugged at the corners of Rodrigues's mouth as he reached into a pocket and pulled out a small black device, tube-shaped, with a connector plug at one end and ringed with ridges along half its length. It was an EIS encrypter, keyed to its owner's DNA, useless to anyone else. "Do you recognize this?"

Sternly reminding himself not to jump to any conclusions, Drew replied carefully, "It looks like Bonelli's. Where did you find it?"

"Bonelli still has his. He's recovering nicely, by the way. This one was recently given to me," Rodrigues told him, adding as he tucked it away, "I've known for some time that you've got one as well, and that not everything that happens out here gets reported to the Authorities on Earth, and what *is* reported may not be entirely truthful. Bonelli made me his second because I'm good at keeping secrets. That was partly why I requested this posting. When the command position came open, I presented a case to Security for having a known quantity in charge, someone who was already respected on Zulu and had proven that he could work with the manager of the Hub. The EIS heard I was interested, took me into the fold, and made it happen. And here we are."

"And here we are," Drew echoed, adding, "And here's our dinner," as Jensen delivered two bowls of steaming hot food to their table.

"Smells good. What is it?" said Rodrigues.

"*Ratatouille*," said Jensen. The Ranger's expression hardened. Before he could say anything, however, the chef explained, "It's an old French word for vegetable stew. In this case, it means carrots, parsnip, celery, diced tomato, pepper squash and zucchini, all locally grown, with appropriate seasoning of the Earth variety. *Bon appétit*." And with that, Jensen spun and bustled off.

Rodrigues was silent for a moment. "So she wasn't cussing at me?"

Grinning, Townsend replied, "I'm afraid not, Paul."

The Ranger gave a philosophical shrug. "I'll apologize to her before I leave." Then he picked up his fork and dived into his meal.

He was hungry. Townsend took a few mouthfuls, then sat and watched him eat, delaying as long as he could before reminding him, "You said we had a lot to discuss. Was there something else?"

"Yes, two things." Rodrigues stopped chewing and laid down his fork. Visibly choosing his words, he said, "First of all, I know that you and Bonelli have a history, and I watched his attitude to Daisy Hub do an about-face once you'd arrived. I don't know what you had on him, or what you threatened him with, and frankly, I don't care. I just want you to know that the tactics you used to deal with him won't be necessary with me. I've been briefed on your mission here and I know how important the Hub is to Earth Intelligence. As a courtesy, I'll order my men to steer clear so you can continue to do your job. However, I have a job to do as well. Zulu will be monitoring everything that happens in this system. If I see or even hear about anything that jeopardizes Daisy Hub or the mission, I'm authorized by the EIS to take whatever countermeasures I deem necessary, with or without your cooperation. Simply put, if there's a threat, I take charge and you take a back seat. That's non-negotiable."

Townsend had been afraid of this. Repressing a shudder, he managed to comment evenly, "I see. And if I'm aware, and you're not, that having a Ranger presence will only escalate the danger, what then?"

"Then it will mean that you withheld critical data from me, preventing me from making an accurate threat assessment. Look," Rodrigues added after a beat, "I'm not trying to be confrontational here. We're on the same side. Bonelli ran the detachment as though it was a street gang, and you're in charge of a bunch of rebels and dissidents, so I understand that things may get a little hairy from time to time. But we're both trained Security officers, and that should count for something. At the very least, we ought to be able to fulfil our respective duties without stepping on each other's toes."

Right, until the day a perceived threat gives you an excuse to board the station in force, bringing a Nandrian fleet into Earth space and triggering an interstellar war.

For now, the Ranger captain was making an effort to be reasonable. Drew decided he could do the same. "We can certainly try," he responded pleasantly. "And you said there was a second thing to discuss?"

"Yes, a personal message. It's from the same friend who sent you your newest crew member, whatever the hell that means. I was told to deliver this word for word, so here goes: The one-eyed man is not what he seems. He's a player looking for a rat." Rodrigues paused and stared quizzically into Drew's face. "Does that make any sense to you?"

Unfortunately, it did. However, the safest answer right now was a puzzled shrug of his shoulders. "Maybe it will later. Earth Intelligence likes to be cryptic."

"Uh-huh," said Rodrigues, unconvinced. He resumed eating. So did Townsend, even though the *ratatouille* now left a burnt aftertaste in his mouth.

Jensen had brought over mugs of his famous sludge to wash everything down. When the Ranger had cleaned his bowl and pushed it to the center of the table, Drew said hopefully, "Can we consider this the new commander's inspection tour? I mean, it's not like you've never been here before."

Rodrigues leaned back in his chair. "What's the matter, Townsend? Have you got a one-eyed man hiding out on the station or something?" he teased.

"Actually, we do," said Drew, pretending to share the joke. "His name is Ahab and he's in the SPA room right now, hunting for Moby Rodent."

The other man laughed.

In the end, Captain Rodrigues received the same orientation tour as Ruby had given Townsend the day he'd first arrived. Thankfully, the one-eyed man, Yoko, and the as-yet-nameless black and white rat all remained safely concealed the whole time. The Ranger could now be satisfied that every part of Daisy Hub was present and accounted for and was being used for its intended purpose — other than the field generator, of course, which seemed to have an agenda of its own — and that every crew member would recognize him the next time they met.

The moment Rodrigues was back inside his shuttle, Drew made for the tube car, activating his wristcomm on the way.

"Lydia, set up a meeting for me with senior staff, an hour from now, in AdComm. And have O'Malley report to me there right away. We've got a problem."

CHAPTER 17

Lydia stood in the triage area of Med Services, surveying an empty room and frowning in confusion. The Doc had asked for a private consultation with her before the staff meeting. In the more than seven standard years that they'd been aboard Daisy Hub together, the Doc had never made a request like this. Intrigued, Lydia had dropped everything and hurried down to H Deck. Now what?

She heard the Trauma room door hum open and a familiar voice behind her: "Good! You're here."

Turning around, she saw a sheaf of printout being thrust at her and automatically held out her hands to receive it. "What's this?"

"That's what I need you to tell *me*," declared the Doc. "Come inside."

Lydia followed her into the pale green alcove that served as Doc Ktumba's office, just off the Trauma room. When both women were seated, the Doc stared silently at her desktop for a moment, her lips pressed tightly together. Then she raised her eyes to meet Lydia's curious gaze and said in a rush, "I told you earlier that both Yoko and the black and white rat had been infected with retroviruses. I've since taken a closer look and discovered that the retroviruses are quite different from each other. I think the one in the rat that Max Karlov brought with him contains an encrypted message, and I need your help to decrypt it."

Lydia glanced over the bars and blanks on the first page of the printout. "And this is the retrovirus's genome?"

"Yes. RNA takes the shape of a single helix, with bases consisting of cytosine, guanine, adenine, and uracil. 'C', 'G', 'A' and 'U'. Put that together with the 'G', 'C', 'T' and 'A' of DNA and you have a pool of base pairs on which to build a cipher. Can you create an algorithm that will search for patterns and groupings and convert them into bits of information?"

"I can try, Doc, but this sort of thing is really O'Malley's forte. Shouldn't you be talking to him?"

She huffed impatiently. "In truth, I'd rather not even be talking to you. If I had the expertise, I'd decrypt it myself. But I don't. My only consolation is that you, at least, know how to keep a secret."

"You aren't planning to let Townsend know about this?"

"It depends on the content of the message. Until we know that, you and I must be the only ones who are even aware that it exists."

—— «» ——

"You're going to love this," said O'Malley with a smug grin. He'd arrived in AdComm ten minutes early for the meeting, strutting like a peacock as he stepped out of the tube car and made his way to a seat directly in front of Townsend's desk. One of these days, thought Drew irritably, the ratkeeper was going to reach too far while patting himself on the back and dislocate his shoulder.

"What did you find?"

"First of all, hats off to whoever created Karlov's creds, because they're brilliant."

"And yet, you spotted the forgery."

O'Malley gave a shrug that Townsend guessed was supposed to convey modesty. "Only because I'm paranoid in addition to being brilliant myself. And because there are advantages to living on the edge of Earth space and receiving database updates bundled into packages. I've configured our system to segregate each package as it arrives, scan it for worms and viruses, and then run a comparison with all our previously recorded data, flagging duplications or discrepancies. That was how I knew *your* creds were bogus when you first arrived."

"So Karlov wasn't there until suddenly he was?"

"Like Athena, sprung full-grown from Jove's forehead. It's a brand-new identity and it's flawless. Fully cross-referenced. Whoever spliced it in was a pro, probably working for some government agency. And if we were on Earth, where updates are constantly streaming through the system, we'd never have twigged to it. This Karlov guy is a plant, boss, I'm sure of it. The only question is, who sent him?"

"No," said Townsend slowly. "The first of many questions is, who the hell is he? Any ideas?"

"Sorry, I haven't got a clue. I checked for people who died at about the time Max Karlov would have appeared, but none of them matched his age or physical profile. And there's no record of anyone remotely resembling him taking passage on an Earth-bound transport from any of the colonies. My guess is that he's a 'ghost' — someone who, for one reason or another, never got entered in the database to start with."

Except that Karlov had supposedly been born and raised on Earth, where not being in the database meant not having a credit account, which in turn meant not having access to housing, proper nourishment, or regular medical care. On a colony world, it was possible to drop off the grid and still have a decent life. People on the margins of Earth's society, however, tended to either die young of illness and neglect or get scooped up and mercilessly exploited by the criminal element. The few that Drew had encountered while working cases for New Chicago Security had been wraith-thin and trailing an aura of despair. Certainly, nobody would describe Max Karlov in those terms. So, he probably hadn't been born on Earth or any of its colonies. And the Doc's genetic testing had effectively ruled out the possibility that he might be an alien.

Townsend felt a sudden tightening in his midsection as a third alternative occurred to him.

According to the message Rodrigues had just delivered, the one-eyed man was looking for a rat. That could only be Yoko. The European gene brokers who had coerced Naguchi into signing over his patents knew how valuable she was. They wouldn't stop trying to acquire her just because their first agent, Nestor Quan, had been thwarted. They would send someone else, giving him a strong incentive to complete the mission successfully — in Karlov's own words, his life. The Doc was convinced that Karlov had been created in a laboratory. What if she was right?

But there was also the matter of that black and white rat which, according to the Doc's theory, must have come from the same lab as Karlov. And what about his disturbing request to practice killing Nandrians in the SPA room?

Nothing about this man was adding up. Which was he — a soldier, as Lydia suspected, or a victim in need of protection, as the Doc maintained? In any case, what was the story behind the condition in which he had arrived on the Hub?

Unanswered questions spun restlessly inside Townsend's mind, threatening to turn the itch in his brain into a full-blown headache and reminding him of an ancient Indo-Asian curse: *May you live in interesting times.*

These were interesting times, indeed. Drew dropped into the chair behind his desk and watched the rest of his senior crew arrive for the meeting. At this point, he knew three things for sure. First, he couldn't tell his crew what he'd been told about Karlov without also revealing its source, and that would blow his EIS cover and very likely cause a mutiny. Second, Rodrigues had said all the right things during his visit to the Hub, but he was still too "by the book" for Townsend's liking. There could be no further sharing of secrets with this man, or of information that might lead him to uncover any. Unfortunately, that included warnings about how the Nandrians would most likely respond should he decide to flex his EIS muscles on or around the station. And third, the Ranger captain must never be shown a reason to believe that there was a threat to the Hub. The Nandrians couldn't be allowed to think so, either. Nor Earth, for that matter. In the unpleasantness to come, there was no one to whom House Daisy Hub could turn for help without starting an interstellar war.

That thought alone was depressing to contemplate, and the grimness was contagious. Each time someone glanced over and met the station manager's eyes, a conversation halted. By the time he got to his feet to address the assembled group, the silence in AdComm was thick enough to spread on a cracker.

"Some new information has come to light," he told them.

"From Rodrigues?" Lydia cut in.

"Most of it, yes. He's now officially the new commander of Zulu. I'm hoping we'll be able to work with him, but only time will tell. Meanwhile, he repeated something to me that Bonelli had also pointed out, using different words: as long as an enemy can plot our location based on our orbit, invisibility alone isn't going to protect us from being fired on or boarded. We have to be able to defend ourselves at a distance. Since we already know that Earth's government is never going to outfit this station with heavy weapons, that leaves us with three alternatives, two of them unacceptable. We are not going to ask the Rangers to be an armed presence aboard Daisy Hub; and we don't dare become a participating House in *tekl'hananni* by asking Trokerk to do it. The first of these is just inviting trouble. The second would be suicidal."

Townsend paused to gauge the reactions of his officers. As his gaze swept the room, he saw Holchuk sitting with his arms crossed and wearing an unreadable expression.

"And the third alternative, Chief?" Ruby prompted him.

"This was suggested by something Rodrigues said. A repulsion field strong enough to deflect weapons fire. If we can make it work, it will at least buy us some time. Repulsion field technology isn't new; every enclave on Earth is surrounded by a one-way barrier to keep out intruders, and every vessel in the Fleet can throw up shields to protect against space dust and debris. Odds are, we already have something like it on the Hub."

Townsend gazed meaningfully at Gouryas and Singh. Gouryas was nodding enthusiastically. Singh's features had contracted, pulling his habitual smirk into a hyphen of disapproval as he slowly shook his head back and forth.

"Which is it, yes or no?" Drew demanded.

"Yes, we have the technology," Gouryas declared. "Our field generator on M Deck establishes a dome-shaped area of gravitational attraction that is stretched northward by amplification relays. Bubbles on top of bubbles. If we reconfigured the Hub's gravity field to free up the relays, we could theoretically repurpose them to create a shield for the outer hull."

"Theoretically," echoed Townsend.

"It would dig into our spare parts locker and reverse the direction of gravity on Decks I through M, but I think it could be done," said Gouryas.

Singh's complexion had visibly darkened. With some asperity he now pointed out, "Aren't we getting ahead of ourselves here? We still have a Nandrian device to figure out—"

"—and a repulsion field could be all that saves us if we're not able to turn off our invisibility cloak before the next ship full of Nandrians shows up and they get offended and start firing on us," Gouryas retorted.

Uttering an exasperated syllable, Singh shot Townsend a look.

Lydia cleared her throat loudly, drawing everyone's attention. "Would it help you to know how we got the Rangers' shuttle through the sensor field without tripping the invisibility switch?" she asked demurely.

"Yes!" both engineers replied.

She told them.

"So, all we need to do for now is program the sensor field to recognize the codes of any approaching Nandrian ships," Singh summed up drily. "Just two small problems: first, we don't know how to program the field; and second, we don't have the codes."

"Not yet," Lydia supplied. "Not until I request them from Nagor."

"Brilliant!" said Gouryas. "And if you can get him to give you a bunch of them at once, we can analyze them—"

"—and maybe use them to figure out how to calibrate the field using the molecular paintbrush," Singh concluded. "It's a slim chance, but it's better than none at all."

A self-satisfied grin had taken up residence on Lydia's face. She'd clearly been spending too much time around the ratkeeper — some of his cockiness had rubbed off on her.

Meanwhile, Gouryas was so excited he could hardly sit still. "Mister Townsend?"

"Yes, go!" he replied, shooing the two engineers toward the tube car door. "Invent! Create!" *Save all our lives*, he added privately.

"Was that it, boss?" asked O'Malley.

He knew it wasn't. With a covert glance at the forbidding features of Security Chief Orvy Hagman, Drew turned his attention to the second major puzzle of the day, the mysterious one-eyed man who, according to Rex Regum's message, had come to the Hub to steal Yoko.

"I had O'Malley here do some digging," he said. "We now know for certain that Max Karlov was added to Earth's database shortly before his arrival on Daisy Hub. It's not his real name."

As Hagman was opening his mouth to speak, the Doc sprang to her feet and cut in ahead of him. "People travel under assumed names all the time. It doesn't mean there's anything sinister going on."

"It might if his true identity was never in the system," said Townsend, matching the sharpness of her tone.

"Never?" Ruby sounded intrigued. "So someone has sent us a one-eyed 'ghost'? This just gets better and better."

"Could he be an alien?" Lydia wondered.

"Absolutely not," declared the Doc. "I've mapped his genome. He's Human, no question."

"This was not an amateur job," O'Malley added. "Not like Major Cisco. Whoever put Karlov's creds online knew exactly what they were doing."

"Now you're saying he's a spy?" bristled Hagman, rising from his chair.

"Can you say for certain that he's not?" O'Malley shot back.

Townsend rolled his eyes toward the ceiling and silently prayed for strength. "Calm down, everyone. We're not ready to stick any labels on this man. We're only saying that the mystery surrounding him seems to be deepening, and until we have answers to our questions we need to be even more cautious around him." He turned to Lydia and asked, "Where is Karlov right now?"

She consulted her compupad. "In the SPA room, sparring with Muhammad Ali. Well, boxing is a form of combat," she went on defensively, "and I wasn't about to—"

"Understood," said Drew. "How is he doing?"

"Too well," she told him, troubled. "According to my readings, he's been hard at it for more than an hour and is barely breaking a sweat."

"What happened to extreme skateboarding and white water rafting?"

Casting a sympathetic glance at Hagman, she replied, "He's given them up for now. When he isn't baking with Nora or interfering with the characters in U-Town, all he wants to do is fight. It's as if he's training for something."

Training for battle? Against Nandrians? A throbbing headache began punctuating Townsend's thoughts.

As an agent, he had two options: turn Karlov or terminate him. Termination was looking a lot more practical at the moment, even though it would polarize the crew and make a permanent enemy of Doc Ktumba.

"Chief?" Ruby prompted.

Everyone was watching him. Townsend cleared his throat and told them, "There's no more that we can do for the moment. You've been brought up to date. Keep doing what you've been doing and remain vigilant for anything worth reporting. Meanwhile, I'm going to try to get some straight answers from Karlov. Lydia, as soon as he's done in the SPA room—"

"—send him to Med Services for a check-up," commanded the Doc, her eyes resting like targeting lasers on Drew's face. "Failure to perspire under stress could be symptomatic of a glandular condition, and I want to verify that Max is in perfect health before the interrogation begins."

Her tone fairly dripped ultimatum. This was the Doc he'd met on his first day on Daisy Hub, the one who could make a charging rhino stop and rethink its plan.

"All right, then," he said irritably. "First the exam, then the questions."

CHAPTER 18

"**Drew? Gouryas and** Singh are asking to meet with you on L Deck. They sound excited," Lydia called to him from her station on AdComm.

"Are they excited with good news, or excited because we're all fried?" he called back.

"Excited with good news, I would say."

It was probably just wishful thinking on her part.

"Tell them I'm on my way. And what about Karlov? Is he in Med Services yet?"

"Nope. Still in the SPA room, still going strong. I programmed the boxing match to end in a draw, so it will last as long as he does."

"It's been three hours. Shouldn't he be getting a little tired by now?"

She gave him a helpless shrug. "I'll notify you the moment the Doc is finished with him," she said, and returned to staring intently at the display on her computer screen. Whatever it was, she didn't look happy about it.

Townsend hesitated for a moment, his curiosity piqued. Then his common sense elbowed it aside. He was already dealing with enough aggravation to ruin the health of five people, and Lydia wasn't a child. If she needed his help she would ask for it. Until then, he had a meeting to attend nine decks below. With a final backward glance, he headed for the tube car.

The first thing Drew noticed when the door opened on L Deck was that the bulkheads and shelving were now turquoise. Not as shocking as hot pink, but still not a color he would want on the walls of his workspace. The second thing he noticed as he approached the drafting table where the two engineers were standing was that Singh was once more smirking archly. So their excitement over the comm really had been a sign of progress? Townsend hoped so. The past few days had been filled with frustration. Any good news would be most welcome right now.

"We were right," declared Gouryas. "Remember when we went on that mission to Zulu and got their field generator to produce the invisibility cloak?"

"As I recall, you painted their entire landing deck purple in the process. And a few other surfaces as well. The Rangers still haven't forgiven us for that."

"Well," began Singh with a dismissive wave of his hand, "we had already hypothesized that the generator would create the field, and that the paintbrush would act as the controller, establishing its nature and parameters."

As though sensing Townsend's growing impatience, Gouryas broke in, "We've been compiling our observations from the experiment on Zulu, searching for anything that might shed some light on our current situation. We've also been looking at the ship identification codes that Lydia procured for us from House Trokerk."

"They've each got a pair of wave frequencies embedded in them," Singh continued. "One is a constant in all the codes, and we're guessing that it denotes the House. The other one varies from ship to ship. In tactical situations, it would make sense for that second frequency to keep cycling, like a password, to prevent an opposing vessel's weapons from locking onto its signal."

"Then how are we supposed to identify their ships when the *tekl'hananni* scoreboard goes up?" Drew demanded.

"Fortunately," said Singh, "we don't have to. Daisy Hub has extended docking privileges to the leading House, not to any individual participating craft. Our sensor field only needs to recognize the first embedded frequency."

So far, so good. Townsend nodded approval. "And how are you coming along with the second half of that problem?"

"Not too well, I'm afraid," Gouryas replied. "However, we've noticed that nothing we did on Zulu and nothing Beale and Oolalong have done here has disrupted the functioning of the Meniscus field on either of the short-hopper landing decks. We think it must be hardwired and on a protected circuit, triggered by the switch that opens the door to space."

"So, even if the invisibility cloak is activated, we can still access and use *Devil Bug*," Townsend concluded. "That could come in handy."

Prompted by a head-jerk from Gouryas, Singh cleared his throat and said, "Actually, we were thinking that if we studied the Meniscus field, we might find a way to separate the invisibility cloak from the sensor field that triggers it."

Townsend felt as though he was back in the ward room at the 33rd Precinct with the hyperactive four-year-olds. He did now what had worked for him back then — sucked in a deep breath and released it slowly, counting to ten as he consciously relaxed his face and shoulders. Then he said, enunciating carefully and with exaggerated patience, "If by study you mean tinker with, the answer is no. The Meniscus field is the only part of this alien contraption that's currently working the way we need it to, and I don't want to risk anyone messing that up."

Just as the four-year-olds had done, Gouryas let out a small, disappointed sound.

Drew's wristcomm buzzed. With luck, it meant he could finally question Karlov.

"Lydia?"

"Nope," said Ruby's voice. "I've got bad news and worse news, Chief. Which do you want first?"

"Give me the bad news," he told her, already suspecting what it might be.

"The scoreboard just went up. Trokerk is ahead by eight, and the *Krronn* and her sister ship the *Nannssi* will be on their way here as soon as their battle damage has been repaired and both vessels are fit to travel. Their estimated ETA is about forty standard hours."

Wonderful. In less than two days Daisy Hub would be receiving twice the usual number of Nandrians. Two ships that might open fire on the station if it disappeared while they were on approach. And if by some miracle it didn't and they were able to dock, Townsend would then have to deliver two welcoming speeches from memory, one of them a first contact script. And there was worse news than this?

He braced himself and asked, "What's the rest of it, Ruby?"

"We've received a commburst from Zulu. Rodrigues wanted us to know that he copied the Nandrian transmission and will be dispatching all three shuttles in time to protect us when our cloaking field deploys, angering the aliens. His words, Chief. He's also sent out a call to the other Ranger detachments in the sector. No responses yet, but he's pretty sure they'll scramble."

This was the icing on the cake: the Rangers and the Nandrians colliding on Daisy Hub's doorstep, giving Karlov the cover he needed to make his move on Yoko. Rodrigues knew from experience what would happen when those three armed short-hoppers approached too close to the station. Clearly, he believed that there was nothing Townsend's crew could do to prevent the aliens from tripping the switch first. Drew hated to admit it, but at the moment, he was right. Before asking the Ranger captain to stand his men down, the station manager would have to demonstrate beyond any doubt that their protection was not needed. Until then, he was stuck.

Townsend turned and saw his mood reflected in the expressions on his senior engineers' faces. Singh's smirk had wilted at the corners, and Gouryas's normally swarthy complexion had visibly paled.

"You heard the lady," he told them. "If you can't find a way to either program or shut off that damned invisibility field in the next forty hours, we're about to have our first interstellar war."

— ‹‹›› —

Lydia Garfield sat at her station, preparing to test the program she had just rewritten — again — and keeping her fingers crossed that the sixth time would be the charm. If the Doc was right, and this extremely long strand of reverse-transcripted DNA was storing encrypted information, then each of its possible base pairs could represent an alphanumeric character, and each character or group of characters might stand for — what? A pixel in a bit map? An Anglo letter or number or symbol? Maybe a letter from one of Earth's older languages? Fortunately, Lydia had given top priority to upgrading the computer systems aboard the Hub. She hated to think how long it would have taken her to run each of these tests on the kludges she had found when she first arrived here.

She pressed the start key. Half a standard minute went by. Then lines began cascading like a waterfall from the top of her screen, some short and curved, others thick and straight. She watched in fascination as they arranged themselves in rows, forming a solid sheet of characters, mostly unfamiliar.

There was more than one alphabet here, and evidently more than one level of encryption. Some of the characters were Anglo letters. Others resembled piles of sticks or an assortment of stylized trees with broken or truncated branches. Her breath caught in her throat as she recognized one of the trees. It looked just like a cookie that she had eaten earlier, a tree shape that Karlov had told Nora was part of his name.

Quickly, Lydia composed and executed a subroutine that would identify the Anglo letters, then copy and paste them to a second document without changing their sequence. If this was a simple case of overlaying multiple messages one atop another, the Anglo text at least should come clear immediately.

Within seconds, her screen had repainted — with nonsense words.

Great. Either there was a third level of encryption or she'd been mistaken about the overlay.

"What are you doing?"

Lydia nearly jumped out of her skin.

"Sorry, kiddo," said Ruby. "I didn't mean to startle you. But what's this? A cryptogram? Must be a tough one — you've been at it for a while. Maybe I can help."

"I don't think so," Lydia began, then gave up as Ruby brought over a chair and sat down beside her. The Doc had wanted the contents of this message kept secret. Lydia weighed the odds of anyone understanding the garbage currently on her screen and decided not to create suspicion by arguing. She shifted to her left to give the other woman a more direct view.

Ruby stared thoughtfully at the jumble of characters for a moment. "That's a word," she said, pointing with an index finger as she pronounced the letters aloud. "Not an Anglo word, unfortunately."

"No," breathed Lydia, riding a swell of excitement, "it's not Anglo. Ruby, you're brilliant."

"Of course, I am," declared 'Mom' with a grin. "Aren't we all?"

— «◇» —

Townsend still had a card or two to play. He rode the tube car north to B Deck to find Lucas Soaring Hawk, the Hub's propulsion expert.

Unlike L Deck, which appeared to be trying on a rainbow one color at a time, Hawk's workshop was shades of gray. It looked dingier in the corners and wherever spare tools and used wipe-rags had gravitated into untidy piles, but it was unremittingly gray everywhere Townsend turned his gaze. The PLS suits hanging beside each of the three airlocks were gray. Even the drop sheets that littered the deck, each displaying an assortment of parts from Hawk's current project, were gray.

Townsend looked up and saw Soaring Hawk striding sure-footedly toward him, skirting the drop sheets without so much as a downward glance. Tall and lithe, the man who had "souped up" *Devil Bug* wore his dark hair shoulder length, securing it in a ponytail at the nape of his neck when he was working, and tying a bandanna around his forehead to keep stray locks from falling over his eyes.

"I was wondering when you would get around to me," said Hawk with a grin.

"You've been monitoring the situation?"

"I know that you've got half the crew working their tails off to keep Karlov from finding out what the other half are doing. So, where do I fit into this?"

"You're my last-ditch guy. We're doing all we can to prevent it, but there's a good chance everything will hit the fan day after tomorrow, putting us in the middle of a battle between the Rangers and the Nandrians. At that point, getting ourselves out of harm's way becomes top priority. Ruby tells me you're the one to see about optimizing engines."

"Ruby speaks the truth," said Hawk sagely.

"It has also been pointed out to me that an invisible object moving at a constant speed on a predictable trajectory may as well be visible. Do our thrusters generate enough power to break us out of orbit?"

"The main thrusters? They can. And someone must have figured that they'd have to at some point, because the Hub's outer frame is specially reinforced to keep everything in one piece during escape velocity flight. However, thruster burn can be tracked, even if we're invisible," Hawk pointed out. "If the Nandrians decide to target us, simply running away under power may not be our best option."

"Actually, that's not all I had in mind."

Hawk cocked his head, intrigued.

"I understand that the Hub can be separated into three sections in an emergency," Townsend continued. "Am I correct in assuming that each of them would then be equipped with its own thrusters and control panel, including communications?"

"I like where this is going," said the propulsion wizard, his dark eyes acquiring a calculating expression. "Tell me more about your plan."

— «» —

"This can't be right," Doc Ktumba declared. "There must be an error in your algorithm."

But Lydia had checked and double-checked each word of her decryption and was prepared to stand her ground, even against the Doc. "It is what it is. And it came here with Karlov, who is genetically Human but different from us on a cellular level. You told me yourself that he could be the result of a laboratory experiment."

"Yes! An experiment conducted by Humans in a laboratory on Earth."

"So, you're willing to believe that Humans would subject other Humans to genetic experimentation, but not that aliens would experiment on Humans?"

"*If* the test subjects referred to in this excerpt are Human," said the Doc, "then it would mean there are two separate branches of the Human race. One of those branches was forcibly relocated to an alien world and left there to survive as best they could, and the other one has been mutated and manipulated to satisfy someone's scientific curiosity — someone, by the way, who might not yet be done tinkering with Humanity. So, which branch of the species do you think we would belong to? Would the Humans of Earth be the test subjects, or would we be the control group? In either case, it would mean we'd been victimized in unspeakable ways — *if* this document is genuine, and *if* you're right about what it says. And in the interests of my being able to sleep at night, I would prefer it if you weren't."

"Well, what about this other text?" Lydia persisted, replacing the Anglo characters on the screen with the sequence of sticks and treelike symbols she had lifted from the decrypted file. "We know that Karlov is familiar with this alphabet. He baked it into cookies in Jensen's kitchen."

The Doc stared thoughtfully for a moment at the display. "I've seen these letters before. Or something like them. They're northern European, and very old."

"Why don't we ask Karlov to read the page aloud for us?"

"No. It arrived here encrypted. We have no idea who, if anyone, was intended to learn its contents, including the courier who brought it to us."

"Then how about asking him to pronounce the letters individually for us?" Lydia suggested. "Nobody can claim their existence was supposed to be kept secret, since he formed them out of cookie dough and even told Nora they spelled out his name. And once we know how to pronounce them, I can feed the information into a database and continue trying out subroutines. Unless you'd rather I stopped?"

Evidently torn, the Doc fell silent. Finally, she said, "Don't stop. Not until you can tell me with certainty when these experiments took place and where, and on whom."

"I gather you still don't want Drew to know anything about this?"

"He's got enough on his mind right now. Besides, if the worst happens and the Nandrians blow the Hub to pieces, it all becomes moot, doesn't it?"

— «» —

Townsend's next stop was the caf on D Deck, where Ruby had told him he would find Gavin Holchuk and Teri Mintz. These two were inseparable lately, except when Holchuk was summoned to a senior staff meeting or Max Karlov needed to be detoured to U-Town to keep him busy. The interactive soap opera had been Teri's passion since before she arrived on the Hub. Now it was Karlov's as well.

In fact, it was the level of realism achieved by the U-Town programming that had given Townsend the idea he was now fine-tuning in his mind.

Gavin and Teri were sitting at a table in the middle of the room, silently basking in each other's company. It was a shame to intrude on their moment. However, in less than thirty-nine hours Daisy Hub would become the epicenter of an interstellar war, and Townsend could practically hear the clock ticking down. He walked over and settled onto the third chair at their table, muttering a brief apology.

Holchuk frowned at the tabletop, then leaned back expectantly in his seat. "What's happening, boss man?"

Teri remained as she was, placidly sipping a brown liquid from one of Jensen's tall mugs. It was too light in color to be java. As though sensing the question in Townsend's mind, she raised her cup toward him in mock salute and explained, "Hot chocolate. Jensen saved some of the cocoa paste you gave him."

The cocoa had come from Bruni Patel. Townsend let himself miss his friend for a moment. Then, meeting the curious gaze of the Chief Cargo Inspector, he got directly to the point. "Two things. First, despite what I said at the senior staff meeting, I'm very suspicious of Karlov. In fact, I think he may actually be here to complete Major Cisco's mission."

Holchuk snapped upright in his chair. "I've felt from the start that there was something off about him."

"I have a plan to sidetrack him, but I'll need your help."

"You've got it," said Holchuk. "Just tell me which airlock you want me to shove him through."

"Gavin!" Teri snatched up his empty cup and made as though to hit him with it.

Townsend put out a hand to stop her. "It's not that kind of plan," he assured her. "Tell me, Teri, on a scale of one to ten, how hooked is Karlov on U-Town?"

"At least an eight, probably higher."

"Definitely higher," Holchuk confirmed. "Seems like it's all he can talk about."

Ignoring the interruption, Teri continued, "He's already been adopted into a fictional family and has identified which roles he wants to play when he interacts with other family members. He's involved with my family as well. When the trial verdict came back not guilty, Max let out a whoop and sent his avatar racing across the courtroom to give Brock a bear hug. I think U-Town feels very real to him."

"That's putting it mildly," declared Holchuk with disgust. "He talks about these characters as though they're living on the station. Now that Angela's pregnant, it wouldn't surprise me if he started knitting little things."

Townsend had to repress a shudder at the image that popped into his mind. "I gather one of the roles he picked was 'protector' or 'rescuer'?"

"Yes, but only because 'avenger' wasn't on the menu," said Teri.

"Perfect."

Now Holchuk was leaning forward, his lips curving slowly into a smile. "Is this another one of your crazy schemes that will make the Doc throw up her hands in frustration?"

"Only if she finds out about it," Townsend told him, "and with luck, she never will." Speaking to Teri once more, he went on, "What does Karlov know about the way U-Town operates?"

Her eyebrows drew together in a delicate frown. "I've explained to him that some of the characters are fictional and the rest are avatars, representing real people, and that all their activities take place in cyberspace."

"Does he know how to tell which characters are fictional and which aren't?"

"There is no way to tell," she said. "Everyone in U-Town is a computer construct, and the avatars have made-up names to protect the privacy of the subscribers who designed them."

"Excellent."

"Just what have you got in mind, boss man?"

"Does it involve Rob O'Malley?" Teri challenged him, her eyes narrowing. When he didn't reply immediately, she went on, "It does, doesn't it? You're going to let him mess with the characters in U-Town. Well, you tell that little hacker that if he kills off anyone I care about, I'll make him sorry he ever started!" *And you too!* said her expression as she stared directly into Townsend's face.

He'd brought U-Town to the Hub so she wouldn't kill him for inviting the Ranger detachment to her concert earlier, and it had worked. Too well, apparently, since he might now have to bribe her — with what, he hadn't the slightest idea — not to kill O'Malley for touching her favorite toy.

"Teri, whatever he does to U-Town, it won't be permanent, I promise. All the files will be backed up, and I'll make sure he restores them after we've wrapped the con. We just need Karlov to believe that one of the avatars belongs to a murderer."

"And who do you plan to cast in the role of this murderer?" she demanded to know. Once again he waited a second too long to reply. "It's O'Malley, isn't it? I knew it! He's going to massacre my family!"

Holchuk was having trouble keeping a straight face. "Drink your chocolate, Tiger," he told her, patting her on the arm. "It'll be all right." Then, addressing Townsend, he said, "So, you're turning the soap opera into a mystery thriller. You don't actually think Karlov will abandon his mission on Daisy Hub to go charging to the rescue of a bunch of characters in a virtual reality town, do you?"

"You said yourself that the line between fantasy and reality seems to blur for him when he's immersed in that program, that he talks about the characters as though they're alive. What I'm hoping is that once his favorites start dying, he'll become obsessed with the mystery and put off snatching Yoko until he's solved it. It's an imperfect solution, but it should buy us enough time to deal with our more immediate problems. Speaking of which—"

"You know, things would be a whole lot simpler if we just shoved him out an airlock."

Townsend gave him a look. "Forget about killing him. If we take him out of play, the European gene brokers will just send another agent, putting us back to square one. Karlov is a known quantity. We have a way to contain him, and as long as he remains in position to carry out his orders, his employers will wait to see what happens. That's what we need right now."

"Fine, then," Holchuk said with a sigh. "But you said there were two things?"

"Yes. Apparently, two ships of House Trokerk were involved in the latest *tekl'hananni* match, the *Krronn* and one other I've never heard of, and they'll both be arriving here in about thirty-eight hours."

"You'll need two different welcoming speeches, then, one per Chief Officer. What have you done lately that could be described as a battle victory?"

Townsend had to think. "I managed to get Rodrigues off the station without letting him find out about Karlov or either of the rats we have aboard. Does that work?"

"It does. Yoko is our *tseritsa*, the symbol of our House, so the Nandrians would consider protecting her to be an act of great honor. All right, boss man, you'll have your speeches, in plenty of time to learn them. I'll make you sound like one of the heroes in those flat-screen videos Lu is always watching."

— «» —

Thirty-eight hours.

O'Malley was waiting for Townsend in AdComm, wearing a smug grin. He had evidently turned up something interesting. The ratkeeper was a natural data miner. In between assignments he did it for fun, and he usually struck pay dirt.

Drew eased himself into the chair behind his desk and gestured to O'Malley to sit down as well. "What have you found?"

"You asked me to look into Harry Mintz. Teri was right. He did have big, important friends."

"He did," Drew echoed. "But not anymore?"

O'Malley's eyes were laughing. "Listen to this, boss. It's a story worthy of U-Town. Harry Mintz was a mid-level white collar in the distribution of drugs off-world. Mostly gray market medicinal, but he had a piece of the recreational pie as well. A couple of years ago, people started dying off-world from taking prescribed doses of medicinal drugs. Space Installation Security launched a covert investigation. Turns out the meds had been spiked with something that boosted their effect. Any prescribed dose became an overdose. Someone leaked the results of the investigation, and suddenly every finger was pointing at Harry Mintz."

"Of course. He was the patsy."

"His Eligibility was revoked to keep him from leaving Earth. Teri had already divorced him at that point. Naturally, the tabs began building up expectations of a big, splashy trial. But it never materialized. According to the database, all charges were quietly dropped and his Eligibility was reinstated."

Townsend smiled. Patsies weren't entirely helpless, as any cop would know. "He must have pulled the plug on his bosses. I remember hearing something about a major drug ring bust on Ginza Hub, shortly before I came here."

"And something else is supposed to have happened around the time you arrived, boss. I found a couple of death notices, one for Harry Mintz and one for Teri Martin. According to the database, they passed away one day apart on Vegas Hub. Digging a little deeper, I came up with a pair of Security files. Put together they're not much thicker than the one on Bruni Patel, but I thought you'd appreciate knowing the details.

"The resident M.E. on Vegas Hub ruled both deaths accidental drug overdoses. No autopsy reports, but circumstantial evidence pointing to cause of death was apparently overwhelming in each case. Quiet funerals, private *shivas*. Strictly a back-page filler."

Dark suspicion began twisting uneasily in Townsend's mind.

Vegas Hub had been where Teri thought she was going when she came out to the airfield that day. Someone had diverted her to Daisy Hub instead and had then faked her death, and probably Harry's as well. Someone with deep pockets and a lot of influence and a vested interest in keeping her — or both of them — alive.

It couldn't be the EIS. Earth Intelligence had staffed the Hub in anticipation of Townsend's arrival. They'd handpicked people with particular knowledge and expertise to operate and protect the station. A previous station manager had even drawn up a list of desirable qualifications and had left it in the bottom drawer of his filing cabinet for Drew to find. Nowhere on that wish list had the words "singer" or "entertainer" appeared.

So, what was Teri Mintz doing on Daisy Hub?

A chill crept across Drew's shoulders as the answer came to him. *Turn him or terminate him.* And if he turns, make the safety of someone he cares about part of the deal.

Teri hadn't been posted to the Hub by her ex-husband pulling strings with the Relocation Authority. She'd been sent here by Space Installation Security as a hostage. If Harry backed out or tried to play them, someone with a kill order would be dispatched to the Hub. Someone Rodrigues might or might not be able to head off. It was not a happy prospect to contemplate.

"So what do you think, boss?" said O'Malley with a twinkle in his voice. "Is Harry Mintz still alive somewhere, using manufactured creds?"

"I've no doubt he is, courtesy of his big, important friends," Townsend mused aloud. "Does Teri suspect any of this?"

"Nope. Anytime she mentions her ex-husband's name, I keep expecting her to spit on the deck. She's convinced he derailed her career out of spite."

"Good. Let's just keep it that way. In the meanwhile, we have a couple of crises to deal with, and I have a special assignment for you, one that I think you'll enjoy."

A speculative gleam came into the ratkeeper's eyes. "Is it a con? It is, isn't it? Who's the mark?"

Townsend leaned forward and lowered his voice. "Karlov. We need to convince him that a serial killer is loose in U-Town, taking out all his favorite characters one by one. This needs to be a mystery, and I want it to be both irresistible and unsolvable. Can you make that happen without permanently modifying any of the programming?"

O'Malley's face lit up. "Piece of cake, boss. There's plenty of space on the SPA server. I can back everything up, then write-protect the original files and work with the backup copy. It won't take long to build a serial-killer avatar — don't worry, I'll make sure it doesn't look like anyone on the station — or, even better, I can hack the programming of one of the existing characters and turn it evil. Or maybe I'll do both and have one of them be a copycat. That'll drive him really crazy. Once the programming is done, I can begin bumping off little VR people right away. Are there any in particular that you want me to terminate?"

Townsend thought for a moment. "Begin with Brock. Make it grisly. After that, it's open season on every character he's friends with. And there's one more thing: I want you to route the U-Town backup through our SPA room."

"Give him the whole experience? That's a lot more work, but not a problem," said O'Malley, practically rubbing his hands together with glee.

"How soon before he can put on his skin?"

"I can lift his physical parameters from the programs Lydia's already written for him, so once I've added the third dimension to U-Town, the rest should be simple. Assuming no glitches, version 1.0 should be available in just about four hours."

"Good. By the way, when the Nandrians arrive, they'll expect to see Yoko at the welcoming ceremony. How is she doing?"

O'Malley's expression morphed from impish to sheepish. "I was going to talk to you about that, boss."

This did not bode well. The Doc hadn't been happy about moving the rat to O'Malley's quarters long-term, but Drew had insisted. He could just imagine what her reaction would be if Yoko came to any harm as a result.

"What's the matter?" he asked warily. "Is she sick?"

"I don't know. I haven't seen her since yesterday."

Townsend stared incredulously into the ratkeeper's face as a torrent of ugly possibilities rushed through his mind. They had been so busy distracting Karlov. Had he figured out a way to complete his mission in spite of them? Or had Karlov himself been a distraction? Was there a second agent concealed aboard the Hub?

Finally, Drew managed to say, "You've lost Yoko? How?"

"When I woke up this morning, her cage was open and she was gone."

"Did Karlov know that she was in your quarters? Could he have sneaked in during the night?"

"Not a chance, boss," O'Malley assured him. "The Doc had me watchdog the room. Ten different alarms would have gone off if anyone had even tried to open the door. Y'know what, though? I'll bet Yoko went walkabout. She does that when she's stressed."

"Excuse me?"

"She's known how to unlock her cage for a long time now. She only stays in it as a courtesy to us. And every once in a while, she lets herself out and goes for a relaxing stroll. Don't worry, boss, she always comes back."

"But — how would she get past the watchdogs and out of your quarters in the middle of the night?"

He shrugged. "Maybe she opened the ventilation grate. Rats are natural escape artists. Even one as large as Yoko can squeeze through incredibly narrow spaces."

"She opened the—!" Drew stopped to take a slow, calming breath before continuing. "So, you figure she's simply wandering around on the station? Unwinding from the stress of being confined to a cage inside your quarters?"

As he heard himself utter these words, he had to stifle the urge to laugh. She was a rat, for heaven's sake! No, he reminded himself, becoming instantly sober, she was the

Überrat — a very old, very large, and very intelligent animal. And O'Malley was the crew member who knew her best. "Okay, then. But you'd better pray that you're right, and that she's smart enough to keep out of sight around Max Karlov. Ruby," he hollered across the deck, "where the hell is Lydia?"

'Mom' hurried over to him. "She's gone to Med Services. What's wrong, Chief? Besides all the other stuff, I mean."

"Can *you* tell me where Karlov is right now?"

"According to Lydia's console, he's in Med Services as well. Oh, and the Doc wants me to tell you not to panic, but when she went into her lab this morning, the black and white rat was missing from her cage. She's probably just found herself a hidey-hole somewhere on H Deck. Yoko does that too, sometimes, when she needs to take a break from being around us crazy Humans."

Townsend shot a look at O'Malley, who was already on his feet and walking toward the tube car.

"I think I'll go check out the evac pods," he tossed over his shoulder.

Yeah, you do that, thought Drew.

— «» —

"Each letter has a name as well as a sound. This one is *fehu*, meaning 'cattle'," Karlov explained. The symbol he was pointing to did look sort of like an Anglo 'F'. If she tilted her head and squinted a little, Lydia could see that it also resembled a squished cow. It was a vertical stick with two other sticks angled upward from the mid-point of its right side. The 'B', the 'R', the 'H', 'I', and 'S' were also similar to their Anglo counterparts, but made up of nothing but straight lines, as though they were normally carved out with a short, sharp edge rather than being drawn with a pen or brush.

Surreptitiously making notes on her compupad, Lydia was realizing just how old this alphabet must be.

"How do you know these letters?" asked the Doc.

"I learned them as a child," he replied matter-of-factly.

"Learned to write them? Or just read them?"

"Both. Why are you so curious about my first language?"

Lydia nearly dropped her 'pad. This was his first language? Before the Doc could reply, she cut in, "It's because of the cookies, Max. They were delicious, by the way. You told Nora that the letters spelled your name. So we were wondering—"

Too late. He'd realized his mistake and put his guard up. Glancing around the lab, he spotted the empty cage on the Doc's work table and did a double take.

"Where is Akiko?" he demanded.

The Doc's eyes widened. "Akiko? You mean the rat you brought with you to the station? I don't know, but I'm sure she's safe."

In a single rapid movement, his large hand wrapped tightly around the Doc's wrist, pulling an exclamation of surprise from her lips. His good eye bored into her face as he dragged her halfway across the table toward him. "You have to find her," he said in a harsh, whispery voice. "She is more valuable than you can imagine."

"I can imagine a lot more than you think," the Doc told him through gritted teeth.

"It's all right, Max," broke in Lydia, "we've already notified the station manager and he's going to order a complete search of the Hub."

"Not good enough," he decided. Throwing the Doc's wrist back at her, he wheeled and stalked out the door. Not until it closed behind him did the two women let out the breath they'd been holding.

The Doc's came out as a groan. She leaned backward, cradling her wrist with her other hand.

Fearing the worst, Lydia asked, "Is it broken?"

"I'm not sure. It's purpling up, so there's definitely tissue damage. I should probably check the bones for cracks. And I'm getting the distinct feeling that we've just opened Pandora's box."

Lydia was already keying commands into the Doc's computer. "That's because we have," she replied tautly, "and her name is Akiko. You can scan your wrist later. Right now we have to save Drew. Karlov is pissed and on his way up to AdComm. I've accessed the tube system and can slow down the car he's in. I just need you to summon the cavalry."

"Oh, I'll do more than that," muttered the Doc, rubbing her bruised wrist.

When Karlov finally stepped out onto C Deck, he found Drew Townsend sitting stern-faced behind his desk, flanked by two members of the Hub's Security force, Ozzie Deniro and Schuyler Tate.

"Mister Karlov," Townsend greeted him, "have a seat. We need to talk."

CHAPTER 19

Tekl'hananni **didn't have** to be a test of physical strength. Sometimes it was a test of moral fiber, or of will power. In Townsend's case, it was evidently a test of nerves. Right now, his weren't faring too well, and the disappearances of Yoko and her sister hadn't helped.

There were just thirty-seven hours left before the Nandrian ships — plural — arrived.

And now this.

Karlov strolled to the chair Drew had indicated and lowered himself onto it. His expression was guarded, but Townsend could guess what was going through his mind. He'd sat across a table from looks like that many times in Security interrogation rooms back in New Chicago.

In the voice he'd always reserved for such occasions, Drew now said, "It has come to my attention that you're not who you claim to be."

"You reviewed my biofile—"

"—and you're not who it says you are either. I warned you when you first arrived that holding back information from me was not a good idea, Max. Or whatever your name really is."

Karlov's face darkened. "We made an agreement. You accepted my protection and I told you the whole story."

"You told me *a* story," declared Townsend. "Half-truths at best."

"Better than the lies that someone else is obviously feeding you," growled Karlov.

"It's someone I trust, and that's more than I can say about you. This is not a conversation, Max. It's your last chance to come clean and save yourself."

"Why should I bother if you're not going to believe anything I say?"

"I will if it's the truth."

Townsend paused to let the implications of that statement sink in. Meanwhile, the two large men beside him, Ozzie to his right and Sky to his left, were playing their roles to perfection. Standing with their legs braced and their arms crossed over their chests, they were a quiet, menacing presence. Karlov had to believe that whatever fate Townsend decreed for him, there was enough muscle aboard the Hub to ensure that it was carried out.

Watching for a tell, Drew waited for the first shadow of uncertainty to cross Karlov's face, then leaned forward and said, "You never knew Bruni Patel, and you never had to fight off his murderers. So tell me, how did you really lose your eye?"

Silence.

Townsend had encountered this before as well.

"You don't want to talk? Fine. I'll talk and you can listen. There's a lot about you that doesn't add up. For example, all those half-healed head lacerations you had when you arrived on the Hub. They weren't inflicted by anyone trying to kill you. Assassins with knives tend to go for the neck or the torso. Or maybe the femoral artery in the thigh. So, either you have the clumsiest barber in creation, or somebody was digging for something under your skin. Was it some sort of implant, Max? Was your eye part of it? Was that why it had to come out?"

Karlov shifted his weight.

Inwardly, Townsend smiled.

"And then there's your apparent fixation on killing Nandrians. They've never visited Earth, which is supposedly where you were born, so there's no way you should know about them. And yet, you do, while knowing next to nothing about the culture of your alleged home world. Frankly, Max, your handlers ought to be ashamed of themselves. They sent you here woefully unprepared. You set so many red flags waving that your cover was certain to be blown."

Karlov had stiffened in his chair. "Are you done?"

"That depends. Are you ready to talk?"

"I wasn't sent here to spy. As I told you, I was sent to protect."

"Yes, by someone calling himself my friend on Earth. But there was another mission that brought you to him so that he could send you to me. We know a lot more than you think. We know you came here to steal, and we know *what* you came to steal. The question is, for whom? Tell me who you work for and I may let you keep your body and soul together."

"I'll tell you something much more important. The rat that I brought you has escaped from her cage."

"I know."

"What you don't know is that she carries a message inside her, something that could change the course of Human history. It's vital that she be located and safely confined, immediately."

Before Townsend could respond, the tube car door opened and Fritz Jensen bustled out onto C Deck. "Oh, my goodness, I forgot to bring you folks your java! I'm so sorry, Mister Townsend!" All apologetic smiles, he carried a pot of steaming brew in his right hand. Three empty mugs dangled from the curled fingers of his left hand. And directly behind him came the Doc, carefully keeping Jensen between herself and Karlov.

Jensen stopped beside Karlov and leaned forward to put the pot and the mugs on Drew's desktop. At once, Ruby appeared and poured herself a java. She picked it up and took a sip. "Thanks, Fritz. It's wretched, as always."

"We aim to please," he replied, taking a step back.

She drank again, then spun and returned to her console, carrying her beverage. Townsend filled the second mug and brought it to his mouth, noting with satisfaction that Karlov's gaze hadn't moved from the pot. They had him. He loved Jensen's java, and they'd just shown him that there was no way this batch could have been doctored.

"Lydia's not here," said Drew casually. "You can have hers if you want." And he poured the third mugful before leaning back in his chair.

Karlov hesitated only a moment. As he reached forward to hook the handle of the mug, the Doc made her move, with a quickness that caught even Townsend off guard. There was no time for Karlov to react. They heard the hiss of an injector, together with his exclamation of surprise. In the space of no more than a second, he went limp and rolled head first to the floor, bouncing off the front of Townsend's desk with an audible thump on his way down. Jensen and the Doc could have grabbed his shoulders to prevent him from tumbling over, but neither one of them had made the effort. In fact, Townsend couldn't help noticing the smile of satisfaction on the Doc's face as she watched Karlov fall. It appeared that Max himself had provided the "damned good reason" she needed to stop protecting him.

"Whatever you gave him, it's certainly fast-acting," Drew remarked, leaning across his desk to stare at the unconscious man sprawled on the deck.

"I wasn't sure how his blood chemistry would react to the sedatives in our pharmacy," replied the Doc. "So, for safety — ours, not his — I just pumped enough into him to bring down a bull elephant."

"You weren't afraid of overdosing him? Not that I disapprove, necessarily, but we do have to keep him alive," he pointed out.

Her smile evaporated. "Mister Townsend," she scolded him, "I am a medical practitioner, bound by the Hippocratic oath."

"My apologies. How long do you think he'll be out?"

"He's not an elephant, so it's hard to say. At a minimum, though, I would estimate five to seven hours."

That was plenty of time for the ratkeeper to work his magic. Townsend signaled to Deniro and Tate. "Take him down to the SPA room and hook him up. Doc, would you give them a hand at the other end, please? And wake him up as soon as O'Malley is ready to run the program."

She'd been about to say something, but changed her mind. "Since you asked nicely," she replied instead, and followed them toward the tube car.

"Ruby, get me O'Malley on the comm. And Lydia. They'll need to work together if we're going to pull this off."

"Right away, Chief."

It wasn't the con he'd originally planned. In fact, it was the Doc's idea, and it was much better. When Karlov came to, he would be trapped in U-Town with no memory of putting on a skin and no way of exiting the program on his own. The ratkeeper's avatar would convince him that his consciousness had somehow been uploaded out of his body and into the Hub's intranet. While Karlov was busy dealing with *that* reality, Lydia and the Doc would be monitoring his vital signs, ensuring that he could be interrogated at greater length later on. At the same time, Townsend and the rest of his crew could turn their full attention to the pressing real-life problems at hand.

— «» —

Thirty-three hours.

After a fruitless search of the station for two wayward rats who obviously didn't want to be found, Townsend stepped out of the tube car and into the middle of a heated argument between Gouryas and Singh on an L Deck that was still far too turquoise for his comfort.

"No matter what you do, there won't be time to test it," exclaimed Gouryas.

"That's all the more reason to focus on something that will prevent the battle," Singh declared. Then, noticing Townsend, the engineer turned and informed him loudly, "All he wants to do now is create repulsion fields." *Thanks to you.* The words hung unspoken in the air.

"Gentlemen, the clock is ticking down," Drew reminded them patiently. "Have you made any progress at all?"

"Some," said Gouryas.

"But I understand you've been working individually on two separate projects because you can't agree on which direction to take, is that right?"

"Yes," they said reluctantly, more or less in unison.

"Then I'm going to change your assignment. I want you to drop everything and build me a bomb powerful enough to blow this station to tiny bits. If there's no Daisy Hub then there will be nothing for the Rangers and Nandrians to fight over. It will be a huge sacrifice, but at least we'll have prevented an interstellar war."

Two pairs of eyes went saucer-wide with shock.

"What? You don't like that assignment? Then figure out which of the other two gives us the best chance of success and work together to make it happen. Am I clear?"

"Yes, sir," mumbled Gouryas.

"Singh?"

"Clear."

"I'll be back to see how you're doing in a couple of hours. Please try to have some good news for me."

Townsend turned his back on the two dazed engineers and returned to AdComm.

— «» —

Thirty-two hours.

"Anything I can do to help, Chief?"

Waiting was not something Drew Townsend did well. Slumped behind his desk, he glanced up and saw Ruby's sympathetic face perched atop his filing cabinet partition.

"You can tell me I'm on the right track," he told her.

"What do you mean?"

"I just keep having this horrible feeling that our *tekl'hananni* might not actually be about solving the problem. What if it's about having the common sense to realize that we can't do it without the Nandrians' help, even with the manual?"

"There's a manual?" she said with poorly feigned astonishment.

"Don't *you* start that," he warned her, his lips quirking involuntarily into a smile.

Ruby walked around the end of the partition to join him at his desk. "Okay. If this whole exercise has been about knowing when to ask for help, I'd say you've got your plan D." She made a face. "Or maybe it's E. There are so many going on that I've lost count."

Townsend straightened in his chair. She was right. He hadn't been formulating a plan — he'd been following multiple leads. Presented with a mystery, his inner field investigator had taken over, compelling him to explore all the various possible ways to solve it, and unwittingly turning Townsend himself into an obstacle for his crew to overcome.

He had no time to kick himself. The tube car door to the left of his desk chose that moment to open, and out barreled the Hub's resident wildcat, Teri 'Tiger' Mintz, under a full head of steam.

"Mister Townsend!" she blustered. "I just tried to visit U-Town, and it's not there! It's gone! Unavailable, says my screen! Where the hell are my characters? If O'Malley has lost a single pixel of my family—!"

Townsend hardened his face and pointed imperiously to a chair. "Sit!"

She was obviously in no mood to follow orders. When her chin had risen to a thirty-degree angle, he pointed again and repeated, "Take a seat, Teri, and I'll explain."

She folded her arms over her chest, remaining defiantly on her feet.

Ruby just rolled her eyes and walked away, shaking her head.

"You showbiz types are so damned temperamental," muttered Townsend. He turned his attention to his computer screen and began mentally counting the seconds, determined to ignore her for as long as it took her to calm down.

When he got to twenty-four, she huffed loudly and plopped herself onto the chair he'd indicated earlier.

"Your characters are stored in protected memory, just as I promised," he told her, still staring at the display on his light screen. "U-Town was completely backed up. The backup copy was modified and is now running non-stop in the SPA room as a virtual reality experience for Karlov. And for O'Malley, who's skinned up and sitting right beside him, playing the part of a fellow prisoner," he added, finally turning to look her in the face. "The original files are all sitting safe and untouched on the SPA server. When the con is wrapped, everything will be restored to the way it was."

"So I can't access the original files because they've been put in storage?"

Hearing this, his brain pounced on an idea: *Original files in storage. Of course!*

But again, it was just one of many possibilities, perhaps worth exploring, perhaps not. If Daisy Hub was going to come out the other end of this situation in one piece, then his first order of business had to be getting himself out of everyone else's way.

"Ruby," he called across the room, "set up a senior staff update meeting in half an hour, my office. O'Malley and the Doc may be tied up, but make sure Lydia and Soaring Hawk attend."

"Roger, Chief."

"And, Teri...? I can't tell you how glad I am that you dropped by."

He gave her the sunniest smile in his repertoire, holding it until the nonplussed diva finally got to her feet and left the deck.

— ‹›› —

Thirty-one hours.

Townsend watched a dozen or so confused and curious people wander into his workspace and mill around for a few moments before finding places to sit. He did a rapid attendance check: Gouryas and Singh, neither of them looking happy; Lucas Soaring Hawk, come straight from one of the thruster wells, it appeared, and still wiping something off his hands with a rag; Lydia, her brow just as furrowed as it had been the last time he'd seen her; Gavin Holchuk, standing in a back corner and surveying the room with a faintly amused expression on his face; Vera Beale and Ray Oolalong, fidgeting restlessly and probably present only at Singh's behest; Jason Smith, kept out of the loop so far but clearly not anticipating any good news; Orvy Hagman, most of his earlier hostility dissipated now that Karlov was temporarily out of the picture; Fritz Jensen, no doubt wondering what a chef could contribute to the discussion but looking pleased at having received the summons; and Ruby, watchfully monitoring the proceedings from her console and ready to jump in whenever necessary.

Townsend stood up and raised a hand to get their attention.

"I've called this meeting because it's time to put our heads together and compare notes. Each of you needs to hear what the others have been doing. Each of you may have information that someone else in the room can use. Working together, we're going to fit all our individual efforts into one master plan to resolve our situation, at least for the time being. Let's begin with update reports. I asked Soaring Hawk to look into two things: breaking the Hub out of orbit if we have to remove ourselves from harm's way, and separating the three parts of the station if it should become necessary. Mister Soaring Hawk, how is that investigation coming along?"

The propulsion wizard stood up, one fist tightly clenched around the rag he'd been using, and cleared his throat. "I've only had time to inspect our main thrusters so far. Those are the ones at the south end of the Hub. Despite the fact that they're hardly ever used, the mains appear to be in good shape. In my opinion, they're all we'll need to achieve escape velocity and get Daisy Hub and everyone on it away from the battle zone. That's provided we keep the station all in one piece."

"And if we break it into thirds?" asked Hagman, frowning.

"Then everything south of J Deck leaves orbit, and anyone caught higher up heads for an evac pod and gets religion."

Silence dropped like a boulder into the middle of the room.

"Maybe you'd better elaborate on that," Townsend advised him.

Hawk sucked in a breath and explained, "The attitudinal thrusters on each section of the Hub can be repositioned to speed us up or slow us down when needed, in orbit. It's how they were designed to operate. We've been doing a good job of maintaining them, and it's possible to reinforce them, up to a point. Problem is, they're physically smaller than the main thrusters and can't generate the same amount of power. Give me half a year and strike Zulu and all the Rangers blind and I can shift the mains around so that each section has a couple. But that would create another problem.

"Earth's government doesn't want us getting any ideas about taking the station for a joy ride, so they've made sure we never have sufficient fuel on hand to actually go anywhere. I keep enough in reserve for the main thrusters to break the Hub out of orbit and send us into space in a direction of our choosing, holding back a ten-second burn so that we can apply the brakes. Divvying up the fuel among the three parts of the Hub would make it impossible for even one of them to escape."

"So, the thrusters at the north end of the Hub can move that section forward and backward?" mused Lydia aloud. "In and out of range of the sensor field, for example?"

She had figured it out, Drew could tell. Her frown was gone and there was a thoughtful set to her mouth.

"Spill it, girl!" called Ruby from her console.

"We got Rodrigues's short-hopper through the sensor field by having him shut down his weapons as he approached," Lydia recalled. "Wouldn't he have turned them off anyway, once he'd docked? Wouldn't any ship have to do that?"

"Brilliant!" exclaimed Gouryas. "We just have to make sure the portal section can be precisely reconnected and the tube car shafts perfectly aligned."

"And the connection will need to be remotely locked and unlocked," added Oolalong.

"We can't use real fuel for practice runs, so we'll need a simulator," Beale pointed out. "Lydia, do we have enough memory for this?"

"Never mind memory. Do we have enough time to pull it all together?" demanded Singh.

Leaps of logic were business as usual for Eligibles, but not everyone on the Hub had technical expertise. Townsend knew what they were talking about, mainly because he'd already thought of it. That was why he'd picked Soaring Hawk to speak first and insisted that Lydia be present. But Hagman was wearing a bewildered expression, Holchuk just sat like someone waiting for an MPV, and Jensen's eyes looked ready to spin in their sockets.

"I gather we have our plan," Townsend declared. Heads began bobbing enthusiastically. "So I can tell the Rangers thanks but no thanks? We've solved the problem and they can sit this one out?"

"Oh, please, do!" said Ruby with a laugh.

"All right, then, people — details," he reminded them. "Soaring Hawk, you'll need to put together a team to prepare the thrusters at the north end of the Hub. If they're not already remotely controlled, they should be."

"They are. The locking mechanisms are on remote control as well, but I'll check everything out to be sure."

"We'll need eyes on the separation and docking process," said Townsend. "Do we have any drones?"

"That'll be me," Ruby piped up, "on *Devil Bug*. I can relay visuals to whoever's working the controls and talk them through the reconnection. Once we're latched together I can scoot back inside, park the shuttle, and hop a tube car up to A Deck. It'll be easy. Like falling off a cake."

Townsend threw her a wry look.

She just grinned.

Life Support Specialist Jason Smith rose ponderously from his chair. "I hate to be the one to rain on your parade, but you've forgotten something important. Separating the Hub is an emergency measure reserved for extreme circumstances. It's a last resort and only meant to happen once, so the separation is accomplished using carefully positioned explosive charges. When they detonate and segments fly apart, things get damaged. Things like air conduits. Power relays. Plumbing. The top and bottom sections have the ability to seal themselves off and become lifeboats, but every system on the remaining part of the Hub is compromised. In short, there can be no reconnection."

"Not yet, maybe," cut in Gouryas, clearly relishing the challenge. He exchanged a look with Singh, who added in a voice filled with determination, "We've got plenty of hands and thirty hours to make it possible."

Townsend smiled. At last, they had a plan and were working as a team. He'd always known that the Daisy Hub crew, pulling together, could find a way to get things done. As long as they didn't run out of time. There was always that.

"Fritz, you'd better put the kitchen on high alert," Drew told him. "Plenty of java and meals available around the clock."

Jensen looked relieved. The rotund chef had probably been worried that someone might ask him to crawl inside a ventilation shaft.

Addressing the entire group, Townsend continued, "Don't forget that we have to be reasonably fresh when the Nandrians arrive, so I would recommend that you stagger the work shifts and make sure everyone gets a chance to sleep at least once between now and then." And there was one more thing: "Mister Holchuk, is there a Nandrian script for a situation in which technical difficulties necessitate a change in routine?"

"I'll add a paragraph to your welcoming speeches," the other man replied. "You'll have them within the hour."

"Then I believe we're done," Drew announced. "Go make it happen."

They looked a lot happier leaving the meeting than they had when they arrived, he noted. Except for Lydia, who remained scowling in her chair.

"Cheer up," he told her. "You may just have prevented the start of an interstellar war."

Her expression didn't change.

"Look, if you're worried about what the Rangers might do—"

"That's not it. Drew, there's something you need to know—"

"Boss!"

At O'Malley's cry, they both started and whipped around.

"You're not going to believe this," he declared as he rushed breathlessly toward them. "I know what Karlov is."

CHAPTER 20

O'Malley was little-kid excited. He was practically vibrating in place.

"You know *what* Karlov is?" Townsend repeated.

The ratkeeper paused for a breath, then explained, "I followed your instructions, just the way you laid them out. When he came to inside the program in the SPA room, I made sure I was inside as well, to greet him. I gave him your story about U-Town secretly being used by Earth's government as a detention center. Then I told him where all those supposedly fictional characters actually came from. I really painted them in shades of dark, boss, especially Brock. I wanted Karlov to wish he'd never tampered with that jury."

"And he bought it?"

"Once he'd recovered from his shock, absolutely! Bought it, paid for it, took it home. He is utterly convinced that we have the technology to separate a conscious mind from its body and trap it inside a computer program. Anyway, I told him that I'd been wrongly convicted of murdering someone from a powerful family on Earth, and then, as inmates tend to do, I asked him what crime *he* had committed to get himself uploaded."

"And he got chatty with his brand-new cellmate?" Townsend frowned. He knew from personal experience that nothing credible came out that quickly in detention.

"He didn't open up right away. Not until we'd pulled a couple of jobs together and he felt he could trust me."

"You teamed up to murder Brock?"

"Nope. I suggested that breaking the law in U-Town might let him vent his frustration and make him feel better. I also told him that since Brock himself was a murderer, killing him might be a good place to start. But Karlov wouldn't go for it. He said only a coward would kill a prisoner in cold blood. Said it while staring directly into my avatar's face, by the way."

Lydia's eyebrows arched. "Sounds very Nandrian to me."

"Definitely a warrior," Townsend agreed.

"It gets better," O'Malley assured them. "He decided we should rob a store. He planned it carefully, making sure none of the other avatars would get hurt. It was a commando operation, boss. Everything about it screamed 'military culture'."

"So he's probably a professional soldier," murmured Drew.

"A government soldier," she agreed. "But which government? And why would they send him here?"

"After the robbery, we did some arson. Burned down an old factory on the edge of U-Town," continued O'Malley. "While we stood watching the structure melt, pixel by pixel, I remarked that it would be a favor to Earth if all the old neglected buildings in the urban districts met the same fate. He told me that there were no abandoned Zones on his world. 'Oh?' says I. 'Then you must be from one of Earth's colonies.'"

"And what did he reply to that?" Townsend asked.

"Nothing at first. He just smiled. Then he looked directly into my avatar's face again and said, 'In a strange way, I guess I am.'"

"That's it?" demanded Lydia.

"It's enough," Drew told her. "If he's not from Earth and he's not from one of our colonies, then—"

"He's got to be an alien," crowed O'Malley, "in spite of what the Doc says. And there's only one alien race in this part of the galaxy that looks just like us."

"He must be Stragori," Lydia concluded thoughtfully. "That would explain a lot."

Yes, it would. According to Nagor, Trokerk had pushed for the alliance with Daisy Hub because Humans and Nandrians had "enemies in common". Could one of them be the Stragori?

By a stroke of sheer luck, the con had become a covert interrogation. Townsend couldn't pass up this chance to learn more about a possible foe. And O'Malley couldn't be allowed to do anything that might jeopardize it, such as breaking character — or, Drew realized with a start, popping in and out of the program. "Where does Karlov think you are right now?"

"Somewhere else in U-Town. I told him that after all the excitement I needed to be alone for a while, and that I'd meet him back at Angela's place. I just figured you'd want to know about him immediately."

"Well, you were right. Go back and see what else you can get out of him. But be careful not to push too hard. You're alone with him in there, and there's no telling what he'll do if he figures out that you're a plant."

"Don't worry, boss. Oh, and I was wondering, has there been any sign of Yoko?"

Lydia jumped to her feet, wide-eyed. "You've lost Yoko?"

"Not exactly. She ran out on me. It's not the same thing," said O'Malley, hastily retreating in the direction of the tube car.

Once the door had closed behind him, Lydia settled back onto her chair with a worried expression on her face. "She hides when she's frightened. Rob says Yoko can understand spoken Gally. Do you suppose she overheard something that scared her?"

"I wouldn't be surprised," Townsend said wearily. "There's a lot going on around here right now that scares the hell out of *me*. I'll have Ruby put out the word to everyone to watch for her. Meanwhile, I believe that you have a simulation to program."

—— «·» ——

Twenty-six hours.

The welcoming speeches that Holchuk had written for Townsend to memorize were delightful works of fiction, full of adventure and suspense. He was just hoping that Drew, son of … *Dammit!* would have the chance to deliver them.

One mistake and he was stuck with that ridiculous name for life. Well, as Ruby had pointed out at the time, it could have been worse. Nervous as he was, he could easily have forgotten his own given name as well. Then what would the Nandrians be calling him? *Dammit, son of Abitch?*

Ruby was alone and at her station when Drew returned to AdComm.

"Has there been any reply from Zulu?" he asked.

"Not a word, Chief. Rodrigues is probably still calming down so he can speak to you in sentences."

"I broke the news to him as gently as I could. Didn't I?"

She made a face. "Gently? That's not the word I would use. But even if he believes that we've actually got everything under control, I doubt whether there's any diplomatic way to tell the local constabulary to butt out and mind their own business." A pause, then, "Do you think they'll keep their distance?"

"A few klicks from the station? Maybe. The other side of the planet? No. I figure we'll have a lot of fast talking to do when the time comes. But if Rodrigues is smart, he'll have called off the other detachments. Has anyone reported seeing either of our fugitive rats?"

"No sightings yet. I doubt that there will be any. It's a safe bet that Yoko broke her sister out of the Doc's lab and is currently showing her all the best hiding places on the Hub. Our *tseritsa* probably knows every corner of the station by now, including the spaces between the decks."

Damn. He hadn't thought about that. "Ruby, we have to find her as soon as possible," he said, struggling to keep his voice steady. "The *tseritsa* of a House is sacred to Nandrians. They believe that if one *tseritsa* dies, every *tseritsa* dies. You know what will happen if we accidentally space Yoko during the separation process."

She blanched as the meaning of his words sank in. "Actually, Chief, I'd rather not even imagine it. I'll assemble a detail immediately to search for her. Shouldn't we let the Doc know?"

"Yes, but we're not going to," he decided. "If anyone needs me, I'll be in my quarters."

— ⟨⟩ —

Eighteen hours.

Too tense to sleep, Townsend had tossed fitfully on his bed for a while before giving up and turning on the light in his sleeping area.

On his instructions, Ruby had begun providing him with hourly progress reports. This mission was mobilizing the efforts of every member of his crew. The Doc and her staff were monitoring Karlov's vital signs and keeping his body hydrated and nourished while O'Malley played mind games with him in the SPA room. Fritz and his *sous chef* were serving up a continuous flow of prepared food in the caf. Lydia's simulator was online and running, helping the steadiest hands on the station practice separating and reconnecting the top third of the Hub. To make that process possible, Gouryas and Singh had thrown themselves and their techs into what amounted to a re-engineering of the space between B Deck and the short-hopper landing deck, in consultation with Jason Smith. Meanwhile, Soaring Hawk was supervising the tune-up work on the attitudinal thrusters and the removal of the explosive charges. And anyone who wasn't already assigned to one of those details was searching every part of the station for a pair of very large, very intelligent rats.

There was still no sign of Yoko and her sister; however, to Townsend's immense relief, everything else seemed to be running smoothly and on or ahead of schedule — *seemed to be* being the operative phrase. There were still more ways for this thing to go south than he cared to contemplate. Images of disaster paraded through his imagination, forcing his stomach into a barrel roll. Every *what if* led to a declaration of war and Daisy Hub exploding in a fireball.

He needed a distraction. Muttering to himself, Townsend threw on a change of clothes and headed to AdComm, where he knew he would find the only other person on the Hub with time to talk.

As he stepped out of the tube car, he found Ruby apparently in the process of dismantling her console. Townsend nearly misstepped. This was a *what if* that hadn't occurred to him — the assistant station manager sabotaging the main control panel. The top of the console was now dangling to one side, supported only by a cat's cradle of multi-colored wires connecting the various dials and buttons on the panel to whatever lay in the console's depths. The barrel roll in his stomach became a death spiral.

"Ruby?"

She glanced up briefly and smiled an acknowledgment, then returned her full attention to the mass of electronic entrails in her hand.

Warily, he approached her and inquired softly, "What are you doing?"

"Looking for the 'off' switch that Gouryas mentioned in one of our many meetings. There isn't one on the panel proper, so I figure it must be under the cowling somewhere."

"Shouldn't Lydia be helping you with this?"

"She is. Was. Detmar found a way to freeze up the simulator program, so she had to rush off." Ruby stopped abruptly and turned to face him. "You thought I did this by myself? I'm flattered, Chief, but honestly, I wouldn't know where to start."

Privately, Townsend doubted that the Nandrians would have given them anything as simple as an on-off switch. However, the aliens might have left something else for them to find.

"It isn't easy having to wait around while other people set things up, is it?" he observed. "When Lydia gets back, how would you like an assignment to fill the next few hours? One that you've already begun."

Intrigued, she dropped what she was holding and leaned back against the edge of the console's shell. "What did you have in mind, Chief?"

"Teri said something earlier that gave me an idea. Original files in storage. She was talking about the U-Town programming, and how O'Malley switched out the original files with the backups. Now the backups are the principal files and the originals are inaccessible."

"Because only one set of files can be executed at a time. That much I do know."

"Right. But both sets are present in the system, and O'Malley can restore the originals at any time. What if the same situation exists for the field generator? What if press-

ing the reset button saved all the previous settings in a protected memory pack or even an entire drive unit somewhere
in that console, and we just need to find it?"

"Hardware put in by the Nandrians as part of the retrofit,
you mean? But left unconnected to any of the controls on the
panel? That makes no sense."

"It's *tekl'hananni*. They're testing us."

"By giving us a puzzle to solve but hiding the most
important piece of it inside another puzzle?"

"They've done it before," he pointed out, "with the
molecular paintbrush. And what do you think your
hypothetical on-off switch would be, if you found it?"

"Probably a red herring. Not unlike what you're
proposing."

"Nonetheless. While you and Lydia are poking around in
there, I'd like you to keep your eyes open for anything that
doesn't belong. A stray wire. A little black box."

"And if our search yields treasure, what do you want us
to do with it?"

"Leave it where it is, but record everything you can about
it. After the current crisis is past, there will be time to figure
out what it is and how it works. Have we had any response
from Zulu?"

"A three-word message: 'Go to hell.'"

Silly Ranger, thought Townsend, *I'm already there.*

— «» —

Ten hours.

Townsend sat alone in the caf, staring into the muddy
depths of a mug of Jensen's java and missing Bruni Patel.
Thoughts of his own mortality had been running through
Drew's mind, bringing with them memories of the man
who had been his only real friend for much of his life. True,
Patel had secretly been working for the EIS when they'd
first met, and Townsend had been outraged to discover that
befriending and mentoring young Drew in the detention
center had begun as nothing more than an undercover
grooming assignment. But the hours he'd spent staring at
the ceiling of his quarters lately had given him a chance to
reconsider. He'd come to realize that the relationship they'd

forged when Drew was eighteen had long outlasted that assignment, growing deeper and stronger over the years than any friendship he had shared with anyone else in his life.

There were no images left of Bruni Patel, not even in O'Malley's data stash. Patel had been wiped from Earth's database shortly after his murder, and the only face that came to Drew's mind now was the lifeless, mutilated one he'd seen on a fellow investigator's compupad. Had Bruni died quickly? Drew hoped so, although the wounds on his forehead and temples and the way his eyes had been removed hinted at torture...

...or the clumsiest barber in creation.

Townsend inhaled sharply, then filed the thought away. Later, he promised himself. There were more urgent matters to take care of right now, but once things had calmed down—

"You need a shave, boss man," said a voice behind his right shoulder. A moment later, Gavin Holchuk dropped onto the chair across from him. "I'm serious. The Nandrians don't understand facial hair. They think mustaches are contagious." When Townsend failed to respond, Holchuk frowned and added, "Have you memorized both your speeches?"

"I know them inside out."

"Let's hope it never comes to that. Ruby wanted me to tell you that all the work has been completed with hours to spare, and Soaring Hawk has declared everything fit and tight and ready for a trial run. They're just waiting for you to come up to AdComm to oversee the operation."

"We can't," Drew told him. "Not yet. We don't dare separate the Hub until both rats are found. If anything happens to Yoko, the Nandrians will open fire on us. If anything happens to her sister, Karlov will probably go *hartoon* and take the station apart, and what's worse, the Doc will never forgive us."

A high-pitched shriek erupted from the kitchen area, followed by dead silence. For a second, both men froze in place, staring quizzically at each other. Then Nora Duvall poked her head out the galley door and bawled, "Get these animals out of my pantry! *Now!*"

"Ask and ye shall receive, boss man," said Holchuk with a faint smile.

CHAPTER 21

Holchuk had not been exaggerating. As Townsend stepped out of the tube car on C Deck, he thought he heard seven people let out a collective sigh of relief.

The main console was back together, he noticed, with Lydia at her own station presiding over the monitoring and recording of the practice session. Presumably, Ruby was already outside in *Devil Bug*.

"Who's on A Deck?" he asked.

"DeVries," replied Jason Smith. "He scored the highest on the simulator."

"We're monitoring the video feed from *Devil Bug* to the light screen on the auxiliary control panel," Lydia explained. "Since the docking archways will be sealed until the Hub is back in one piece, there's no need for anyone but the operator to be present on A Deck during the procedure."

"This is a dry run, using minimal fuel," added Soaring Hawk. "Out half a klick and then back."

"How far away will DeVries have to go to meet the Nandrians?" Townsend asked.

Lydia paused and looked up from her console. "Rodrigues's short-hopper tripped the invisibility cloak at a distance of seven klicks, so to be safe, we're sending A Deck ten kilometers ahead of the rest of the Hub. When the Nandrian ships have docked, DeVries will reverse his thrusters for a couple of seconds, then adjust the rotation of A Deck to match ours when the rest of Daisy Hub catches up. That's what he's been practicing, at least," she added. "We'll have to see how well it works in real space." She pressed the comm button on her panel. "You're a go, Will. Separation in sixty-four seconds."

The air in AdComm was charged and expectant. Not a syllable was uttered, not even a breath exhaled as everyone stood staring intently at the light screen on Lydia's console. Meanwhile, Ruby kept *Devil Bug* hovering abeam the juncture just below B Deck, focusing her forward viewcam with machine-like steadiness. It appeared that 'Mom' had been practicing as well.

Drew could feel tension seeping into his neck and shoulder muscles, making them ache. Waiting around, even for just a standard minute, was definitely not one of his favorite things to do. It gave him time for self-doubt, for second-guessing his decisions. That was probably what the people around him were engaged in right now. Mentally reviewing every step they'd taken over the past few hours, wondering what they might have missed, what they should have done differently. It didn't help that the image on the screen showed a nearly solid expanse of outer bulkhead. It revealed a seam in the metal, but nothing that even remotely resembled a latching mechanism.

The tube car door hummed open and shut, and a couple of seconds later Holchuk joined the group.

"Sorry to be late," he said. "After dropping the rats off with the Doc, I had to talk Teri out of marching into the SPA room and meddling in O'Malley's con. You can thank me later, boss man."

"You found Yoko?" asked Singh.

"Yeah," Holchuk replied distractedly. "She and her sister were in the kitchen, having a late-night snack. Nora nearly threw a fit when she saw them half in and half out of her cookie bin."

Holding up a hand for silence, Lydia counted down. "Five. Four. Three. Two. One. Now, Will."

"Unsealing the sections," said DeVries.

The Hub shuddered. It made a groaning noise that raced up and down Drew's spine, chilling and unnerving him. For a moment, he could swear that the stressing of metal bulkheads sounded just like a cry of pain, as though the station were a living creature that could feel itself being ripped apart. When silence fell again, a sense of dread hung in the air, and uneasy looks crisscrossed the room. There was a reason that separation was not meant to be an everyday occurrence.

"Thrusters forward full, five seconds," came DeVries's voice again.

"There she goes," murmured Soaring Hawk, and all eyes returned to the light screen.

The gray seam had become a crack. As they watched, the gap widened, forcing Ruby to zoom out in order to keep both sides in view. Deck A kept moving until it was nearly a Hub's-length away. Then they heard DeVries say, "Reversing thrusters and braking."

Like a liner many times its size, the top section of the Hub gradually slowed its forward movement, finally gliding smoothly to a halt.

"Perfect," breathed Singh.

"We're not done yet," Soaring Hawk reminded him. "He still has to fit the pieces back together and lock them down."

"Ruby, you're on," said Lydia.

The angle on the screen shifted, revealing color-coded markers that the engineers had placed on both sides of the gap. Using these as guides, DeVries would attempt to match the severed ends of the tube car shafts exactly, thus bringing everything else into proper alignment as well.

Drew mentally crossed his fingers.

"Adjusting attitude," DeVries reported.

Townsend caught a flash at the corner of his right eye. It was the comm light on Ruby's console. An incoming message. Of course. With his luck, it was probably a Nandrian ship, letting him know that they were just around the corner and would be arriving momentarily. Reluctantly, he tore himself away from the group and crossed to the main comm panel to take the call.

"Townsend," barked Rodrigues's voice, "what are you and your merry band of lunatics up to now?"

"Just trying to avert the outbreak of interstellar war, Captain. And how is your day going so far?"

After a moment of ominous silence, Rodrigues growled, "We're seeing Daisy Hub in two pieces on our screens."

Drew couldn't help himself. "Yeah, we broke the station. Sorry about that. But don't worry, Paul — we're putting it back together."

He could practically hear the steam escaping from Rodrigues's ears. Drew let himself enjoy the moment. Then his common sense cut in. Twitting the Ranger commander was not the best way to secure his cooperation.

"Okay, Paul, listen. Our plan is to have the Nandrians dock outside the range of the sensor field so they won't have to shut down their weapons. They'll be here in about eight to ten hours. What you're seeing on your screen is a dry run. We're making sure everything will work."

"That's all?"

"That's all. They won't get insulted, and we won't need protection. But we do appreciate your readiness to provide it."

"Promise me you haven't damaged the Hub beyond your crew's ability to repair it."

Once again, the urge was irresistible. "Damaged it?" Drew declared. "Hell, no! We've improved it."

Rodrigues muttered something in Euranglo under his breath. "All right. It goes against protocol, not to mention my better judgment, but I'll stand my men down and let you handle this on your own. Call me back when it's over. Make sure you're sober. We need to talk."

With perfect timing, Drew severed the commlink with Zulu as applause burst out behind him. Evidently, the reconnection had gone as planned.

"One hour before the Nandrians are scheduled to arrive, we send him back out there," said Soaring Hawk. "And we hope that having two Nandrian ships attached to A Deck doesn't make a difference to the operation. We're out in space, so it shouldn't, but..."

There was no need for him to complete the thought.

— «» —

Eight hours.

Every time Drew let himself consider the possibility that Bruni Patel might have been an alien, like Karlov, his brain began to itch. What if Karlov had been telling the truth earlier about government agents coming after Bruni and then himself, only the government in question had been the Directorate on Stragon? That might explain why the New Chicago Security investigation into Patel's murder had been so quickly and thoroughly shut down: alien-on-alien violence would have been considered none of the Earth High Council's business. And if Karlov's purpose in being sent to Daisy Hub had truly been to protect — which could well be the case, judging by his reaction to discovering that the black and white rat was missing — then Townsend had just made a tactical error of monumental proportions.

He knew he ought to get some rest, but his thoughts kept running in ever-tightening circles, making it impossible for him to fall asleep. As soon as he'd arrived in his quarters, Drew pulled the playback device and encrypted datawafer out of their respective wall compartments and settled down to read. There had to be an answer on that wafer, something that he'd missed before, or that his mind had simply balked at taking in because he'd been so furious — at Olivia for abandoning him, and at Rex Regum for tearing open old wounds and making him ache and bleed all over again. Well, Olivia had made her choices and Drew had survived them, and the bleeding would have to stop now.

Because this wasn't just about Drew Townsend anymore. It was about Daisy Hub, and possibly also about Earth itself.

— «◊» —

Six hours.

"Drew?"

Townsend's eyes snapped open. He was sprawled on his back in bed, with the playback device lying beside him. He'd been dreaming, something about running around with a net, trying to capture fragments of his homework assignment after Olivia had laughingly torn it up and tossed the pieces into the air. A second later, the details had slid off the edges of his memory, leaving him with nothing but a residual feeling of betrayal.

"Drew? Are you awake?" Lydia's voice over the wallcomm sounded small and tentative. "You know I wouldn't bother you if it weren't important."

"What's the matter? Are the Nandrians here already?"

"No, it's — it's Rob. You'd better come down to Med Services right away."

O'Malley was in Med Services?

In an instant, Townsend was on his feet and heading out the door.

Lydia sat curled up on one of the chairs in the Doc's triage area, hugging her knees to her chest and looking even paler and more distraught than she'd been the first time they'd met. He eased himself down beside her and asked, "What happened?"

Her eyes welled with tears. "It's my fault," she said, choking on the words. "Karlov's avatar lit Rob's avatar on fire."

"How is that your fault?"

"I'm the one who set the sensory output values for the program. Rob wanted the U-Town experience to be as realistic as possible, so I boosted them to the same level as the other SPA activities. When Karlov shoved Rob into the flames—" Her face crumpled into a portrait of misery. "He felt everything. He was screaming. I got to him as soon as I could, but—"

Townsend went cold all over. "O'Malley's dead?"

"Mr. O'Malley is sedated and resting comfortably in the Trauma unit," said the Doc, stepping into the triage room to join them. "He went into pain-induced shock when Karlov's avatar burned him — or rather, his avatar — alive. If we can use that term when discussing avatars," she added, frowning.

Tears were flowing freely now down Lydia's cheeks. "I'm so sorry," she whispered. "You warned him that Karlov was dangerous. I should have realized something like this could happen. I should have reduced the sensory intensity levels. But he was having so much fun!"

Townsend and the Doc exchanged a look of understanding. It was always fun, until somebody got hurt. Thankfully, in this case only the pain had been real.

A sudden thought occurred to him. "Where's Karlov now, Doc?"

"He's snoring peacefully in the bed beside O'Malley's," she replied. "Lydia had to abort the program, so I gave him another massive sedative injection."

"Any idea why Karlov tried to kill him?"

"No, but I'm pretty sure *you* might have one," she replied tartly.

In fact, he had two. First, O'Malley must have tried too hard to pull information out of Karlov, outing himself as a plant. And second, Karlov must have figured out that their consciousnesses were still inside their bodies, and that he could terminate the interrogation by forcing an end to the SPA program.

"Doc, how long can you keep Karlov unconscious?"

"For as long as you require. Can I assume that you would prefer not to have to think about him again until after the Nandrians have left the station?"

"At least until then. And I'll want to debrief O'Malley as soon as he's sufficiently recovered to talk."

"It may be a while, Mr. Townsend," she warned him. "The counselor has already begun working with him, but he's been badly traumatized."

Drew looked at Lydia, still resting her chin on her knees and looking as though a casual touch might break her into a thousand pieces, and thought, *He's not the only one.*

— ⟨⟩ —

Two hours.

The prolonged waiting was taking its toll. The atmosphere on C Deck was taut, almost to the snapping point. Drew had given up on the idea of returning to his quarters to rest and now sat at his desk, mentally reviewing his speeches. Ruby was at her console, occasionally breaking into a little dance step when standing still became too difficult. And, ignoring the Doc's advice, Lydia had arrived a few minutes earlier and taken her place at the monitors as well.

Privately, Townsend was glad, and not just because her presence would be needed in AdComm once the separation process began. Seeing the redness around her eyes took him back to the day he'd arrived on the Hub, shortly after Karim Khaloub's death. She'd blamed herself then and she was blaming herself now; and even though O'Malley, unlike Khaloub, had survived and would eventually make a full recovery, the fact that he was a personal friend could only worsen the guilt she was feeling. This was not a good time for Lydia to be alone with nothing else to occupy her thoughts.

A light began blinking on the main console. Ruby pounced. A second later she called out, "I'm receiving a signal from the *Krronn*, Chief. ETA in one and a half hours."

— «» —

It was show time.

The separation and reconnection had gone like clockwork, without so much as a flicker from the invisibility field. Now came the hard part.

Drew stood in the middle of A Deck, his gaze shifting between archways 4 and 8 as a cold sweat tattooed his skin. The Nandrians had complied with his carefully worded request and had docked with the separated portion of the Hub, but he had no idea what their mood would be when they came through those portals. The last time he'd been in a situation like this, there had been a phalanx of dock workers at his back. Today, all he had was Holchuk, Ruby, and the Überrat. Twice he'd tried to pick up Yoko — it was customary for the highest-ranked member of a House to be holding the *tseritsa* whenever a first contact was made — and twice she'd bitten him and slithered frantically out of his arms to take refuge in her cage on the deck.

"Yoko," he muttered darkly, "your timing stinks."

"You know, she's always been uncomfortable around you, boss man," remarked Holchuk. "Maybe she knows something the rest of us don't."

"It'll be all right, Chief," Ruby assured him. "A live animal can't be expected to be as obedient as a stick of wood."

Holchuk took instant exception. "Their *tseritsa* is a living staff," he corrected her sharply, "a branch from the sacred tree on their original home world."

"If you say so," she replied, rolling her eyes.

Rodrigues was right. The Humans on this station were crazy. The rats were the only ones showing any common sense.

At the sound of a docking portal unsealing, Ruby and Holchuk spoke together:

"It's number 4."

"It's number 8."

Townsend's jaw dropped. It was both of them. Six huge aliens lumbered through the archways, three to either side of him. The Chief Officer of the *Nannssi* was even taller than Nagor, and half again as broad in the chest. And wafting on his breath was a distinct aroma of citrus.

Drew swallowed hard. The Nandrians had been drinking. "Holchuk?" he murmured uncertainly.

The other man leaned close and whispered, "Careful, boss man. See the markings down the left sleeve of his uniform? That one's a Third Shield, superior in rank to everyone on this deck but you."

"But *I'm* a Third Shield."

"You were, before we became a House. Now you're a *Hak'kor*. Stand tall," Holchuk hissed into his ear. "Everyone defers to you now. But that doesn't mean you can do things out of order."

Fair enough, thought Townsend, his lofty new position making him feel a little light-headed. He would begin with the first contact speech, directed to the higher-ranked Chief Officer, and proceed from there.

"Greetings, honored guests from the House of Trokerk, and welcome to House Daisy Hub. Daisy Hub has a glorious history dating back to—"

"We already know it," Nagor cut in. He was swaying a little and apparently having some difficulty keeping his eyes focused. The other Chief Officer slowly turned his massive head and impaled him with a cold stare.

Townsend froze, remembering after a moment to close his mouth, as a single thought filled his mind: Had Nagor just insulted the other Chief Officer? Was Nandrian blood about to be spilled on A Deck?

The moment stretched out, thickening the air with tension. Then the second Chief Officer emitted the snorting, wheezing sound that was the aliens' version of laughter. Warily, Townsend began to relax. "With respect, *Hak'kor*,

Nagor ban Nagoram, Fifth Shield of House Trokerk, has heard this story many times. He recounted it to us while we were repairing our ships," the Nandrian said. "I am Agnosk ban Sitgaram, Third Shield of House Trokerk. Please honor us by continuing on to the good part."

Drew stared a question at Holchuk and received a helpless shrug in response.

All right, then, he thought with growing unease. They had evidently skipped to the introductions.

Townsend drew a steadying breath and began. "It is my honor to introduce myself. I am Drew, son of ... *Dammit!*—"

He was interrupted by a sudden chorus of snorting and wheezing. Drew's stomach dropped as he realized that all six aliens were laughing themselves silly over his name.

The good part, he thought sourly. *Of course.*

Glaring at Holchuk, Drew muttered under his breath, "You told Nagor, didn't you?"

The other man shrugged again. "I might have used it as an example while explaining about Human nervousness."

"They have to respect me or we're all fried, remember? Your words," Drew reminded him sternly.

"...spoken when you were Third Shield. Now you're First Shield. And they do respect you, boss man — as much as they're able to respect anyone after imbibing several glasses of lemon juice."

"Besides, Drew," Ruby chimed in, "isn't it good to know that the Nandrians have a sense of humor?"

"Hear me, *Hak'kor*," bellowed the big Chief Officer, commanding instant silence and attentiveness. "We had heard of the Human love of fun, and we are grateful that you deemed us worthy to witness this demonstration of it. Now, please honor us by telling us your true name."

At last, a chance to set the record straight! Pulling himself up to his full height, Townsend threw out his chest and announced, "I am Drew, son of David, First Shield of House Daisy Hub."

He paused for a moment to recognize how satisfying it was to hear himself speak those words. The Nandrians paused too, as though it were a normal part of the ceremony.

After that, the rest of the introductions proceeded smoothly, in traditional prescribed order: first, Chief Officers Agnosk and Nagor announced their full names; then Drew identified Ruby as his second in command and the Nandrians took turns introducing their seconds; and finally, Drew presented Holchuk as his third in command and Agnosk and Nagor followed suit.

"You come here victorious from *tekl'hananni*," said Townsend, following the script. "Please honor us with a telling of your triumph."

With that, Nagor and Agnosk launched into an energetic account that bounced back and forth between them, growing wilder and more improbable with each shift of narrator. By the time they were done, their two ships had defeated an armada of over twenty vessels from five different Houses, leaving half of them drifting in pieces in the asteroid belt of a distant star system; and Agnosk had leaped valorously into space, wearing nothing but his armor, to rescue Nagor from certain death after an enemy ship had broken up while he was in the process of boarding it.

The Nandrians fell silent and stood watching Drew expectantly. It was his turn. He might be a high official in their eyes, but his tale of victory had to match theirs, or he would be considered a poor host or, worse, would not be respected as an authority figure aboard his own station. Mentally keeping his fingers crossed and mustering all the theatricality he possessed, Townsend delivered the speech Holchuk had written, with just a few impromptu modifications. Rodrigues and his shuttle were now five entire Ranger detachments, bristling with weaponry and approaching the Hub at flank speed aboard a formidable fleet of heavily armed ships. With impressive wit and guile, Townsend had single-handedly ensured that none of them could dock or get close enough to board. When one of the Rangers had slipped past him onto the station, intending to make off with Daisy Hub's *tseritsa*, the fearless *Hak'kor* had then chased the intruder from one deck to the next, finally overpowering him in Soaring Hawk's workshop and ejecting the Ranger through an airlock. In so doing, Townsend had saved the honor not only of Daisy Hub, but also of Trokerk.

At the end, the Nandrians bared their lower fangs in approval. Drew had to resist the urge to take a bow. He was now a *Hak'kor*, after all, and the First Shield bowed to no one.

Closing remarks were brief. Drew invited the two Nandrian crews to come and celebrate their victory aboard the station. Following the script, the two Chief Officers accepted, praising him for being an excellent host.

On a signal from Drew's wristcomm, Lydia opened both docking portals wide, and a stream of big alien warriors began pouring through them, snorting and wheezing and headed for the tube cars. The three Humans remained standing in the middle of the deck, safe and untouched, as the Nandrians swarmed around them. When the crowd had thinned out, Holchuk turned to face the newly-minted *Hak'kor*, wearing an expression that was equal parts pride and amusement. "Well done, boss man. You understand."

"Yeah, I have my moments," he conceded wearily. "By the way, Holchuk — an airlock?"

The other man shrugged. "It's what a Nandrian would have done. Besides, I just felt that *some*body should go through an airlock today, and you won't let me space Karlov."

Beside him, Ruby snapped to attention, her cheeks dimpling. "Permission to go down to the caf and join in the Human custom of fun, sir?"

Drew waved her toward a tube car, thinking of all the work he still had to do. First, O'Malley had to be debriefed. Lydia would want to be present, if only to assure herself that he really was going to be all right. Then, and only after the Nandrians had left the station, Townsend could resume interrogating Karlov. Meanwhile, there were reports to prepare for the Space Installation Authority, Space Installation Security (Covert Ops), and Earth Intelligence, each one carefully worded and omitting all mention of Houses, *tseritsas* and a certain one-eyed Stragori.

— «» —

"Agnosk begs a favor from the *Hak'kor*."

Startled, Townsend glanced up from his light screen and found Holchuk standing in front of his desk. He'd been so busy with his report that his brain hadn't registered the sound of the tube car door opening.

"He begs?"

"From the *Hak'kor*," Holchuk repeated.

"And he sent you instead of coming himself?" Not that Drew was particularly anxious to be joined in AdComm by a seven-foot-tall reptilian warrior, drunk or sober. However, Agnosk was a first-time visitor, and Townsend had reason to be hyperconcerned about Nandrian protocol at that moment.

"Normally the *Kalufah* would be the go-between," Holchuk explained, "but Ruby's not available, so I'm standing in. It's unorthodox, since I'm technically in the Fifth Shield of House Trokerk. However, you did introduce me as your third in command, so—"

"Wait a minute. He said he wants a favor?" Drew cut in, struck by a sudden thought. "But isn't it the Nandrian custom to state a need and let the other person decide how to meet it?"

"When honor is involved, yes. But this is more about his personal curiosity."

"And what exactly is he curious about?"

"He would like to speak with Karlov."

Townsend sat bolt upright in his chair. "How does he know about Karlov?" he demanded. "Did you—?"

"Not a word, boss man. But you have to understand something. They may look like big, lumbering brutes, but the Nandrians are not stupid. They've been partying with our crew for the past several hours—"

"—and something was bound to slip out," Drew supplied ruefully. "So, they know we have him. Terrific. What happens if I simply say no?"

Holchuk thought for a moment. "You'd be within your rights, of course. But he could then ask you to explain why, and you'd have to give him a reason, since denying a respectfully made request without cause is considered to be an insult."

"Okay," declared Townsend. "Karlov is a prisoner and I'm in the process of interrogating him. How's that for a reason?"

"Prisoners are shackled and kept in the brig," Holchuk pointed out. "Or they're made as uncomfortable as possible and barraged by questions. Where is Karlov right now?"

Reluctantly, Drew replied, "Asleep in Med Services."

"So, that excuse won't fly. Have you got a more plausible one up your sleeve? Because, trust me, the truth will not work in this situation. We have twice the usual number of Nandrians aboard, carousing on every deck but this one, and they're all drunk on lemon juice. The ones that aren't passed out are staggering around with hair-trigger tempers and battle-ready reflexes, making life interesting for Hagman and his Security team. Confessing to harboring a Stragori spy who's been training to kill Nandrians would probably be the last mistake you ever made, especially since Daisy Hub is also in the middle of *tekl'hananni*. As I see it, if you want to keep the peace on this station, your one and only option is to find a way to grant Agnosk's request."

He was right. Townsend blew out a frustrated breath and thought hard. He wasn't yet ready to wake Karlov up, and shipping him off to the brig on Zulu would create more problems than it solved. "All right," Drew decided, overruling the misgivings that had already begun turning his midsection to soup. "Tell Agnosk that I'll give him two minutes with Karlov, but not until the current celebration is over and all the other Nandrians are aboard their ships and ready to depart."

"That should work," said Holchuk. "I'll let him know."

CHAPTER 22

There were five patients, all Human, sitting in the Doc's triage area when Townsend walked through the Med Services door. The sight of them sent a shiver down his spine. Thankfully, Will DeVries was not among the injured. The crewman would need to be healthy and alert when it came time to move A Deck beyond the sensor field for the Nandrian ships' departure.

"What happened to them?" Drew asked the Doc, frowning.

"A battle re-enactment in the caf got a little too realistic. I wasn't there, but apparently there was a difference of opinion among the Nandrians over which ship had scored the winning point, the *Krronn* or the *Nannssi*. A fight broke out between the two crews, spilling out of the caf and into the corridor, and not all of our people were able to get out of the way in time."

"I trust someone broke it up?"

"When Hagman's team showed up, the senior Nandrian officers finally intervened. I suspect this sort of brawling is just business as usual aboard a Nandrian vessel," remarked the Doc. Pointing with her stylus, she added, "In any case, Ramez, Fehr, and Flanagan are waiting for regen for broken bones and torn ligaments. They'll be out of action for an interval following treatment. The other two have superficial injuries, what we in the medical profession sometimes refer to as 'boo-boos'. Nurse Fermi is preparing to kiss them better as we speak. And what can I do for you, Mr. Townsend?"

"I need to talk to O'Malley."

Her features contracted in silent warning. "I asked Lydia to take him back to his quarters to rest. That's what *he* needs most right now."

But Drew couldn't back down. "The Nandrians know about Karlov and one of the Chief Officers has asked to meet with him. It's imperative that I find out what O'Malley learned about him before Karlov tried to— Before the incident," he amended.

Her eyes widened slightly as she took in the significance of his words. However, the stiffness of her posture and the set of her mouth sent a clear message that her priorities weren't about to budge, not for him or for anyone else.

"Mr. O'Malley is in a very fragile state right now," she informed him. "And even if he weren't, the trauma is still fresh in his mind. The brain edits memories that are too painful to recall, so I doubt whether you'll get anything useful from questioning him at this time."

"Nonetheless, I have to try, Doctor."

A pause, then, "I know," she said with a sigh. "I gather you'll want me to wake Karlov for this meeting with the Nandrian?"

"You'll have to," Townsend told her grimly. "Just make sure he's tightly secured to the bed. It's perilous enough having a bunch of drunken Nandrians careening all over the Hub. We don't need an attempted murderer running around loose as well."

— «» —

By the time Drew left Med Services to find the ratkeeper's quarters on F Deck, the party was all but over. Most of the Nandrians were already back aboard their respective ships, sleeping off the citric acid in their systems, and the handful of aliens still on the station were in no condition to make trouble.

As the Doc had predicted, O'Malley wasn't much help. However, he couldn't have been *too* traumatized — behind the wounded plaintiveness of his voice was an unmistakable note of indignation.

"He knew, boss. He must have known the whole time that it was just another SPA program, but he kept stringing me along. He conned me!"

"I know. He's probably been conning all of us since the day he came aboard the Hub."

Somehow, that would have to stop. Field Investigator Drew Townsend had been forbidden to use physical abuse when interrogating a suspect. But this wasn't the 33rd Precinct, he reminded himself, and covert operative Townsend was authorized by the EIS to do whatever it took to complete his mission, including torture a captive if he believed it would obtain results. Townsend was determined to drag the truth out of Max Karlov, and not philosophically opposed at this point to using torture to do it. However, there was one major problem: he'd been sent to Daisy Hub to get a bunch of mavericks and misfits working together as a team, and torturing Karlov was certain to break that team apart.

Two things had been drilled into Townsend during his EIS training. The first was that the mission always took priority. The second was what to do if anyone got in the way, and this was the mantra that was repeating insistently in his brain: *Turn him or terminate him.*

"What now, Drew?" Lydia wondered.

"At this point, what choice do we have? We put two very strong and dangerous alien beings face to face and keep our fingers crossed that they don't try to kill each other."

— «» —

The following morning, as promised, Agnosk was ushered into Med Services by Hagman and Deniro. Nandrian celebrations were stressful affairs. After a solid day and a half spent escorting drunken alien warriors back to their ships, the Security officers looked both weary and wired. Agnosk had evidently stopped at the caf for a proverbial "hair of the dog". He might have had the telltale yellowish cast of a hangover when he woke up, but he was green and mellow as he stepped through the Trauma room door.

Townsend and the Doc stood to either side of Karlov's bed, prepared for trouble. Drew was keeping a channel open to AdComm and had given Lydia orders to seal the docking portals if she overheard anything that suggested a fight had broken out in Med Services. Meanwhile, the Doc was focused on the smaller picture. A pair of sedative-loaded injectors sat on a tray at her elbow in case one or two someones needed to be knocked out.

Karlov lay back against the raised head of the bed, his eyes half-closed, seemingly unaware of the padded leather cuffs on his wrists and ankles — until he noticed the Nandrian standing near his feet. Karlov's eyes opened wide and he jackknifed to a sitting position, pulling frantically — and futilely — against the restraints.

"You!" he exclaimed.

Agnosk made the snorting, wheezing sound and bared his lower fangs. "I heard," he said. "I suspected. I was right." Turning to face Townsend, the Nandrian added, *"Hak'kor,* I heard that you had captured a spy. With respect, it seems that we were both deceived."

Townsend's jaw had dropped. He closed it, exchanged a bewildered look with the Doc, then ventured, "He's not a spy?"

"This one is a warrior of sorts," said Agnosk.

"I'm a soldier and a moderate," Karlov corrected him. "Just because we don't adhere to some strict ancient code—"

"Does he have honor, Agnosk son of Sitgar?" Drew cut in urgently.

"This one does, *Hak'kor.* He fights well for a Stragori. But he would not survive a warrior's *tekl'hananni."*

Not many of us would, thought Drew. Aloud, he declared, "I need to know what is going on here. Evidently, the two of you are acquainted. How?"

"We first met at the *ssalssit essendi* between our Houses," Agnosk replied. "Like yours, his people found a way to make the ritual egg exchange possible in order to cement the alliance."

"So, the Stragori are not an enemy that Trokerk and Daisy Hub have in common," Drew reasoned. "Instead, Trokerk is an ally that Daisy Hub and the Stragori have in common."

Agnosk bowed slightly from the shoulders. "You understand. And, with respect, *Hak'kor,* I am needed on my ship."

Of course. And Townsend was needed up on A Deck, where there was still the leave-taking ceremony to go through before DeVries could move the *Krronn* and the *Nannssi* outside the range of the sensor field and send them on their way. But Drew had many questions, to which he was now certain Karlov had the answers. At the earliest opportunity, he decided, they would have to have a very long and thorough conversation.

— «·» —

Once again, the separation and reconnection went without a hiccup. When the Nandrian ships had departed, most of the senior staff accompanied DeVries to the caf for a well-earned reward from Jensen's private distillery. Hagman and Deniro excused themselves to finally get some sleep. The Doc checked O'Malley over and declared him fit to return to restricted duty. After that, Holchuk escorted Karlov up to AdComm to answer some questions, with Lydia at her console and the Doc hovering nearby serving as additional witnesses to the discussion.

Karlov's recuperative powers were astonishing. Watching him step out of the tube car and stride to the guest chair waiting for him in front of Drew's desk, no one would ever suspect that not too many hours earlier, this man's body had been flooded with the strongest sedative in the Doc's pharmacy.

"*Ssalssit essendi*," Townsend repeated, staring thoughtfully at him. "So, there's a formal alliance between Trokerk and the Stragori."

"Has been for some time," Karlov replied, then returned in the same conversational tone, "And you're a *Hak'kor*. So, Daisy Hub has declared itself a House and is also allied with the Nandrians. Does your friend on Earth know about this?"

Instead of answering, Drew countered, "Does he know what *you* really are? What your actual mission is aboard Daisy Hub? Remember, I cautioned you earlier about the consequences of withholding information."

A smile tugged at the corners of Karlov's mouth. "Yes, you did. Perhaps I should have issued the same warning to you."

Perhaps he should have, Townsend privately conceded. Not that it would have made a difference, since Agnosk's endorsement was the only reason either of them had to trust the other right now, and it was a shaky sort of trust at best.

"I knew you weren't capable of uploading a living consciousness into a machine," Karlov continued. "Still, it was an impressive show."

"And you demonstrated your appreciation by murdering the avatar of the crew member who shared the program with you," Townsend informed him sternly. "Burned him alive."

"Ah! That explains the restraints. My sincerest apologies. Unfortunately, I had no way of knowing that I wasn't alone in there." He turned to address the Doc. "Is he going to be all right?"

Absently massaging her wrist, she replied with a scowl, "Eventually."

He dipped his head, visibly relieved. "I'm curious, Mr. Townsend. If you're a *Hak'kor*, then you've been through *ssalssit essendi*. Given the rather primitive level of your scientific technology compared to ours, how did you manage to fulfil the egg exchange requirement?"

"How did *you* do it?"

"Our scientists blended the two genomes, creating identical twins with the physical characteristics of both species. We kept one child and gave Trokerk the other. Your turn."

"Our scientific technology isn't as primitive as you think. We're exchanging clones of our respective *tseritsas*."

Suddenly attentive, Karlov demanded, "You have a *tseritsa*?"

Drew leaned forward. "It's not a living staff. It's a rat." In a low, intense voice, he added, "The one you came to steal."

Karlov's eyebrows shot up. "The rat is your *tseritsa*? But it would have to be—"

"Immortal," supplied the Doc with a faint smile. The smile broadened, becoming positively smug, as a shocked expression swept across his features.

"It's not a trick," Drew assured him. "Yoko has already lived eight times longer than any rat normally would. She's the result of years of scientific experimentation by one of the most brilliant Human minds of this century."

"And that explains a great deal," said Karlov thoughtfully.

Standing behind him, Holchuk clapped a hand on the other man's shoulder, then put his lips close to Karlov's ear and inquired, "Are you saying you didn't know why you'd been sent to Daisy Hub to steal her?"

"No, I always knew why the Directorate wanted me to collect her — and, believe me, if they'd known she was your *tseritsa* that order would never have been given. But now that you've explained her true nature, I understand why the radical faction would be so interested in her."

Townsend and the Doc traded confused looks. "You'd better explain that," Drew told him.

"On Earth, you have the Relocation Authority," said Karlov. "It's a group of individuals who decide for the entire population where you will live, where you will work, whether you will travel, and how well and easily you will live. And many Humans wish it didn't exist."

It wasn't a question. In the stunned silence that followed his words, he continued, "We have much the same situation on Stragon, with the Directorate. Most of our people feel that it no longer serves a useful purpose, but there is disagreement over what action to take. The radical faction wants to eliminate the Directorate altogether, simply pull the plug. The moderate faction, the one I belong to, is pushing instead for controls to be put in place that would limit its power over our lives. Lately, support for the radical faction has been growing."

"And why should the politics on Stragon be any of our concern?" said Drew.

"Because the battle between the two factions has spilled over onto your home world as well. Human and Stragori society have a great deal in common."

The Doc cleared her throat loudly and said, "Yes, we do. And you know the reason for that, don't you, Mr. Karlov?" To Drew, she continued, "I took a closer look at Akiko, the black and white rat that he brought to the Hub. She was carrying an encrypted message in the form of a retrovirus, which Lydia was able to partially decode."

Lydia had quietly crossed the deck and slipped unnoticed around the end of the filing cabinet partition. Now, as all eyes turned toward her, she approached Townsend's desk and dropped a printout in front of him. "I'm sorry, Drew," she said. "We should have told you earlier, but there was so much going on—"

Waving her silent, he quickly read through the text. He read it a second time to be sure he understood it. Then, deliberately replacing the page on his desktop, he took a calming breath, noting distractedly that everyone else in the room appeared to be holding theirs. Once he knew he could trust his voice, he asked, "Do we know where this message came from, and who the intended recipient is?"

"The method of encryption is one that Nayo Naguchi was working on before he died," replied the Doc. "He would only have shared it with someone he trusted. As for the recipient, I'm not convinced there is one. The information was most likely sent here for safekeeping only, in which case we were never meant to decipher it at all."

She gave herself too little credit. Or perhaps she was just being careful about what she revealed around Karlov. Well, thought Drew, for good or ill, this particular cat had crawled too far out of its bag for any of them to be worrying about what a Stragori agent did or didn't overhear.

"But you did decode it, Doctor," he pointed out, "and now I have even more questions for the man who has been so zealously protective of the animal that carried it here." Getting to his feet, Townsend leaned over his desk, glared at his guest, and demanded in a voice that felt and sounded as though something punishing was being pulled through his throat, "Which are we, Karlov? Is Humanity the control group, or are we the ones who were left behind to be experimented on?"

For a long, tense moment, they watched Karlov debate with himself whether to answer. Finally, he said, "We were the control group. And to answer your next question, we know this because the word *stragori* means 'control group' in the language of the race that conducted the experiments."

"So I was right," murmured the Doc. "Genetically, the Stragori are Human."

"But only genetically," Karlov informed her stiffly. "In all other respects, we are alien to each other, and the Directorate—" He fell silent.

"The Directorate wants to keep it that way. Am I right?" Lydia sank slowly onto the chair beside him. "But you don't agree. You've been dropping hints about who you really are — who the Stragori really are — ever since you arrived. You knew what that document said. You wanted us to make the connection with ancient Earth. That's why you baked those cookies."

Predictably, his spine went rigid with denial; but Townsend was skilled at reading tells, and Karlov's good eye was giving him quite the opposite message.

"So, the Stragori are genetically Human. How long have you known?" Lydia asked gently. "You personally, I mean. When did you find out that Humans and Stragori are the same race? Did you know it when you first arrived on the Hub? Were you aware before you got here that your mission was to steal science from fellow Humans? Was that why you slipped up and said too much every once in a while? Because you wanted us to stop you from carrying out that mission?"

Staring straight ahead, Karlov sat tall and replied firmly, "No. I'm a loyal soldier, and a soldier follows orders without question."

"Of course, you do," she soothed, "until you receive one that clearly came from an irrational mind, an order that flies in the face of reality. An order that you can't carry out without violating everything that makes you who you are. Is that why the Directorate has fallen into disfavor with the Stragori people? Because it has lost touch with reality? Because its orders no longer make sense? Like stealing science from a race that is technologically inferior to your own?"

Now he turned his head and glared directly into her eyes. "The Directorate is not insane. It has a tighter grip on reality than you do. And you have no idea how much you owe it." Again, he fell silent.

"Then enlighten us," Townsend commanded, moving to stand in front of his desk and taking over the interrogation once more. "You keep claiming that you're here to protect, but you refuse to tell us from what. So far, we've seen you commit assault and murder, and you've admitted to planning a theft. By what twisted definition could that possibly be considered protection?"

Karlov's cat had all four feet on the ground now, and the expression on his face said he knew it. Exhaling a gusty breath that seemed to force him back against his chair, he told them, "You want the truth? All right. If anyone on Stragon knew I was telling you this, I would be executed without a tribunal. Where do you think the blueprint for the Reorganization came from? Why do you suppose the powers of the Relocation Authority were expanded to permit a rapid colonization program? Pandemics were decimating your population on Earth. Each one diminished your race intellectually and creatively. Humans had to go out into space, as quickly as possible, in order to preserve your future. So, the Directorate placed agents on your world to ensure that it would happen.

"There have been Stragori on Earth for a very long time, Mr. Townsend. As we are now learning, some of them belong to the radical faction. They're actively working against the Directorate, and they're looking for Human allies to join their cause."

"And you said they're interested in Yoko?" the Doc interjected.

"They're interested in anything they can use to prove that the Directorate is on the wrong path," said Karlov. "The radicals obviously know what you have here on Daisy Hub, since they've already made one attempt to acquire Yoko."

"And you were assigned to make a second attempt," Holchuk pointed out, scowling. "I don't see much difference."

"I guess you wouldn't, not at this end. But there's a huge difference on Stragon. There are moderates and radicals with competing agendas in every segment of Stragori society, and many have chosen not to advertise which side they're on. The first agent the Directorate sent here finally revealed himself to be a radical. You know who I'm talking about."

"Nestor Quan?" Drew replied. "He claimed to be working for a European gene broker. We sent him away empty-handed."

"With Nandrian assistance," chimed in Holchuk.

"You're in a difficult position," Karlov conceded. "Revealing your alliance with the Nandrians and Yoko's status as *tseritsa* would eliminate the threat of any further

Stragori incursion; however, it would probably draw a hostile response from your own planetary government, once word got back to Earth."

"And that's why the alliance is secret, and will remain that way for as long as possible," said Drew pleasantly. "Unless you plan to betray us?"

Behind Karlov's chair, Holchuk had begun mouthing the word *airlock*.

The alien grinned. "Not at all. You wanted to know by what definition my presence aboard your station constitutes protection. I'm giving you an answer. I'm a moderate, sent by the Directorate as part of a plan to protect Humanity."

"By taking Yoko?" the Doc reminded them indignantly.

The grin broadened. "By keeping her out of radical hands in whatever way turns out to be the best. As long as the Directorate stands, your future remains assured."

So, not only was Yoko a living staff, she had also become a political football. Wasn't *that* just wonderful, thought Townsend darkly.

"One more question," Lydia said. "If the Nandrians are your allies, why have you been so keen to practice killing them?"

The grin spread to Karlov's good eye. "It's simple. In thousands of years, no non-Nandrian has ever scored a point in *tekl'hananni*. I plan to be the first."

— «» —

Anyone who thought the worst was over was kidding himself. As the others would soon find out, the hard work had just begun.

Lydia and the ratkeeper were waiting for Townsend in the caf as ordered, sipping from huge mugs of Jensen's most potent brew. As he joined them at the table farthest from the door, Lydia pushed a third java, already poured, in front of him. He lifted it and took a slow swallow, studying O'Malley's expression over the rim of his cup. The kid had aged. Not physically, with gray hair and wrinkles, but it seemed to Drew as though the blaze that had consumed the ratkeeper's avatar had also burned away most of his youthful cockiness. It was a saddening thought.

"How are you feeling, O'Malley? Are you ready to work?"

He shrugged. "I'm a little numb and tingly here and there, but the Doc says it will pass."

"Good. I've got three jobs for you, and one of them's a con."

That reignited the spark in his eyes. "The same mark?"

"I figured you'd appreciate another crack at him. First of all, though, you need to restore U-Town to the way you found it, or Teri is liable to put you right back in the Trauma room. She's in full-blown withdrawal right now and giving everyone grief."

O'Malley chuckled. "Sure thing. And the second job, boss?"

"Were you serious when you told me you'd hacked the Galactic database and begun copying records to our system?"

"Absolutely. We're up to nearly thirty percent."

"I want you to find out all you can about the Stragori home world, Stragon. I want everything Karlov told us today checked and double-checked, and I want you to let me know immediately if there's any kind of discrepancy."

Lydia's eyes widened briefly. "You don't trust him. Even after Agnosk said—"

"Agnosk was talking about honor. Karlov just came right out and told us where his loyalty lies, and it's not with Earth or Daisy Hub. I think we can be fairly certain that he still hasn't told us the whole truth, about anything. That's where the con comes in."

"What's my part?" said O'Malley.

"Essentially the same as it was before, but minus the SPA room and the arson. By now he knows that you're the one he set on fire in U-Town. He'll be expecting hostility from you, maybe even revenge, so his guard will be up. You'll need to give an award-winning performance in order to get past those watchdogs. Convince him that you're not carrying a grudge, that you realize he's part of the team now. After all, Daisy Hub is a small place and you'll probably end up working together at some point, so the best thing to do is let bygones be bygones. Once you're past his defenses, keep your eyes and ears open. Don't be too friendly or ask too many questions — that's how you got in trouble before. Karlov relaxes and lets information slip out from time to time. Just be easy to get along with and listen carefully to everything he says."

"And double-check it before reporting anything to you. Got it."

As they watched O'Malley leave the caf, Lydia murmured to Drew, "Karlov isn't the only mark this time, is he?"

Townsend feigned horrified indignation. "Why, Ms. Garfield! I'm shocked that you would even suggest — whatever it is you're suggesting!"

Arching a knowing eyebrow, she took another swallow of her java.

"Now let's talk about you," he said.

She arranged her features into an expression of puzzlement. "What about me?"

"You're a trained interrogator, Ms. Garfield." When she didn't respond, he continued, "In my years as a field investigator, I questioned hundreds of suspects. I had one of the highest confession rates in the precinct, so I was obviously good at it. But the way you softened Karlov up earlier today was impressive. You slipped into that conversation as cold and smooth as ice and took his legs out from under him, and you did it without once raising your voice or even moving a muscle."

"Are you complimenting me on my technique, Drew?" she said, flashing him a grin.

He gave her an appraising look. "I'm just wondering what other surprises you might have in store for me."

She reached across the table and laid a hand over his. "Well," she told him, "if things continue the way they've been going, I'm guessing you'll be finding out soon enough."

With that, Lydia got up and left as well.

Alone at the table, Drew took a thoughtful sip of his java and let a single realization fill his mind: They'd survived. There were still mysteries to solve, and the worst danger lay ahead of them, but for at least the next short while they were all safe. The Daisy Hub crew had dug deep and managed to pull a bunch of rabbits out of their disparate and extremely divergent hats. War had been averted. Secrets were still protected, his own in particular. And — both comforting and disturbing to contemplate — it appeared that Humanity, like Drew Townsend himself, had "friends in high places".

The Stragori might not want to rejoin the Human race, but — if Karlov was to be believed — they were determined not to let it die out, either, not as long as the Directorate had a say in the matter. They had taken over Earth, secretly shaping and directing Humanity's progress. Sending Humans out to proliferate among the stars.

According to Karlov, the Directorate's motives had been nothing but altruistic. Everything had been done for the benefit and protection of the Human race. Whether or not that was true remained to be seen. Life was full of uncertainty right now, and Drew had no doubt that the future would be an unfriendly place. Nonetheless, for the moment, they were safe. Daisy Hub would fight another day, with or without alien assistance. And for Drew Townsend, that was more than enough.

EPILOGUE

As **Barry Novak** pulled into his parking spot beneath the Kings' headquarters in the Zone, a figure stepped out of the shadows and stood waiting in front of the hologram-protected elevator door. It was Nayo Naguchi. Cursing inwardly, Novak paused to compose his features before leaving his PV. He was returning from having tea with Madame Vargas for the third time in a week, and the outcome was not something he wished to discuss outside of a clean room.

As though sensing the reason for his reticence, Naguchi boarded the elevator with him in silence and stood beside him, facing frontward, for the duration of the eight-floor trip. Novak led the way out of the car and down the hall to his private office, each footstep seeming to inflate the anger and tension inside him a little more.

Once the door was closed behind them, Naguchi sank onto one of the falsahyde chairs. He looked Novak up and down, then said, "She didn't go for it, did she?"

"No. The moment I mentioned that he was Stragori, her mind slammed shut, and nothing I've said since then has been able to reopen it. She wants the EIS to have nothing to do with him."

"So now what?"

"She's ordered me to terminate him."

"Of course, she has. I repeat, so now what?"

"So now Nestor Quan dies," Novak informed him stiffly.

"Changed your mind about giving him a new identity, have you?"

"He dies, Nayo. Termination is final. A body will be found and identified."

"Like mine was? Don't spout the party line to me, Barry. In all the years we've been associated, I've never known you to let a direct order stand in your way. And neither has she. She's probably *expecting* you to disobey this one." The corners of his mouth quirked briefly. "So, if you really wanted to surprise her—"

"Surprise isn't exactly the effect I have in mind," Novak declared darkly.

A light flashed repeatedly on his desktop.

Naguchi raised an eyebrow. "Shall I leave so you can answer that?"

"Not necessary. It's a status report from Rodrigues. Nothing urgent."

"You gave him a direct channel?"

"And a mission. We've known for a while that Madame Vargas has eyes and ears on Daisy Hub, someone who reports directly to her and takes orders only from her, including carrying out hits on targets of Vargas's choosing. So, I'm making Paul Rodrigues my eyes and ears on Zulu. It may be hours away from Daisy Hub, but the Ranger platform and short-hoppers are all heavily armed. And once he discovers the identity of Vargas's plant..."

"Termination?"

Novak scowled. "You know that's not our call. It's up to Townsend to decide."

"Sure it is," Naguchi murmured, his face now wearing an inscrutable mask. "And my name is really Randall Chin, and Nestor Quan has only our best interests at heart. Be honest with yourself, Barry — how far do you actually trust Drew Townsend?"

"As far as I need to," came the unhesitating response. "And if he remembers his years on the street, that's how far he'll trust me too."

— ⟨⟩ —

Juno Vargas took a mouthful of Earl Grey tea and closed her eyes, savoring its citrus notes for a moment before she swallowed. Behind her, the clean room door opened, then closed again.

"I'm sorry to be late. I had to be certain I wasn't followed."

Angeli crossed to the armchair and sank into it, letting out an *aah* of relaxation. The long braid of hair was now twisted into a knot at the nape of her neck, making her look even older than her forty-five years. But there was an entire revolution in her eyes, like an ember on the cusp of bursting into flame. The news would be good. It always was, when Angeli brought it.

"You're not *too* late," Juno told her. "There's still half a pot left." She leaned forward and filled the second cup on the silver tray, then turned the tray and slid it closer to her guest. "So," she continued, "how did it go in Vancouverville?"

"Long story short, Earth for Terrans has a new chapter on the west coast, twenty members strong. Before I left, they'd already identified four suspected Stragori agents, one of them on the District Council, no less. There are two main street gangs, and I spoke with both their leaders, separately and then together. They're willing to support the Reformation, but they want something in return for their loyalty."

"Let me guess," said Juno with a mirthless smile. "They want to keep their power?"

"Their turf," Angeli replied, mirroring her expression. "Same thing."

Of course, thought Juno. The generous deals that Dennis Forrand had offered as enticements to those who could help him build the Earth Intelligence Service were, unfortunately, well beyond her own resources. As a result, in places like Vancouverville and Havana there had been no clean slates and fresh beginnings, just bargains with uneducated thugs and criminals who guarded their paltry spheres of dominance with the ferocity of a dragon protecting its hoard of gold.

"What did you tell them?"

"I pointed out the benefits that everyone would enjoy if the Reformation was successful and that nobody would receive if it wasn't. I informed them that they could either take part or take their chances. Then I left."

"And when push comes to shove?"

"Hard to say. The Vancouverville bunch could go either way. I should have better luck with Hickman in Greater London next month. He's calling all the gang leaders together for a summit meeting to hear our proposal." A pause, then, "It's a shame Barry Novak won't come onside. I understand why you've chosen to keep your brother in the dark about this, but wouldn't it be better if the organization presented a united front?" Juno pretended not to hear her. Swallowing her exasperation, Angeli tried again. "What if I had a talk with Novak? I'll bet I could persuade him to reconsider."

Juno made a face. "You'd be wasting your time. The man consorts with Stragori agents. In fact, he's trying to make a deal with one right now. I thought Forrand was bad, hiring a Stragori to look after my brother in detention, but Novak is worse. Would you believe that he had the nerve to come in here and suggest to my face that the EIS formalize an alliance with one of the Stragori factions?"

"How did you answer him?"

"I turned him down flat, of course. An alien race is headed for civil war and he wants to put Earth smack in the middle of it? It's insane."

Angeli cocked her head and remarked, "And it's the Stragori. And you still trust him?"

Cool gray eyes found her face and rested there for a moment.

"Strange though it may sound," said Juno with a tiny shrug, "you and Barry Novak are the only two people I feel I *can* trust right now."

"Even though he 'consorts with Stragori agents'?"

"He can consort all he likes. I know who they are. And when the time comes, I'll be the one who orders the hits. Once the Stragori are gone and the Reformation is launched, there will be only one side for the EIS to be on — mine. And if he knows what's good for him, that's where you'll find Barry Novak as well."

If you enjoyed this read

Please leave a review on Amazon, Facebook, Good Reads or Instagram.

It takes less than five minutes and it really does make a difference.

If you're not sure how to leave a review on Amazon:

1. *Go to amazon.com.*

2. *Type in The Relativity Bomb by Arlene F. Marks and when you see it, click on it.*

3. *Scroll down to Customer Reviews. Nearby you'll see a box labeled Write a Review. Click it.*

4. *Now, if you've never written a review before on Amazon, they might ask you to create a name for yourself.*

5. *Reviews can be as simple as, "Loved the book! Can't wait for the Next!" (Please don't give the story away.)*

And that's it!

Brian Hades, publisher

About the Author:

Born and raised in Toronto, Arlene F. Marks began writing stories at the age of 6 and can't seem to stop. Although she's been published in multiple genres, her first love has always been speculative fiction. Her work has appeared in H.P. Lovecraft's Magazine of Horror, Onder Magazine, and Daily Science Fiction. Her science fantasy novel, The Accidental God, was nominated for the 2015 Stephen Leacock Medal for Humour. Arlene lives with her husband on Nottawasaga Bay but spends an inordinate amount of time in the Sic Transit Terra universe. She welcomes visitors to her website:
www.thewritersnest.ca